The Miracle of
Pelham Bay Park

❧❦❧

ALSO BY ANTHONY MANCINI

Minnie Santangelo's Mortal Sin
Minnie Santangelo & the Evil Eye

The Miracle of Pelham Bay Park

❧

Anthony Mancini

E. P. Dutton · New York

Published in the United States by
E. P. Dutton, Inc.
2 Park Avenue, New York, N.Y. 10016

Library of Congress Cataloging in Publication Data
Mancini, Anthony.
The miracle of Pelham Bay Park.
I. Title.
PS3563.A4354M5   813'.54   81-12495
AACR2

ISBN: 0-525-03058-1

Published simultaneously in Canada by
Clarke, Irwin & Company
Limited, Toronto and Vancouver

Designed by Nancy Scarino

10 9 8 7 6 5 4 3 2 1
First Edition

For Maria

Acknowledgment

My special thanks
to Owen Laster and Jane Rosenman,
who had faith.

The Miracle of
Pelham Bay Park

Prologue

The girl comes out of the bakery with a warm round loaf tucked under her arm and skips in the shimmering morning across Westchester Avenue. As she touches the far curb she begins in an angelic soprano to sing: "Whistle while you work. Hitler is a jerk. Mussolini is a weenie and the Japs are even worse."

The jingoisms sound anomalous on the rosebud lips of a little girl who has just received Holy Communion. They jangle in the echo of the Sanctus. Her braided brown hair flaps on her shoulders as she skips. The monogrammed wafer glows like an ember in her belly.

Pelham Bay Park looms green ahead, veiled in mist, cast in morning light. She enters the park and the babble of finches merges with the rumble of the nearby el. Canvas shoes touch wet grass, nostrils fill with the sweet mingled essences of May. She wears a blue school jumper and white blouse. Her slender body is dwarfed by straight trees that pillar the cloudless dome of sky. In nature's sanctuary she stops singing.

She ambles now, picking buttercups, observing the stately pageant of worker ants, until finally she sits on a bench to perform a daily ritual. From her jumper pocket she produces a fistful of unshelled peanuts.

Soon she is visited by three mendicant squirrels, each of whom gets an equal share of the nuts doled out one by one with cooing words. The animals sit on their hind legs, devouring the food in the posture of orants come to life. Now the sun breaks through the trees and she squints through eyes still somewhat attuned to the darkness of church. Her pale face is warm and the wafer still glows inside her. She basks, feeling wonderful, curiously expectant.

She runs out of peanuts and the squirrels flee into the trees. It is also time for her to go. Seeing the animals eat has whetted her own appetite already primed by fasting. Nothing but water and her workbound father's stubbled cheek had touched her lips before they received the host at seven o'clock mass this morning.

Stretching languidly, she rises from the bench. A tongue of flame flickers where *Gesù* reposes. She hoists her sagging wool stockings and heads for home.

She crosses the weedy football field, dodging scattered rain pools deposited overnight. She sighs. What a fine, glorious day. Despite her hunger she wants to prolong the stay in the park. The bracing spring air is like sweet sacramental wine. But her brother awaits his slice of bread to dunk into the *caffè latte* and her mother will fly into a rage if she is late. So she continues homeward, cheeks aflame with some rampant mysterious pleasure.

Her senses are recalled to church where these feelings were first sown. She hears again the deep swell of the organ, sees the whorl on the hardwood pew and the chipped tunic of the plaster angel. She hears again the toot of Sister Mary Barnabas's pitch pipe before the children sing.

"Daughter of the mighty Father, maiden patron of the May,
Angel forms around thee gather, macula non est in te."

Her voice pealed above the listless drone of her schoolmates, rang with conviction. She lifted her fervent eyes to the statue of the Virgin as she sang.

"Macula non est in te. Macula non est in te."

She prayed passionately, with a native faith in the power of prayer. She prayed for her brother, Mario.

"Macula non est in te. Macula non est in te."

The hymn ended and the hushed parishioners shuffled up
to the altar to receive the sacred host. The girl found herself in
a motley file of communicants, old and young.
Right in front
of her was Basil Two-Times, the retarded boy, chewing his
tongue and smiling brightly. To her left was Mrs.
Feeney, the
Irish dowager with the snooty expression, stepping delicately
as a camel up to the altar rail.
The girl felt buoyant on the path to receiving the sacrament. She felt as ever poised on the brink of an adventure,
about to partake of a sumptuous feast of the spirit. It was as if
she had received an engraved invitation to the seder called the
Last Supper, so vivid and literal was her faith. She knelt at the
marble railing and lifted her eyes to the high cupolated ceiling
that was adorned with biblical scenes. Out of the corner of her
eye she caught the glint of the golden chalice. The murmuring
priest drew nearer. Her eyes shut tightly and her lips parted.
"Domine non sum dignus."

The girl's recollections dissolve at the appearance on the
grass before her of a brown grosbeak, hopping, apparently
grounded by an injured wing. Uttering a stunted cry of alarm,
she stoops and gently picks it up. Then she sees the lady.

She stands in a nearby clearing, bathed in a mandorla of
morning light. She wears a plain white Mother Hubbard and a
red rose in her raven hair. She draws closer and her features
come into focus: she is beautiful in a markedly Levantine way
with creamy brown skin and black almond-shaped eyes. Despite
her simple dress she has the easy assurance of the well-born
and a gliding, regal gait. She comes toward the girl.

A hush descends over the park. The birds stop chattering
in the leafy trees, the morning loses its voice. The lady smiles
as she approaches.

She stops about four feet from the girl and stands beside
a knotted oak in which the girl remembers her brother had
once carved his initials. In silent communication the lady looks
at her. She immediately hands over the injured bird. The lady
softly kisses the bird and holds out the cup of her hand. It
flutters away. The girl drops the loaf of bread on the ground
and falls to her knees.

The lady smiles again. It is a radiant smile, warm as the rearing sun. The girl feels awestruck but unafraid and, a little nervously, returns the smile. She waits, not knowing for what. The lady speaks in a high fluty voice. "Rise, my child. God loves you."

She rises, her heart brimming with an ineffable joy. "Mario," she manages to say. "My brother . . ."

The lady's look of tolerant disapproval silences her. "You have work to do," she says.

The girl humbly bows her head. She is as prepared as her forerunners for a commission to heathen regions, to act as envoy between pope and prince, to embrace lepers or feed the pyre. She waits, saucer-eyed, heart pounding.

The lady speaks again. "These are bad times. War rages in Europe. The fires of faith burn low. Tell everyone that you saw me, the thornless rose, and ask them to believe. It is a difficult job, my daughter, for I leave no girdle to Thomas. Yet it has to be done."

The girl stands in silence, mystified by this speech. Now a moment comes when time and space seem to merge and the lady seems balanced between the grassy humic earth and evanescent clouds. She is gilded in light from the early sun which seems suddenly to get a boost of power, making it look near enough to pluck, a fiery orange in the ardent sky. Then it all dissolves and the lady is gone.

For an eternal minute the girl stands fixed to the spot. Presently the chorus of birds and crickets resumes and the earth rotates again. Dumbly, like a puppet limbering up, she stirs herself. The look of awe is still etched into her face. She glances around her.

The mist has lifted over Pelham Bay Park, a patch of green in the northeast Bronx where an eleven-year-old girl searches the green for a loaf of bread. In its place she finds a spray of red roses beaded with moisture.

1

Reading the morning paper I came across Lucia's obituary and choked on a jelly doughnut. After completely disgorging this sinful breakfast upon my sister's Limoges I slowly reread the unhappy news. And, as the sun winked through the Limerick curtains, I wept.

A priest's tears are not holy water, my children. Especially not the salty flow of an old glutton like me. These sprang from the same geyser of regret and guilt that afflicts anyone who reaches old age still puzzled by final matters and convinced that somewhere in the past an important signpost was missed. But now the way was charted and there was no turning back.

Lucia Buonfiglio is dead. My tears blot the newspaper right beneath her photo taken in the days of "the miracle," when she was only eleven. Here is that familiar face with freckles sprinkled like cinnamon over the bridge of a noble Sicilian nose. Here are the same blue eyes limpid with trust. Here is the face that has haunted my dreams for the last forty years.

I was always a poor hagiographer but I must remark how much she resembled her namesake Santa Lucia of Syracuse. Those eyes, those lucid pools of light that gave men no rest! Unlike the organs of the namesake, they were not plucked out. Now they are lidded forever, dazzling their imperviable Maker, while my own lusterless, glaucomatous peepers are washed in brine. *Confiteor:* I loved the girl.

5

This is no time for the confessor to confess. There is too much work to be done.

I stare at the wreck of the jelly doughnut, averting my eyes from the newspaper page on which the obituary is printed. Outside my window the day slowly ripens into sultriness. The street is lined with Victorian clapboard houses, standing proud as matrons under the great knotted elms. Catherine will soon be returning from the market. I can't let her find me like this. I pluck a Kleenex from the box on the desk and dab my eyes.

Get a grip on yourself, Owen Fogarty, you slobbering old sacerdote. You needn't cry on her account. She finally got what she wanted—the martyr's palm. The confessor must now do penance. Instead of beads, I will mumble this narrative. Though the form will be literary, the purpose will be ecclesiastical.

I must break silence. Surely her death releases me from the obligation of confessional secrecy to which she has bound me all these years. Finally I can lift the veil of shame from her memory. And more.

I will write my nephew, auxiliary bishop of the Archdiocese of New York, including my story as the basis of a formal request for her beatification and canonization. Yes, I will promote sainthood for Lucia Buonfiglio. I will urge the Vatican to convene a *processus*, a trial that can be conducted only after the subject's death, exploring—what is the official phrase?— "the virtues and miracles of persons proposed for public veneration." Indeed, she who has been reviled will be reverenced, I vow. There is still time in the neap of my life for at least one agonal victory, even if I am nothing but an overweight grizzled sophist with an excessive fondness for Irish whiskey. What have I got to lose?

Why bother, you might ask. She is dead and gone, and isn't sainthood a quaint institutional relic of a bygone time? Isn't the whole thing just another excuse for me to fritter my dwindling supply of days?

I am tempted to agree. But, somehow, the image of my holy client shores up my resolution. The story of her extraordinary life must be made public. If sainthood has any meaning at all, it derives from the *exemplary* function of canonization. Today we need saints and martyrs as much as ever. For they teach us how to live and die.

You may also ask what qualifies me as narrator of her life, her virtues and miracles? And why sponsor the cause of an insignificant Italian girl who has left us only a few yellowed clippings of articles about purported miraculous events in the Bronx? My qualifications as chronicler, I contend, are beyond dispute. My position as her student counselor, as direct witness to many of the events I undertake to describe and, above all, as her confessor, put me in a unique position to tell Lucia's story. Only she herself would have had a better vantage and her pretty lips, like her eyes, are sealed forever. So it is up to this old, infirm and sinful man to set the record straight.

As to my skill, I fear the narrative will be peppered a bit too liberally with the pedantries and prejudices of a man who has held the shepherd's crook in the uneasy grip of frustrated scholar and philosophe. I beg, too, indulgence for the limited use of poetic license that I have decided to make. In mitigation, may I say that I feel highly qualified from the vantage of the confessional box to fathom and take soundings of her psychological mechanism, trusting that such an approach will give to the ecclesiastical jurists a rounded Giottesque picture of this mosaic of events.

Surely the newspaper and magazine accounts of the time hardly conveyed the happenings accurately and roundly. Most of the stories sprang from the active but distorted imagination of *Bronx Home News* reporter Albert Dunlop, whose byline was the signature of deceit. This paragon of objectivity in fact controlled events more faithfully than he recorded them, but that is getting ahead of my story.

Mother Church also owns no true record. Her earthly representatives, of whom I am a particularly reprehensible example, behaved quite without dignity much less sanctity during the whole affair. In fact, the heirs of the Fisherman might still find it expedient to suppress the story I am determined to spill. Forty years is but an eyeblink to an institution accustomed to regarding the world *ab aeterno*. In other words, some reputations are still liable to be tarred, some pet mythologies to be punctured, some egos to be bruised and, most importantly, perhaps some heads to be cold—bare of the coveted mitre. But damn the torpedoes . . .

I also have personal reasons for undertaking this project, many of which will become evident as the story unravels. Not the least of them, I venture, concerns the need to fortify the sagging ramparts of an arteriosclerotic priest's faith, which was a shaky thing in the best of times but is especially pregnable now in old age. In the popular mind it is laymen not priests who return to the fold as the chill descends. But it seems that senility brings to us anointed ones just as many if not more tests of faith, scruples and doubts, particularly about perhaps having wasted one's life in the service of an ill-tempered, vain and demanding dowager. By recounting Lucia's exemplary story I frankly hope to recoup some of the indulgences I have squandered in the Boss Lady's name. I hope also in the process to aspire to belief. It is axiomatic—and this, if I may tip my hand, is one of the lessons of Lucia's life—that no miracle can be wrought without faith. She taught us even more: faith itself is a miracle. I too wish to perform a miracle as the candle is snuffed. I wish to die with dignity.

The flesh is weak. I nibble guiltily at the more palatable portions of the jelly doughnut. A delaying tactic, for it is time to lay fingers to the keys of my venerable Royal—the modern scribe's quill.

Finally it occurs to me that the events related in the following story may test the reader's credence. Amen. Read with the raised eyebrow of the Devil's Advocate but keep an open mind. Emulate Dante in the dusky wood and regard me as a shade magnanimous, a guide to wonderful sights.

Of course, this caveat applies only to the lay reader. As for the esteemed jurists of the pontifical court, belief in miracles is presumed.

2

Positio Super Introductione Causae

M y Jesuit training predisposes me to a sense of order so I launch my story at the beginning, that is, at my first face-to-face meeting with Lucia without the obstacle of the confessional grid. The clarity of my memory of this meeting is in itself a minor miracle. While my recollection of yesterday comes across dimly as if, in the phrase of Saint Paul, through a glass darkly, my picture of that faraway time is incandescent; it emerges from the tunnel of years like a bath of daylight.

I was sitting in my office in the old school, the small red-shingled building that served the educational needs of Saint Bonaventure's parish quite well until the postwar baby boom prompted one of those massive "building drives" trumpeted endlessly from the pulpit before the wicker baskets were passed around still another time by seasoned extortionists of the Holy Name Society, and the big new school was constructed complete with butterfly backboards two blocks away. I was sitting at my varnished mahogany desk, swiveling indolently and indulging in a favorite—as you may have noticed—pastime: reading the newspaper. I was young then—thirty-five or so—and cut, so I thought, quite a dashing figure as a red-haired curate in a flowing cassock, darling of the widows who roosted like blackbirds on telephone wires at my side altar each morning. Actually a good-sized paunch already was blooming under my cassock, transubstantiated in part from chocolate doughnuts, a

9

box of which I habitually kept in the upper left-hand desk drawer where my fingers now reached as I scanned the headlines.

It was a day in early May that would have been etched in my memory in any case. As a confirmed Hellenophile I remember my deep sadness at the lead article in the newspaper announcing that the swastika had been planted on the Acropolis. Three columns over, Churchill was quoted, branding Mussolini a "whipped jackal," and a short article low on the page reported Missouri Senator Harry Truman's sharp questioning of Army generals about the nation's state of war readiness. I had already reached the sports pages and was engrossed in a story about Joe Louis training to meet Buddy Baer when I heard a soft and deferential voice.

"Excuse me, please, Father."

I blushed, disposed of the remainder of the doughnut and peered over the top of the newspaper.

She was noticeably small for her age, a dark girl with delicate bones and braided hair, sleek as an otter's coat. Her blue eyes contrasted appealingly with her dusky skin. She carried a ragged leather book bag. "If you're busy," she continued apologetically, "I can come back another time."

Her voice had a reedy quality, a tuneful vibrato coarsened, I speculated, by a premature tonsillectomy and it came from a birdlike body just big enough to contain it. At first glance the child provoked my interest. She had an indefinable aura. I folded my newspaper, assumed my best paternal manner and gave her full attention. "I'm not busy, young lady. Not at all. Just reading the paper." She seemed nervous so I smiled to put her at her ease. "Would you like a chocolate doughnut?"

She shyly shook her head.

I suppressed feelings of relief mingled with guilt. There were only two left. "What's your name?" I asked.

"Lucia Buonfiglio," she replied in smooth Italian, deliberately avoiding the Anglicized pronunciation favored by her teachers and classmates.

"What grade are you in?" I asked as she stood fidgeting before me.

"Sixth."

I nodded sympathetically. "One of Sister Mary Rachel's little charges. She makes you toe the line, eh?"

Her cheeks became tinged with color.

"How are your marks?"

"Fine, mostly," she said.

"Do you have trouble with English?"

"Oh, no," she protested with unusual readiness, breaking out of her cocoon of shyness. "I was born in America just like you."

I chuckled. "Were you now? Well, I was born in Galway, I'll have you know."

The remarkable eyes widened. "Is that somewhere in France?" she ventured.

"No. Ireland."

"Oh," she said, dropping her fringed eyelids. Then it came to me, who she was. I linked the face to the familiar voice, a voice that had whispered to me so often in the confessional box those minor sins and scruples of her innocent age.

I urged her to sit down. She sat across from me and looked unblinkingly at my bland and homely face. Her demureness gradually ebbed. Despite her youth and self-effacing manner she had unusual poise and a kind of grace. I suppose you could call it charisma in the classical sense of the word—a spiritual gift of personal magnetism. Before speaking again I coughed. Was I shy before an eleven-year-old?

"Now then," I began in a pompous manner, "what can I do for you?" It sounded hollow. I seemed to be unnerved.

"I have something very important to tell you," she said, rather sententiously, I thought. "I don't know how to say this. You're a priest but still I'm afraid you won't believe me."

I swiveled the chair, marveling at this oration. "Lord, what could it possibly be? Out with it, child. I'll believe you."

She still hesitated, her small cameo face wrinkled with indecision. Finally she managed to produce these words: "I have seen Our Lady."

This announcement floated between us before I finally comprehended what she was driving at.

"I mean the Blessed Mother," she stammered. "I saw her. I guess you would call it a vision."

I was mute. I was not tempted to laugh. The proclamation had been made in too serious and direct a manner. My automatic skepticism was tempered by the ring of conviction in her voice and manner.

"You don't say," was my clumsy reaction.

"I do say." She folded her small hands in the lap of her jumper uniform, volunteering no more information, waiting for me to make the next statement. I finally asked: "Where? Where did the vision take place, my dear?"

"In Pelham Bay Park."

"When?"

"Yesterday morning as I was returning from mass."

"I see," I said, recovering my composure. A note of skepticism crept into my tone. "Do you attend mass on weekdays?"

"Every day."

I leaned backward and stuck my hands through the slits in the cassock into my trouser pockets, assuming what I fancied to be a casual Solomonic pose. "I see," I said again, as the chair squeaked. "You are very devout, aren't you? Do you often have visions?"

She frowned. "Of course not. This was the first time in my life."

"Well—tell me about it, okay? What did she look like? What did she say? How do you know for certain she was Mary, Mother of God?"

"I just know." She batted her eyes. "She was very beautiful. She had black hair and she was dressed all in white."

"Did she say she was the Blessed Mother?"

"No. She called herself 'the thornless rose.'"

"Ah, the thornless rose. And where had you heard that expression before?"

"I never heard it before." Impatience had elevated her voice.

"Not even from Sister Mary Rachel in catechism or Bible history?"

She knitted her brow for a moment. "Not that I remember."

"And how is your memory? Do you have a good memory?"

"Oh, yes. I'm very smart in school, as I told you. I get all

12

A's. Except," she added, blushing, ". . . except in conduct. In conduct I get C's."

"No kidding," I said, truly surprised.

"Sister Mary Rachel doesn't like me," she said, looking gloomy.

"And why not?"

She shrugged. "She says I have hubris."

"Indeed."

"It's a Greek word she taught us. It means I'm too big for my britches."

"I see."

She shrugged again. "She always scolds me in front of the whole class. She quotes a poet about me. She says, 'A little knowledge is a dangerous thing.' "

" 'A little learning,' " I amended. "Alexander Pope."

"She says 'knowledge.' "

Now I shrugged. "No matter. Is she right? Do you have hubris?"

"I don't know. In my heart I don't think so."

"Perhaps you're a little outspoken, eh?"

"I take after my father. I say exactly what I think."

I cupped my chin in my hands and gazed directly at her. I said, "Now tell me more about the vision. Did the heavens open or something? Did her feet crush a serpent's head?"

Detecting sarcasm in my voice, she scanned my face. But it was deadpan.

"It wasn't that way at all," she said. "It didn't seem like magic or anything. It didn't seem like a miracle. She was just there, natural like. It was like meeting an Oriental queen in the middle of the Bronx, that's what it was like." She had spoken rather breathlessly. She glanced at the water cooler behind my chair. "May I have a drink, Father?"

After swallowing a paper coneful of water she continued. "Every morning after seven o'clock mass I spend time alone in the park. It's the only time I have to myself—I mean all to myself. After school, you see, I have to take care of my brother Mario. He's sick, you know. When I go, the park is usually deserted. It's my own special place then. Full of animals and friendly spirits and nice smells. I feed the squirrels and pick flowers and talk to God. It's like going to church twice: once to the man-made church of stone and marble and then to the God-made church of grass and earth.

"I was on my way home across the football field when I found a bird with a broken wing. As I picked it up I saw her. All of a sudden she was there, walking toward me, and my heart immediately identified her. Nobody had to tell me who she was. She was the most beautiful woman I have ever seen, even more beautiful than Rita Hayworth or Deanna Durbin. She wasn't like a ghost or anything. She was real. I mean, when she smiled I could see spittle in her mouth and . . . and there was a spot of red color in her cheeks. There was no serpent under her feet, no, Father. And no halo around her head. But I knew she was the Mother of God from the minute I laid eyes on her."

This monologue left me speechless. Now her uncompromising eyes, those blue searchlights, scanned my troubled features for a telltale reaction. Would my ruddy face betray the disbelief I felt? I yearned for a chocolate doughnut but settled for filling and tamping my pipe instead. "What happened next?" I asked in a soft, chastened voice.

"A miracle."

I puffed solemnly.

"She communicated to me without speaking a word. It was like her mind had a direct channel to mine. I handed the bird over to her. She kissed it and it flew away."

"Then what?"

"I knelt but she told me to get up. She spoke in words this time, and in a wonderful voice, just like the sound of a waterfall. Soothing and beautiful. She said that God loves me."

"I'm sure he does, young lady."

"I tried to tell her about Mario's sickness but she hushed me up, like she already knew about it. Then she told me that I had work to do."

At this point her eyes grew watery and her cheeks reddened. "She said that I must tell everyone that I have seen her, the thornless rose, and ask them to believe. But she also said something else, something I didn't understand. I can't remember the exact words but it had something to do with how difficult my job would be because this time she left no girdle to Saint Thomas." She looked puzzled and repeated the last phrase: "No girdle to Saint Thomas. What did she mean?"

I had no reply but a baffled look. "What happened next?"

"She vanished into the sun."

"Come again?"

"She went back to heaven, I guess." Her face became glum. "You don't believe me."

"I didn't say that," I said, pipe smoke wreathing my embarrassment.

"But you don't," she retorted sharply and sadly. Then she was silent, thinking intently.

"Let's put it this way," I protested. "I don't disbelieve you. I haven't made up my mind yet. Give me some time to think about it."

This seemed to satisfy her, at least momentarily.

"Whom else have you told?" I asked.

"You're the first, Father. I tried to tell my mother but she wouldn't listen."

"I'm flattered. Why did you choose me?"

"Sooner or later I have to tell everyone. That's my job. But I knew I had to pick the right person to break the news to. Somebody who wouldn't laugh. Somehow you seemed like the right one."

I made a courtly little bow and then asked, "Why didn't you tell your teacher?"

"She would have been furious. She would have accused me of lying, of committing a sin. I said she doesn't like me but it's more than that. For some reason my presence is like an insult to her. I only have to say good morning to make her look as angry as an owl."

"Now, now," I admonished, although my own infrequent reflections on the nun's character had confirmed this judgment. "You mustn't speak disrespectfully of your teacher."

Our eyes met and she seemed sadly resolute. "I'm sorry but I'm just telling the truth."

I could not debate the point. Her candor and intelligence had completely disarmed me. I was convinced that, if she was not a true visionary, she certainly was something more than a hysterical and imaginative child. Frankly I found the whole matter intriguing and a welcome break from the drone of parochial affairs. This remarkable girl was, if nothing else, a fascinating psychological subject. I wanted to know more about her. So I asked: "You didn't tell your family about this?"

She looked sad and reflective. "I wanted to tell my mother, as I told you. But she was so upset when I didn't bring bread home for breakfast that I never got the chance."

"And why didn't you bring the bread home?" I asked through gusts of pipe smoke. "Did you forget?"

She shook her pigtailed head. "Our Lady changed the loaf into red roses. She made another miracle."

I made a mental note to consult reference works in the rectory library. The details of this so-called vision sounded familiar, echoed themes from stories of the Assumption and other scenes from Church tradition. What was going on here? My instincts told me that the kid was no charlatan. Although my reading of Freud in those days was discouraged by the Church I still was vaguely aware of possible psychological explanations for her behavior. Something about this girl made me rule out completely any conscious deception. Or did I? I glued my gaze to her, contemplating the possibility that her angelic appearance deceived me, that this dewy freckled face masked a liar.

"Where do you live, Lucia?" I asked.

"Bayside Avenue."

"You have brothers and sisters besides Mario?"

"I also have a half-sister. Rosemary."

"How sick is your brother?"

"Very sick," she answered in a tone of quiet resignation. "The doctor says he won't live to become an adult. He has Cooley's anemia. It's a bad blood disease."

"And you love him very much?"

She nodded fervently.

"Of course you want him to get well."

"Of course. I pray for him every day."

"Do you often think that a miracle will happen to make him well?"

"I pray to Jesus and the Blessed Mother. If they wish to,

they can cure him." She gazed into my eyes. "Isn't that so?"
I flushed at the direct challenge to my faith. "Yes," I replied hesitantly. I continued the questioning: "Do you sometimes dream about the Blessed Mother performing a miracle to save Mario?"

She looked troubled. She knew what I was driving at.
"No," she said.

"Are you a very imaginative child?"

Now furrows appeared in her smooth brow. "I saw Our Lady, Father. I saw her."

"You're a good girl, Lucia. Faithful and devout. Do you know what the 'power of suggestion' means?"

"I saw her, Father."

"I'm not implying that there was no one at all in the park the other morning. Perhaps a stranger . . ."

"She cured the sick bird. She turned bread into roses."

"Maybe the bird regained its strength and the bread got lost in the grass. There are many possible explanations."

"Don't you read the Bible, Father? Don't you believe in visions and miracles?"

Her words stung. She reminded me of Thoreau's phrase about ministers who spoke of God as if they enjoyed a monopoly on the subject. "Yes, I believe," I replied sheepishly. "But they are not everyday events."

"Are they someday events? If they can happen in olden times why can't they happen in 1941? God is still with us."

"I often wonder."

Pipe smoke curled around my head and silence reigned between us.

"Do you believe me?" she finally asked.

Again I was flustered. I stammered: "My child, it's not . . . it's not important whether I . . ."

"Oh, but it is. Our Lady commanded me to make people believe."

"I have an open mind. But you can't make people believe just by asking them to."

Her eyes, pools of innocence, widened. "How then? How do you make people believe?"

It was disconcerting to be stumped by such a basic question

17

about my profession. "If I only could answer that. I am not a sage or a saint but a simple parish priest. Faith is a mystery, a gift from God. One must seek grace . . ."

As platitudes sprang glibly from my lips she brooded in Sicilian beauty. It was as if she swiftly took my measure and now was humoring me. Yet I could not stem the flow of drivel, the steady trickle of evasion and ratiocination.

". . . a wise man named H. L. Mencken calls faith an 'illogical belief in the occurrence of the improbable.' It's as good a definition as any."

She sighed. "You don't believe me. I must find a way to make people believe." Dejected, she rose from the chair.

I rose too. "And if I did believe? Then what?"

"Others might believe. I must make many believe."

"And then?"

She stood there, sallow hands tugging at her knitted cardigan. She looked puzzled. "I don't really know. I guess I'll have to wait for instructions."

"So you expect to see her again."

"I think so."

"At a specific time? Did she make an appointment?"

Again her face betrayed annoyance at my mocking tone. "No. I just think she will appear to me again, that's all."

I tapped the bowl of my pipe on the ashtray and glanced at the Gothic-numbered wall clock. It was three-thirty, time to get ready for the poker game with Father Moore and the seminarians. "Let me know what happens, okay?"

She nodded demurely.

"In the meantime I would advise you not to go around talking about this. You know, not everybody is as open-minded as I. God only knows what they'd say or do. At best you'd be ridiculed."

She pointedly withheld comment on this advice. She picked up her book bag and undid the clasp. "Before I go I want to give you something."

I smiled absently.

She took a small object out of the bag and laid it on the desk. "Good afternoon, Father Fogarty," she said with dignity, and walked out the door.

I picked it up. The petals, once satin-soft, were turning brittle to the touch, shrinking in the remorseless stream of time. The scarlet coat was trimmed with purple now, the royal hue it wore as it faded with majesty from this form into a new and secret life. It had no thorn.

3

❧ ❧

That evening I lost over five bucks at poker to young Tomlin, the pockmarked seminarian whose motives for wanting to don the soutane were, in my judgment, highly suspect. *Mea culpa.* I couldn't get my mind off the little girl. As soon as I got home I went straight to the rectory library to prepare for a bit of research in apocrypha and hagiography.

In my room later, over two Swiss cheese sandwiches and a glass of milk, I dipped into several volumes of the Catholic encyclopedia and various lives of the saints. Before long I found the reference I was seeking. The legend of the Girdle of Saint Thomas was connected in art and apocryphal writings to the Assumption of Mary. As the Virgin was being assumed bodily into heaven she was often depicted handing down her chastity belt to the apostle Thomas, doubting Thomas, who once again required proof of a miracle. This was a fairly esoteric detail for an eleven-year-old. I wet my thumb and continued reading.

Ah, here it was: "The rose without thorns." This was a frequent symbol of Mary, who was free from original sin. It probably stemmed from a legend spun by Saint Ambrose, the honey-tongued Bishop of Milan. He wrote that a thornless rose grew in the Garden of Eden. After the Fall it sprang thorns to inflict pain along with the perfume of pleasure on sinful mankind. Another obscure touch for an inventive little girl. I drank the milk to the dregs and closed the books.

The window near my desk overlooked Weir Creek and Eastchester Bay now mirroring the full moon, a rippled yellow specter in the black depths. Boat hulks bobbed in the cradling tide. It was time for bed.

I tossed and turned on my mother's linen sheets. I couldn't concentrate on my bootleg copy of *Finnegans Wake* and thrust it back under the pillow where the housekeeper, Mrs. Carney, wouldn't see it when she woke me in the morning. Moonlight bathed the room. Could Lucia, at her tender age, be a faker? Could she have such a precocious knowledge of traditional myths and miracles? Was she perhaps the victim of an elaborate and cruel hoax? The questions buzzed like mosquitoes in my brain.

The big question remained submerged. Why was it so hard to accept the other possibility? Were we purveyors of religion all infidels at heart? Why hadn't I pursued my boyhood dream and become a riverboat captain? Finally a dreamless sleep descended.

Lucia was up at dawn as usual. As she put on her school jumper she too looked out a window at boats in the bay brushed gold by the morning light. She awoke, as always, alert and clearheaded. She braided her hair, rinsed her teeth and said her morning prayers before the plaster statue of Saint Lucy that sat on the dresser.

Her parents were already downstairs in the kitchen, wrapped in silence. Ettore Buonfiglio sat at the enamel-topped table, reading *Il Carroccio* and sipping a concoction of egg yolk, milk and coffee. His cocoa brown eyes were still misty with sleep. His second wife, Serafina, sister of his late first wife, Gemma, hovered sulkily over the sputtering gas stove, cooking peppers and eggs for his brown bag lunch. Idly, she poked the food in the skillet with a spatula and from time to time threw him glances of annoyance.

Ettore was a brown and muscular man of forty, a skilled bricklayer with an avid interest in politics. As he gripped the newspaper his biceps strained against the cotton shirt-sleeves. Displeasure was carved into his rugged face. He was reading a day-old editorial in the Italian-language sheet criticizing FDR for a "slap on the beautiful face of Italy" in the President's statement a few months earlier about the old country's declaration of war against France. Roosevelt had said: "The hand that held the dagger had struck it into the back of its neighbor."

The language used by Roosevelt made the bricklayer's blood boil—the picture it painted of Italians brandishing knives. He was in passionate agreement with the philosophy expressed in the editorial, that FDR's choice of words had besmirched the honor of a noble race many members of which had helped put him in office. Ettore himself, a loyal Democrat since the day he got his citizenship papers, had voted for Roosevelt in 1932 and 1936. He did not consider himself a Fascist but a patriot and heartily disagreed with Pope Pius XI's description of Mussolini as the "man sent us by Providence." He was too sharp-witted not to recognize that Il Duce was the *pagliaccio* of international politics. But Ettore's grandfather had fought with Garibaldi's Red Shirts in Sicily and his pride was stung by Roosevelt's words. He, like many of his compatriots, felt grateful to America not only for giving him his daily bread but for fighting side by side with Italy during the Great War and helping to liberate much of the country from Austria. But he smarted under the lash of discrimination, rankled, for instance, at the Immigration Acts of 1921 and 1924 that restricted Italians.

He sipped his eggnog and muttered under his breath. Bah, American propagandists. If the United States was entitled to the Panama Canal and Puerto Rico and the Philippines, why couldn't Italy pass through the Suez Canal and have Malta and Corsica? They used a double standard. He turned the page in disgust.

Serafina took little notice of his grumbling. She was a weary dispirited woman. A panorama of unmade beds, dirty dishes, soiled clothes, scuffed floors and potato peelings obscured history and politics and blocked her vision of the higher things in life. Her dusky beauty, once the envy of her native village, had faded with time and worry and her youthful illusions had fled at a premature age. Tart by nature, she had soured completely as a result of her son's illness.

The doctors called it thalassemia major, or Cooley's anemia. Words for languid eyes that watched other children play. They talked about a deficiency of red corpuscles. Serafina saw only the pallid cheek and knees revolving listlessly around the hub of a tricycle wheel.

The doctors prescribed therapeutic transfusions. This meant monthly expenditures of boyish tears and hard-earned dollars. They said it was a sickness borne over Mother Sea, afflicting children of Mediterranean blood. To Serafina it was a curse.

There was no known cure.

She sprinkled the peppers and eggs with spices. She grumbled, "Who left the icebox door open all night, that's what I wanna know." She sniffed over the skillet. "The milk is-a spoil and these eggs . . ." She shook her head. "These kids, *per la morte di Dio.*"

Silently as a sprite, Lucia had entered the kitchen and stood at the sink filling a glass of water from the tap. "Morning, Mamma," she said after drinking.

Serafina did not return the greeting. "Have some crumb cake for breakfast," she urged. "You' thin as a rail."

"You know I can't eat before communion," she said evenly. "Is Mario still asleep?"

"I'm shoo God don't want you to starve to death," Serafina said, removing the food from the skillet and placing it deftly between two slices of leftover Italian bread.

"I won't starve. Is Mario all right, Mamma?"

"He's joost tire', that's all," she said wearily, wrapping the sandwich in wax paper.

At that moment Rosemary entered the kitchen, yawning and flopping her slippers. She headed straight for the coffee pot.

"Look who's up," said Serafina sardonically. "*La principessa.*"

"Lee' me alone, huh?" said Rosemary, drinking the coffee straight.

"What happen? You have a nightmare?"

She ignored the taunts and sat at the table with her father, who was still glumly reading the newspaper. "Morning, Pop," she slurred. "You still here?"

He scowled. "Car's late. It always happens when it's Peppino's turn in the car pool."

Rosemary was dressed in an orange silk robe that she had bought at discount at Alexander's on Fordham Road, where she worked as a sales clerk. She was nineteen, buxom and pretty, and wore her glossy black hair in stylish waves. Her job and contributions to household expenses gave her an air of haughty independence. She also kept steady company with Peter Giusti, whose father owned the butcher shop on Saint Raymond Boulevard.

She sipped and sang: "Hut-sut Rawlson on the rillerah and a-brawla, brawla, soo-it."

Ettore angrily looked up from the newspaper. "Stop that noise," he grumbled. "You call it moosic?"

She pouted. "I call it *mu*sic," she said, deriding her father's accent which was not as heavy as his wife's because he was out in the world more than she.

Rosemary turned to her stepmother. "Can you cook me a fried egg?"

Serafina's face wrinkled up. "What's-a matter? You cripple? I look like a servant?" Still, she took an egg and cracked it on the skillet. It spluttered in the pan.

Lucia pecked her mother on the cheek. " 'Bye, Mamma."

"Don't forget the bread this morning," Serafina called after her.

When Lucia returned from mass Ettore and Rosemary had already left for work and Serafina was upstairs making the beds. Mario was sitting at the kitchen table, toying with a cup of *caffe latte*.

"Hiya, Buddy," she greeted him by his nickname. "I have fresh bread for you."

He looked at her with eyes big as saucers in his pale face. "I'm not hungry," he said irritably.

She smiled tolerantly. She knew the source of his ill-tempered behavior. It was almost time for his transfusions. "Come on, soldier. It's still hot from the oven." She grabbed a jagged bread knife and cut the round loaf deftly across her chest. "I'm starved myself."

A bar of sunlight touched his slender fingers as they drummed the enamel-topped table with impatience. He was small too for his seven years and birdlike in appearance. "Okay," he said, relenting. "I'll have a small slice."

Eagerly she sat down at the table and smeared butter on his slice. "Atta boy. You need your nourishment for schoolwork."

"Can't go to school," he said dourly, nibbling at the bread like a wren, pecking crust under a bobbing pointed nose. "Have to go to the doctor." He made a face. "I hate it."

"I know, Buddy. But the transfusions give you strength."

Now he dunked the bread into the mug. "How come the other kids get to go to school? How come they don't need transfusions? How come I get tired all the time?" The anger in his eyes veiled a pleading look.

She looked down at the tiles. "You're sick, Mario. You know that."

His voice cracked. "Why me?"

"Only God knows."

His eyes smoldered. "Did God make me sick?"

"I don't know how to answer that."

"I hate God."

She had a stricken look. "You don't mean that."

"Yes, I do."

"It's a sin to say that, Mario. You've reached the age of reason."

"I don't care if it's a sin. I don't care."

Her face softened. "God will forgive you. He loves you even if you say you hate him. He sees your heart. A good father loves his children, no matter what."

His eyes were glazed with welling moisture. "I didn't mean it."

"I know you didn't."

He buried his face in his hands. "Will I ever get better?"

She came around the table and enfolded him in her arms. Her fingers ruffled his silky hair, her breast absorbed the tremors of his body. She raised her wet eyes upward, as if searching the cracked-plaster ceiling for the answer.

"You *will* get better," she said, tasting salt from the stream of tears. "By the Mother of God, you will."

4

※ ※

Sister Mary Rachel was a rather beautiful woman. She was tall and graceful and had the kind of ripe figure that even the severe lines of the clerical habit could not disguise. The clean lines of her regular features were, if anything, enhanced by the frame of wimple and headdress which gave a pleasing geometric cast to her face. But her blue eyes could glint with cruelty behind her rimless glasses especially when, as now, they beheld Lucia Buonfiglio arriving late to school.

She towered over the girl, hands on hips, mouth tightly shut. "So glad you could make it today."

Lucia flushed and lowered her eyes as titters rippled through the classroom. "I'm sorry, Sister."

"'I'm sorry, Sister,'" the nun mimicked, causing the wave of laughter to swell. She stilled the merriment with a glare. Then she turned to Lucia. "Have you an explanation, young lady?"

Lucia's eyes were still lowered. She had stayed home longer than she had realized to comfort her brother. But that was not a legitimate excuse so she kept silent.

"Well?" the nun demanded.

Lucia shook her head. "No," she said in a barely audible voice.

The nun's face too was red, but with anger mingled with an odd suppressed pleasure that deepened the color. She loomed like a dark colossus over the trembling girl. "I suppose you think you're too smart to benefit from my English lessons, eh?" She paused. "Answer me," she barked.

"Yes, Sister. I mean, no, Sister."

A long hard silence reigned. "You will stay after school," the nun said, "to wash the blackboards and empty the trash baskets. After that you will write one hundred times, 'I will not come late to school.' I'm letting you off easy. Go to your desk."

To a chorus of whispers Lucia hurried to her seat.

"Quiet," the nun commanded, tapping the desk with a yardstick. When the tumult had subsided she said, "Before we were so rudely interrupted, Maureen Hayes was diagramming a sentence. Return to the blackboard, Maureen."

As the hum of classwork resumed Lucia put her books into the desktop, took out her marble-covered composition book and filled her fountain pen from the inkwell carved into the desk. She dimly heard the scratching of pens and the singsong of Sister Mary Rachel's voice but could not focus her concentration on the subject. The reprimand still filled her with shame and her brother's unhappiness also occupied her thoughts. Above all she was consumed with worry about what she perceived as a heavenly commission to spread the word that Mary had come to Pelham Bay Park. So far she had told no one but this priest about the vision and she was sure that the Blessed Mother was disappointed in her performance so far. How could she expect her prayers for Mario's cure to be answered if she was so faint-hearted, if she failed the Mother of God Himself? Her lateness to school bruised her conscience all the more although she was well aware that Sister Mary Rachel needed little provocation to show her dislike for her.

Despite the distractions, Lucia survived the English lesson without being called upon. During the following history class, Sister Mary Rachel (who taught all sixth-grade subjects) asked her a question about the Lewis and Clark expedition which the girl answered correctly and succinctly, eliciting no more than a grunt from the grudging teacher. Catechism followed. In this class the teacher would hold a verbal quiz on the life of a specific saint about whom she had lectured on the preceding day. Yesterday's subject had been Catherine of Siena.

The nun walked up and down the aisles, solemnly posing the questions and tapping pupils on the shoulder with the yardstick for the answers. Many children stood mute and others gave incorrect replies and Sister Mary Rachel became more and more furious. Her face looked hard and cold under the hanging lamps.

"Disgraceful," she said gravely. "You should all be ashamed of yourselves."

A sepulchral silence descended.

Then Joey Fazio burped out loud and Sister Mary Rachel slapped him resoundingly in the face. The corpulent sulky boy's face grew red as a tomato but he did not cry although it was obvious from the way he continued to wince that the slap still stung. He blew air into his fat cheeks until they looked like big red balloons but still he did not cry.

Soon the nun had recovered her composure and usual flinty expression. The lesson resumed. She posed more questions about Saint Catherine's journey to Avignon and finally her agate-hard eyes fell on Lucia. The girl was ordered to her feet.

"You don't seem quite with us, young lady. Are you paying attention?"

"Oh, yes, I am, Sister," she answered readily.

"We'll see." She fired a question: "What are stigmata?"

Lucia did not hesitate. "They are wounds Our Lord received when he was nailed to the cross and pierced by a spear as they miraculously reappear in the limbs of a saint or mystic."

Without praising the rote answer the nun let fly another question: "In what year was Catherine of Siena born?"

"1347?"

"Is that a question or an answer?"

"1347."

Another salvo: "When did she die?"

"1380."

"Which Pope did she persuade to come back to Rome?"

"Gregory the Eleventh."

The other children marveled at the speed and accuracy of her answers but the nun looked displeased. "Sit down," she ordered.

The very sight of the girl set her teeth on edge. She could not fathom the cause of this antipathy but she was not prone to speculate on it either. She didn't question her instincts. She knew only that the girl always activated her volcanic temper. Had she delved more deeply she might have discovered the source of her pleasurable hatred. If only the girl were impious and dull instead of devout and bright the nun might have had an easier conscience, a convenient cloak for the odd illicit impulses that Lucia kindled beneath the black robe. What a sweet face the girl had to mask a rebellious heart. She continued prowling the aisles and barking questions.

Lucia, for her part, was puzzled and saddened by the teacher's obvious dislike of her. She prayed for a way to win her over but she refused to play the serf. There was a core of resolute pride beneath the girl's submissive exterior. She had the pliant strength of a young tree. She would bend but not break under the buffeting storms of the nun's unjust anger and this quality only served to further infuriate the teacher.

The morning wore on. The teacher concluded the quiz and began to lecture on the life of Mary, immediately riveting Lucia's attention. The nun now sat at her desk under an ivory crucifix. As she spoke she tapped the yardstick to emphasize various points in the lecture. The late morning sun reflected off her spectacles. She spoke of the Presentation of Mary in the temple, when the Virgin was consecrated to the service of God—an event which inspired the name of the Presentation nuns, the order to which she and the other teachers in the school belonged. She spoke of the Virgin's betrothal to Joseph of the House of David, of the Annunciation by the Archangel Gabriel that she was to bear the Messiah, of the Visitation to her cousin Elizabeth when she was pregnant with John the Baptist, of the Nativity, of Mary's Passion at the death of her divine Son, of her own death, called the Dormition, and of her triumphant Assumption into heaven. Fact or fable, related though it was by the unpleasant teacher, this story captivated Lucia. Her inner picture of the Pieta was as strong as if she had been standing before Michelangelo's masterwork. She wept.

Suddenly she felt her head being yanked backward.

"Ow," she yelled involuntarily.

Dickie Powers had pulled her pigtails again.

Sister Mary Rachel glared at her with obvious venom. "Stand up!"

Lucia stumbled to her feet.

"Now what was the meaning of that outburst?"

Lucia was mute. She would not tattle.

"Answer me," demanded the nun.

"I . . . I can't." She would not lie.

The nun's face puffed up like a blowfish. "The impudence! What do you mean you can't?"

"Please, Sister. It wasn't my fault."

"Then why did you disturb the class?"

Lucia could not utter a word in her defense.

All color drained from the nun's face. "You're an illmannered, rebellious child."

The girl bowed her head.

"And sinful too."

This brought her head up sharply. "No, Sister. Please." Her face became contorted. "Oh, I'm so sorry."

"How dare you make noise when I'm talking? Especially when I'm telling the story of Mary, Mother of God. It's like spitting on the Virgin's veil."

Lucia gasped for breath while the class buzzed with whispers at this remark. "Oh, heavens, no, please don't say that." Tears sprang to her eyes.

The nun sneered. "Crocodile tears," she said contemptuously. "Wipe your eyes and stand up straight." Her eyes narrowed and she growled, barely audibly, "You Sicilians are all alike. Sinners and gangsters, the lot of you."

Lucia stopped crying. The trembling that had shaken her limbs now ceased. She suddenly got from some unknown reservoir an infusion of courage. And she knew what she had to do.

"I would never spit on her veil," she said calmly. "I have seen her."

The nun was puzzled into immobility. "What do you mean?" she finally asked.

"I have seen the Blessed Mother. I have had a vision, like Saint Catherine and Saint Joan."

"How . . . dare . . . you," the nun fumed.

"Yes, Sister," she said, passionately now. "The Mother of God appeared to me in Pelham Bay Park. She told me to tell everyone that she has come and so I'm telling you."

The class burst into nervous laughter but now the words poured forth in a torrent. "She said she was the thornless rose. We must have faith in her."

"Liar," the nun shouted.

"I'm not lying. God has chosen me."

"Blasphemer," she said, gripping the yardstick.

"No," the girl said firmly.

The nun made a visible effort to calm herself. Lucia's steady refusal to back down from the announcement had greatly unsettled her. She was not used to such intransigence. Needless to add, this was the first time in her ten years of teaching that a student had claimed to have had a mystical experience. She didn't quite know how to handle the matter. She knew one thing for certain: she could brook no mutinous behavior from any of the little rats or discipline would break down completely. She would have to make an example of this girl.

"So Our Lady has appeared to you, has she?" She spoke in a low controlled monotone. "So you fancy yourself a saint, do you?"

"No. You can't be a saint before death. But I am a tool of God . . ."

"Shut up," she shouted, silencing the murmuring class as well as Lucia. "I will tolerate no more such sinful talk. 'Pride goeth before destruction,' young lady, 'and a haughty spirit before a fall.' Come to the front of the classroom. Now march!"

Fear made Lucia's heart flutter and she tripped as she walked down the aisle. She knew what was coming and steeled herself for it.

"Three on each hand," said the nun ominously. "And each time you dare pull back you get another one."

Lucia stood erect and silent. She saw a wren alight on the classroom window ledge.

"Now hold out your left hand," the nun ordered, gripping the yardstick.

Lucia shut her eyes and held out the shaking hand, knuckles upward. She heard the quick rustle of the nun's robe as the yardstick struck. One.

The hand burned with pain. The impulse to pull back had been strong but she resisted it. Tremors ran through her thin body down to her fingertips but she held out the hand again, this time palm upward. She knew the routine. The ruler fell. Two.

Her hand was on fire and tears stung her eyes. She wanted to cry out but the shout caught in her throat. Again she held out the hand, knuckles up. Three.

The third blow had been delivered with even greater force than the other two and the flaming hand crumpled like burning paper.

"Now the other hand," said the nun. "Palms up."

Gingerly she held out her right hand. The habit swished. One.

Pain still stung the hand at her side when the right hand received the blow. She winced but kept the hand fairly steady. The palm throbbed as blood rushed through the arteries. She turned her knuckles upward. Two.

This time the girl doubled over, grabbing her wrist, muffling a cry in her throat. "Please, Sister," she said. "I think my finger . . ."

The nun's stony glare silenced her. She again held out her hand. Three.

The hand was a limp shaking mass of hot pain. The ordeal was over now but the ache remained, especially in the right index finger which was already swollen. Lucia stood there, rocking her shoulders back and forth, stifling tears, waiting.

"Go back to your seat," the nun commanded.

"I think my finger's broken. My index finger . . ."

"Back to your seat," she shouted.

Fifty pairs of wide eyes followed Lucia back to her seat. Pain was chiseled into her ashen face. The lunch bell then resounded through the hushed classroom.

Instead of going home for lunch Lucia went by herself to the nurse's office. The finger had been broken. As the nurse applied a splint the girl felt more relief than pain and an odd sense of satisfaction. She had suffered a little but so what? She had performed her duty. She had planted the seed. She felt like Theresa of Avila or Joan of Arc. The finger throbbed with pain but her heart pounded with happy excitement. She felt that she could face anything, the flames of scorn, the rack of ridicule, anything. Faith would flower and Buddy would be saved.

5

❧❧ ❧❧

I Postulator envision the gloating smile of the Promoter of
Faith as he struts like a pheasant before the stony visages in
the Congregation of Rites. I hear him scoff in the summation
of *animadversiones*—a broken finger? Is this the substance of the
positio super virtutibus? Is this all she suffered *in odium fidei?* Far
more is required before unveiling the image and chanting the
Te Deum. Far more must be established before publishing the
Apostolic brief and celebrating the pontifical mass in the hol-
low-toned basilica under a shower of clerestory light.

I concede the objection. So the narrative continues.

The episode was told to me in the confessional box where
Lucia, haunted by scruples, came one rainy Saturday evening
about five days after her finger had been broken. Her words,
muffled and diffident, floated through the cross-hatched cage.
She couched the story in formulas of Penance but I shall attempt to reproduce it in a more palatable way.

She had gone fishing that afternoon under the Hutchinson
River Bridge where the waters ran into Eastchester Bay. Three
hours had passed without a nibble and the sun sat low on the
horizon. She felt languorous and serene, for once untroubled
by recent events. She smelled with pleasure the briny odor of
the marshes, heard the lament of the gulls and felt at peace.

Soon, though, storm clouds gathered over City Island. She
pulled in her line and, after removing hook and lure, wound it

around the bamboo pole. The sky darkened abruptly, like a room where the lamps are suddenly extinguished. It crackled moodily with distant thunder. She shivered in her cotton dress. By the time she reached Hutchinson River Parkway it was spattered with raindrops. She was running for shelter in a copse of trees when she saw him cycling toward her and hallooing over the thunderclaps.

They arrived simultaneously at the grove of cedars. "Hi, Lucy," he said, braking the bike and climbing off. "You got caught in the rain, you got caught. Me, too."

Basil Two-Times was so named for this habit of repeating phrases. He was sixteen and backward, so to speak. Peach fuzz bristled in his angular chin and his slack mouth formed an affable smile. Rain pelted their leafy canopy.

"Hello, Basil," she said, smiling back at him and surveying the dark roily skies. "God makes a storm in no time flat, doesn't He?"

Eyes glistening, he looked up at the turbulent clouds. "I love the rain," he said. He turned his vacant gaze on Lucia. "It makes me shiver, it makes me." His mouth lolled like a puppet's.

She combated a sense of uneasiness. She was one of the few neighborhood children who did not openly deride Basil Two-Times and she stood in mortal fear of offending or hurting him. But he disquieted her, especially now as they huddled together under the branches, listening to the tattoo of the rain.

"Whatcha doin' here?" he asked.

"Fishing," she said, clutching her elbows for warmth. The wet dress clung to her long haunches and she was ashamed.

"I was at Split Rock caddyin'," he said proudly. "I got a job, I got. Did you know that? Sometimes I make fi' dollars a day."

"That's nice."

"I could buy a lot of things, I could. I could buy you a present." There was an avid look in his eyes as he waited for her reaction.

"That's . . . that's very sweet," she stammered. "But I don't need anything."

An expression of eagerness was stamped on his otherwise bovine face. Saliva appeared at the corners of his mouth. "You cold?" he asked.

She nodded vigorously, hugging her arms. Strands of hair were matted to her forehead and her braids were coming loose. He didn't offer her the slicker he was wearing. "You look nice wet, you look."

She glanced at the road, which glistened like a lake in the rain. She tried to mask the flush of color in her face. The downpour had abated now to a steady pit-a-pat. "I'd better go home," she said.

The fixed smile faded from his face. "You'll get more wet, you'll get. You'll catch cold. Don't you catch cold from the rain? That's what my mommy says."

"I'll catch cold standing here," she said.

Suddenly his face grew animated, as if he had been struck by a sudden thought. "I know a hut, I know. It's in the woods near the golf course. I go there sometimes when I'm huntin' squirrels. Ever hit a squirrel with a slingshot? It's a lotta fun. We could go to the hut and get dry. Nobody lives there but the spiders."

She fought against a feeling of revulsion. "No. I don't want to go there."

"The spiders won't hurt you. I can kill them."

"No, please. I don't want to."

His face darkened. "So you'll stay wet, you'll stay."

Now her fathomless sympathies had been tapped. She didn't want to add to his burden of hurt. She gently touched his arm. "I'm sorry, Basil," she said. "It's nothing personal, you know. It's just that I have to get home."

He noticed the splint and bandage on her finger. "What happened?"

"Nothing really. Just broke my finger."

"Does it hurt?" he asked avidly.

"Sometimes. Just a little, though."

"Gee, how'd it happen, huh?"

"It was an accident," she said, thinking this was not a lie. She felt that the nun had meant to punish her but not to break her finger.

"I broke my ankle once, I broke. Fell off the bike." He grimaced in recollection. "Boy, did it hurt."

"That's too bad, Basil."

"Then my mother hit me too. She said I should ride more careful, I should." His vacant eyes grew flinty with barely bridled anger. "I hate her sometimes, I do."

"You shouldn't say that."

"When I'm bad she says she'll send me away, she'll send. She'll put me in the crazy house where I belong. She won't though. I'll beat her up and run away."

"You wouldn't."

His eyes flashed. "Yes, I would. I can beat her up, I can beat. I'm strong."

"You should forgive her if she's mean to you," she advised. "It's better that way."

While he pondered this suggestion with an absent expression under his knitted brow she looked again at the slanting rain. "I have to go home," she announced once more.

"I'll give you a lift," he offered. "On the frame bar of my bike." He saw hesitation in her eyes and quickly added, "I've done it before, I've done it. It's real easy."

"No, thanks."

"It's because you don't like me."

"No, Basil, that's not it at all."

"Then why? You think I'm a dimwit, you think. Like everybody else."

"That's not true. I think you're nice."

He smiled in an odd way. The rain now was a misty drizzle. "You hold the fishing pole and we can put your bucket in the bike basket." He tapped the metal bar that connected the saddle to the fork. "You can sit here, you can sit. I'm strong. I can pedal good."

After hesitating yet another second she decided to do it. She put the fishing bucket into the basket as he climbed onto the saddle. He smiled and again tapped the bar invitingly.

She gripped the fishing pole and sidled up to the bike. Her dress clung to her flesh. As she hoisted herself up to the bar she felt his hand brush against her buttock. She flushed crimson.

"Here we go," he cried, standing up and pedaling into the rain.

The bike raced down the slick parkway. There were no cars in sight. Lucia gripped the pole in one hand and the handlebars in the other. She shifted her weight uneasily on the bar. Her braids had come loose and the wind lashed her streaming hair. She felt frightened and mortified.

His chest strained against her shoulder as he pumped the pedals. He grunted and breathed heavily. There was a texture to his breathing that suggested more than physical effort. His knees now and then brushed against her wet shanks.

The gleaming trees fled backward as they crossed the bridge and headed toward Westchester Avenue. He leaned hard into the rain, pumping vigorously. His pelvis thrust closer to her squirming hips. She felt a knot of flesh, both soft and hard, like a bunch of grapes, in his pants, pressing against her backside and she began silently to cry.

"Stop the bike and let me off."

He kept pedaling and panting, pretending not to hear.

"Stop," she implored. "Or I'll jump."

He choked out the word: "Why?"

"Please," she said. "Oh, please." She sobbed audibly.

He braked the bike and she jumped off. Her sandaled feet thrashed through puddles as she ran toward Bayside Avenue.

Without breaking stride she glanced back at the rain-soaked figure on the bike. Even through tears of humiliation he seemed to the relentlessly sympathetic girl a forlorn and pitiable creature, forming a macabre silhouette of loneliness against the electric and tempestuous sky. She ran harder and harder and tears and rain mingled on her cheeks.

She sat on the bed, combing out her hair. She wore a terry-cloth robe over her freshly bathed body and wool socks on her cold feet. The paroxysms had subsided now, replaced by murmurous breathing, high and barely controlled like the whine of wind through pines. She followed a high-pitched course of reflection: she had cleansed her body but what of her soul? Confession, the purgatorial rite, cleansing and cathartic. She would follow the angel pilot to the second kingdom and puri-fication. But first one final physical act.

The scissors lay on the dresser. She gathered up her wavy, waist-length hair and picked up the bevel-edged blades. Her hand was steady.

6
❦❦ ❦❦

The crowd roared like a roused animal. It was only the first round and Baer had Louis hanging over the ropes headfirst. Now the champ was flat on the apron. In the June heat of Griffith Stadium 25,000 prizefight zealots shouted themselves hoarse, encouraging the young giant to come in for the kill.

Sitting by the radio Ettore Buonfiglio did not echo the call. He never forgave Buddy's brother Max Baer for dethroning Primo Carnera in 1934. So he was rooting for Louis, black as he was. *Avanti, campione.* Chop him down like a tree.

Lucia sat in an armchair by the screen door, basking in breezes from the bay and reading a book. She grimaced at the sounds coming from the radio, the husky voice of communal bloodlust, the urgent clang of metal, the grunts of combat and crunch of flesh and bone. She tried to block out the sounds and concentrate on the book, a biography of Saint Augustine by Rebecca West. Bright as she was, it was heavy reading for one her age. She just couldn't focus and shut the book with a loud clap.

The noise startled her mother, who was rocking on the porch swing just outside the screen door. "Loo-chee," she demanded, "what happen?"

The girl rose from the armchair and went outside to join Serafina on the porch which was bathed in an amber light. "Oh, nothing, Mamma," she said. "Just closing my book."

Serafina inspected her daughter's face. "Sound joost like a gunshot." She swatted her cheek. The porch was infested by mosquitoes.

Pouting, Lucia sat in a wicker chair. "That prizefight. It makes me so sad."

Serafina huffed. "Let 'em beat each other's brains out for all I care." She waved a straw fan in front of her gloomy face.

They sat there serenaded by crickets and the lulling voice of the summer night. The palm-leaf fan whispered before Serafina's chalky ravaged face. Across the street the waters of the bay lapped murmurously on the rocks, a sad crooning song in their ears. The fan swished, swished, and swished.

"What's the matter, Mamma?"

Serafina was silent, her eyes riveted to the brackish bay water which shimmered in the dappling moonlight.

"Please, what's the matter?"

Serafina turned to face her daughter. The fan stopped. She looked at Lucia lingeringly, blending love and bitterness. Then the expression softened. "It's Mario," she croaked.

In the fifth round the kid with the Star of David sewn on his satin trunks still pursued the shuffling and bobbing Brown Bomber. The crowd surged to its feet when he opened a gash over the champ's left eye. Rivulets of blood trickled down Louis's tawny face now contorted with anger and pain. He stalked his muscular adversary as the round ended.

Newly fledged crickets danced and fiddled on the muddy banks of Eastchester Bay. The maritime air was perfumed with honeysuckle and roses. Lucia wept softly.

The rustle of the palm-leaf fan resumed. "He says they will continue the transfusions joost in case it makes a difference. But . . ." Serafina bit her thin lower lip, bit it hard and punishingly. "What's the use anyway? What's the damn use? All the money's gone. Maybe we must sell the house."

Lucia dabbed at her eyes. "How long do they say, Mamma?"

The woman wore a pained but defiant expression, free of both sorrow and hope. "Maybe a year. Maybe less." She displayed the stoicism of her Sicilian ancestors who bore earthquakes and famine.

"They could be wrong," Lucia said. "Doctors sometimes make mistakes."

Serafina smiled a thin smile. "Stop kidding you-self."

"We'll pray," Lucia said.

Serafina snorted.

"Oh, you must have faith, Mamma. The Holy Mother will help him."

Serafina's derisive laughter rippled through the scented night.

In the sixth round Louis came crouching out of his corner, a wounded bruin, deceptively dangerous. Referee Arthur Donovan danced around the combatants, who poked each other with tentative blows. Then Louis exploded with savage combinations and sledgehammer jabs. A right to the jaw put Baby Baer on the canvas.

Ettore leapt to his feet, tensing his own steely muscles and punching the air. "Knock 'im cold, you sweet black son a muh bitch."

At the count of seven Baer regained his wobbly feet. Immediately Louis's right hand connected again, toppling the tall youngster. As the count reached ten Baer again found his feet and sought balance. Donovan waved the fighters on. But then Baer swayed and fell. He was out.

Ettore picked up the radio set and kissed it. "That's five bucks Herskovitz owes me. I could kiss you black ass."

Weeping, Lucia swept past her father and rushed up the stairs to her room. He hadn't even noticed her.

She lay on her back on top of the covers and stared vacantly at the ceiling. Outside the window a whippoorwill cried unseen. Her body was immobile even though the tears flowed. Lamplight illumined her dark cropped hair and sparkled in her liquid eyes. The tears streamed without effort, without outward emotion, as if they came from a spigot. Her mind raced. She could scarcely believe what her mother had told her. Whimpering softly, she caressed her scalp under the thatch of hair that had grown only a little since she had mown it three weeks earlier in a frenzied act of propitiation. Her confessor had soothed her scrupulous conscience with assurances that she had not sinned. But the news about Mario had rekindled the fire of guilt that burned under her blooming breast. Was this her penance for mounting the bike? Would her brother have to suffer for her transgressions? Her thoughts raced in the noisy summer night, fueled by doubt and fear, emotions reflected in her sweet telltale face, bathed in moonlight, translucent as porcelain.

Our Lady had abandoned her, she thought in a febrile state. The alarm clock on the night table ticked, a monotonous voice of recrimination. She failed in her mission. Her young body burned on the griddle of her consuming conscience and she began to thrash about on the bed.

Soon she grew still again. Quiescence, cold and fearsome, stole over her limbs. She realized what was happening. Her faith, this treasured thing, was disintegrating right then and there. Was she mad? Who was the lady she met in the park? Who was that impostor in white, flatterer of her sinful and prideful nature? Did it ever happen at all? Was she mad, mad, mad, mad?

Take my Vergilian hand. Let me lead the red-hatted tribunes down the pudic path of a girl's dreams where things are reversed like photo negatives, where man may be the fancy of a shade. Come with me to the darksome wood and see what flared up in Lucia's troubled brain.

Bloodied boxers danced and feinted there. The blind, the deaf, the dumb, the lame, lepers and demoniacs reared as spectral supplicants before her inner eye. Sister Mary Rachel flapped around in the guise of a vampire bat. Basil Two-Times was a gangly marionette pedaling back and forth across a makeshift stage.

Now from a distant quasar of her mind came a great light, pulsing then bursting into fireworks. She saw Christ spiked to the cross and coming toward her in a stream of light. An impulse like a magnet pulled her toward Him. She sat up somnambulistically in the bed. Then from the scars of His wounds five shafts of blood shot toward her, to her hands, her feet and her side where the Roman soldier's lance had entered. The five wounds seared with pain.

She awoke, beaded with perspiration but calm. Though

racked with bodily pain she felt serene. She looked out the window. The silver moon was fading in the rush of dawn. She looked down at her body. She had slept with her clothes on. She stumbled out of bed to get a drink of water, to rinse the taste of bitumen from her mouth. Stillness reigned in the house. She returned to the bed, doubled over with pain. She hurt all over, in her hands, feet, side and groin. What was the matter?

Excitedly she examined her hands. It was just as she suspected. She hurriedly removed her stockings and inspected her feet. Here too were the marks of her answered prayers. She wriggled out of her jumper and slip. Yes, right below the rib cage. Oh, the blessed pain! There was a triumphant smile on her face. The gift of faith had been restored to her. Our Lady had not abandoned her. It was all true, all flesh-and-blood real like the sticky liquid that oozed from those tender wounds, like the scarlet kiss of Christ.

She sank back into the bed and slept.

7

Serafina shook her daughter by the shoulder. "Wake up, sleep-head. You missed mass."

Lucia surfaced from the depths of sleep and sat bolt upright in bed. "Oh, no!" She rubbed her eyes and looked through the window at leaden daylight, the grayness of a gathering storm. "What time is it?"

"Eleven," said her mother, picking up clothing strewn over the floor. "You threw your clothes all around. What's wrong with you?"

"Why didn't you wake me?" she moaned. "There's no late mass on Saturday."

Serafina looked at her through narrowed eyes. "What's wrong? You didn't even wear your nightgown."

Lucia was silent. The memory of last night flooded back, quickening her pulse. Did it really happen? She lacked the courage to look at her hands.

As she folded the discarded clothing Serafina's face was a gargoyle of displeasure. "Don't answer me. I'm only your mother, that's all." Her face registered shock now as she saw the bloodstains on the sheets, big brazen blotches of red, unfolded like overripe roses. "What's this?" she demanded.

"Don't be afraid, Mamma." Lucia was determined to tell her mother all about it now, about the vision of Mary and the wounds of Christ and the work that God had summoned her to perform. She was determined to enlist her natural mother as an ally in the mission assigned her by her spiritual mother. "Don't be afraid. I'm blessed. It is the blood of Christ on these sheets."

And she poured out the whole story to Serafina, who listened with a blank expression for a long time. She sat on the edge of the bed, brooding as the child chattered on. When she was through, Serafina said, "Get up."

Lucia looked at her questioningly.

"Get out of bed," Serafina ordered.

Lucia obeyed. She was dressed only in underpants. Her angular shoulders jutted forward and curved down to her chest, still concave and vulnerable, dotted with the puckered buds of her nipples. She shivered in the cool gray morning air.

"Take down your pants," Serafina commanded wearily.

Lucia stepped out of her underpants, more obedient than ashamed. She felt mortified as her mother examined her pubic area.

Serafina finished probing and motioned her daughter to put her pants back on. The woman shook her head from side to side, clucking her tongue.

"The blood of Christ, eh? What a foolish girl you are. Don't you know anything?"

Lucia was sitting on the bed, blushing with shame and confusion. "What do you mean, Mamma?"

"About life, I mean. Don't you know anything about life? It's about time you got saints and virgins and Christ out of your mind. You got to grow up sometime."

"Please, Mamma."

Serafina looked stern. "You have a wild imagination. Stop dreaming. You not a baby anymore."

"I'm not dreaming," Lucia said softly but firmly. "I have seen the Virgin Mary and I have received the stigmata."

Serafina snorted in ridicule. "You became a woman last night."

Lucia was mute. At first she didn't understand but soon it dawned on her. She looked down at her hands. There were no wounds, no scars, nothing.

Serafina reached the door. "Make your bed and come to breakfast," she said.

For the next two weeks Lucia suffered under the flagella of doubt and worry. Mario was growing more listless every day. His eyes were round and haunted. Lucia still went to mass every morning, still prayed, chanted hymns and lit candles regularly. But her faith seemed to wither as the season grew sultrier. She performed the rites of devotion mechanically, with only a fraction of her usual fervor. Her worries were so distracting that her schoolwork suffered too, and final exams were approaching. She hardly cared. She felt estranged from God and His Mother and very unhappy.

In June all the students had to attend a mass in honor of the Sacred Heart to whom the month was dedicated. Everywhere loomed effigies of the passional Christ, on calendars and holy cards, in classroom and cafeteria. He was invariably depicted as a handsome ascetic with auburn tresses and beard. He wore a faint smile, veiled by suffering, and pointed with his forefinger to his breast where there lay exposed on his robe a russet heart bleeding from the pricks of a crown of thorns. His vermilion smile haunted Lucia.

The students filed into church. They genuflected in unison to the click-click of the principal's tin frog. They entered the pews which were separated by grade, sat down and waited for the mass to begin. Scattered coughing ruffled the silence.

Lucia thumbed through the missal in what was for her an unusually absent mood. It was oppressively hot. From her front pew vantage she could see flies swarming like mocking apostates around the tabernacle. The organist played in the background.

The congregation rumbled to its feet as the priest and altar boys entered from the sacristy. Lucia became immediately alert. One of the altar boys was Basil Two-Times. Flustered, she used her missal to try to follow the mass. The flames of guilt and confusion had been fanned in God's own house.

As the mass progressed she made a firm effort to tame her maverick feelings by focusing on the passion of Christ, tapping her fountainous supply of empathy for His suffering. She imagined what it must have been like to feel the lash of the Roman scourger and, worse, the sputum of the mob. Her head pounded too with the pain of the thorns bristling from the crown of mockery. Her shoulder was bruised by the bark of the tree that He had been forced to carry, her knee skinned from the fall. She felt Veronica's soothing cloth and then the spikes piercing the flesh of hands and feet, the lance plunging into the rib cage. She tasted vinegar on her parched lips. She almost experienced the sweet deliverance of death.

The Sanctus bell rang, dissolving these thoughts. Beads of sweat had formed on her white brow. She looked toward the altar. Basil Two-Times caught her eye and smiled with pride. While he moved around the altar he gathered up the skirt of his cassock daintily and performed his missal duties with an air of great officiousness. A wave of nausea swept over her. She fought it off and resumed praying.

She riveted her eyes to the statue of the Sacred Heart at the side altar, focusing on the plump bleeding heart. Her heart too felt filled to bursting with blood and sympathy. Her school beret felt tight on her head like a wreath of thorns. Shafts of sunlight streamed through the arched windows and illumined her damp face, giving it a strange pellucid quality. The intensity of her praying grew.

The time came to receive Holy Communion. Sister Mary Rachel rose from her place in the pew and motioned to the first child in the row. The children solemnly began to file out, hands forming tents of prayer. They streamed out of the pew in one body, a caterpillar of communicants. In a virtual trance Lucia brought up the rear.

She passed Sister Mary Rachel without noticing the cold steel of her gaze. Mumbling a litany of prayers she knelt with the other children at the altar rail. She prayed in near-ecstasy, oblivious to all her surroundings except the bobbing ciborium and the image of the Sacred Heart. Basil held the paten for the priest but she didn't notice him now either. She was consumed with an inner passion. She had entered her Gethsemane. The ciborium came closer.

The wafer clung to her tongue as she bowed her head in prayer. After a long time she rose from the altar rail and began walking back to the pew. Without chewing, she swallowed the small wafer. Suddenly her knees wobbled. She staggered down the aisle. As she reached the pew pains stabbed her hands, feet, side and temples. Her clothing felt damp. She fell writhing to the tile floor.

The congregation gave a collective gasp. In mid-motion the priest stopped dispensing communion and his mouth dropped open. Sister Mary Rachel balled her fists and glared in disbelief.

8

Unfortunately I was not an eyewitness to the remarkable event just described so I am not competent to give direct testimony before the learned curiales. On the afternoon in question I was—and I'm too old to be embarrassed about it—nursing a sherry hangover.

But many parishioners who were present told me all about it in gory detail later. Under questioning Lucia herself had but a faint memory of what had happened. The version of the parishioners, students, and teachers, while admittedly subject to the inevitable embellishment of collective fantasy, was nonetheless consistent enough to be credible on the major points. Many of these witnesses, by the way, are undoubtedly still alive and available for summons by the sacred congregation.

After she fell to the church floor Lucia soon stopped writhing and entered what appeared a cataleptic state. While the children and teachers stood dumbstruck, Father O'Herlihy rushed to her aid. But he soon was stopped dead in his tracks by what he saw.

Blood was everywhere. It stained her stockings and jumper. It gushed forth from gaping wounds in her hands and at her temples. Her very eyes, wide and blue as the Mediterranean, were bleeding profusely.

Yet she seemed to be in no pain. There was a rapt, even beatific expression on her ashen freckled face.

In a few moments the bleeding stopped and Lucia emerged from the ecstatic state. The nuns cleaned her up and rushed her to the office of Dr. John Papajohn, two blocks away. Papajohn's nurse, Sophie Mariano, a black-eyed beauty with a taste for gossip, helped dress the wounds. Which leads us to Albert Dunlop. In the interests of objectivity I will try to restrain my dislike of the man.

In 1941 Albert Dunlop was a star reporter for the *Bronx Home News,* now defunct. He was forty-two years old. He had curly brown hair, a ruddy complexion, pointy faunlike features and—to put it bluntly—a Faustian heart. Externally at least, he was a model of order amid the chaos of the city room. His clothes were always crisply pressed and uniform: he invariably wore a shirt, tie and sleeveless V-neck sweater under a tweed jacket. He affected the look of an English squire. The left arm of his jacket was tucked into the pocket. Dunlop had misplaced the arm somewhere in the forests of the Argonne.

The fingers of his right hand were long and manicured, graceful as a courtesan's. With them he laboriously typed his stories—stories that often made the front page of his newspaper. They were successful not for grace of style or syntax. In fact Dunlop's writing prowess—or lack thereof—prompted a colleague to observe maliciously that the one-armed reporter wrote with his feet.

Still his stories usually made the front page for he was skillful in another way. He was, in the lingo of journalists, a consummate "pipe artist." In other words he was not reluctant, if it suited his purpose, to invent the facts.

He was doing that right now, pecking away with his elegant right hand at the black Smith-Corona typewriter that dominated his small well-ordered desktop. This time he was making up a story about a Bainbridge Avenue auto mechanic named Anthony Hess to whom he gave twenty dollars to say he was the cousin of Rudolf Hess, the Nazi minister who had recently parachuted into Scotland on a personal peace mission or act of lunacy. Dunlop paid the mechanic, a German immigrant, to say that the Nazi leader had been a notorious homosexual in his youth. Hess, locked up somewhere in Britain, was not likely to deny the story or sue the *Bronx Home News.* So

52

Dunlop had no fear of exposure as he pecked out his lies with his long and lonely hand.

He wrote "thirty" at the bottom of the page, signifying the end of the story, and plucked the copy from the typewriter. He didn't bother to blue-pencil his crippled prose. He was not afflicted with self-doubt. Whatever he wrote went straight into the hands of avid editors and usually landed on the page one form in the composing room. And the editors often rewarded him with pats on the back, free ballpark tickets and Christmas bonuses. Albert Dunlop's byline sold newspapers.

He smiled with satisfaction and handed the article over to a waiting copy boy. He glanced at his wristwatch: seven-thirty. Dunlop, a man with a predilection for plump women, smiled again. He had a date in half an hour with one as plump and juicy as a ripe peach. Her name was Sophie Mariano.

She felt uncomfortable sitting alone in the cocktail lounge on Fordham Road. In those days only one kind of woman did that. He had promised to be there first but he was late as usual. She should have known better than to get mixed up with a newspaper reporter.

Sophie nursed a gin fizz, trying to ignore the stares of the men. Under her breath she cursed Al Dunlop. He treated her shabbily. Why did she put up with it? She sighed into the carbonated drink: because she was sold on the skunk and, let's face it, the passing of years had a way of increasing her tolerance.

She didn't look thirty, she thought, gazing into the mirror behind the bar and fluffing her banana curls. She was very pretty and knew it. Everybody told her that she had beautiful skin, white as milk, soft as satin, still unlined. Her hair was dark and plentiful, cascading when unbound all the way down to her waist. Her figure could be called bountiful and she had the kind of breasts that turned men into infants.

One of these sucklings had been sitting at the other end of the bar, downing boilermakers to screw up the courage to approach her. He finally did.

"Buy you a drink?" he asked with a lopsided leer.

"Beat it, buster. I'm waiting for someone." She had said

this without even looking at him, without seeing his waxed mustache and pomaded black hair.

The rebuff brought color to his cheeks and an insult to his lips. "Who ya waiting for? Ya pimp?"

Suddenly he yelped in pain. Dunlop's remaining arm, the knuckles on the hand of which he had dug into the man's ribs, was very, very strong. "Get lost, cocksucker," Dunlop said.

The man whirled around, poised to fight. But something in Dunlop's eyes, eyes that had seen unimaginable horrors in northeastern France, deterred him. Then he noticed that his adversary was an amputee and this gave him a face-saving exit.

"No harm meant," he said and was gone.

Dunlop snapped his fingers at the bartender. "Irish whiskey."

Sophie brooded over her gin. "You don't have to use language like that around me. Where you been, anyhow? You're late."

He flipped a five-dollar bill on the bar. "What language? You mean 'cocksucker'? That's the only kind of language his type understands. Besides," he added, smirking, "you know what it means, don't you?"

She blushed. "That's not the point." She turned to him in a fury. "Oh, you make me so mad sometimes."

He smiled and sipped his drink.

"Why are you late? If you were on time these creeps wouldn't bother me."

"Had a late story. Sorry."

This crumb of apology placated her. She finished her drink and he ordered another one for her. She was quick to anger, quicker still to melt. She wanted him so much to be the right fellow for her. She didn't even suspect that he was already married.

She toyed with the swizzle stick, sticking out her petulant lower lip, growing expansive toward him, falling back into the comfortable habit of endowing him, the debonair one-armed newspaper reporter, with romantic qualities that were alien to his real nature. "Where you taking me tonight?" she asked, bouncing her big butt on the stool in happy expectation. "Let's go to the movies, okay? I wanna see the new Gary Cooper film, *Sergeant York*. It's playing at the Paradise."

He stiffened. "Forget it," he snapped. Dunlop needed no reminders of the Battle of the Meuse-Argonne.

She pouted but recovered quickly. "Then how about *Road to Zanzibar?* I hear it's real funny. It's playing right around the corner."

He downed his drink, grimaced and ordered another. "I'm too tired. I thought we'd go to your place, whip up an omelet and fool around."

Blotches of anger appeared on Sophie's flawless skin. "You never take me anywhere anymore," she whined. "Please, Al. I wanna go out. I work hard all day. I need some relaxation, some fun."

"Sure," he said. "We'll have fun at your place."

"You mean *you'll* have fun." She continued to pout. To Sophie sex was a matter of joyless submission—which suited him just fine. "Can't we eat out at least?"

"Okay. We'll stop off at the White Castle."

She rolled her eyes. "For this I missed 'The Goldbergs'?"

He looked at her with open cruelty. "Forget it then."

She knew what he meant. Plenty of other trout in the stream. And this approach never failed to panic her. She slipped an arm around his waist and massaged his ribs under the sweater. "I understand, honey. You're tired. Mamma understands."

He made no reply, just gazed straight ahead in that cold flinty way, smug in the knowledge that he could bend her to his will. He lit a cigarette and savored the straight fiery whiskey.

She continued to massage his ribs and coo, "Yes, Mamma understands. She understands . . ." Her waxy face in the bar mirror looked desolate.

Duke Ellington was playing "Moonglow" on the Victrola. He lay on top of the covers, smoking, basking in satisfaction. He wore black socks and nothing else. She tossed and turned on the bed, her abundant flesh shimmering like pale jelly. He was so distant and uncommunicative, she thought. Why did he never whisper endearments and confess his secret fears? Why did he never really make love to her? She did everything he wanted, performed every carnal act to please him. She might even have enjoyed it if he responded with more than the complacent passivity that he always displayed. He took her lovemaking for granted and it depressed her so.

She tried to engage him in conversation. "Whatcha working on?" she asked. "An interesting story? Another scoop?"

"Nothing much," he said curtly, blowing wreaths of smoke at the ceiling. "Same old stuff."

"Your job is so interesting and exciting," she said. "Wish I had a job like that."

"Yeah," he said absently.

She nestled her head on his chest. His body grew rigid. He didn't like it one bit when she became all lovey-dovey. He continued smoking moodily.

"My job is so depressing," she said, snuggling closer to his poker-stiff body. "All I ever see is sickness, blood and death. It's so depressing."

"Uh-huh," he said, his mind wandering to the trenches near Verdun.

"That Dr. Papajohn, I gotta hand it to him, though, He's always so calm and philosophical. I don't know how he does it."

He squashed out the cigarette.

"You should have seen him today when this girl was brought in. Boy, what a strange case she was!"

He remained silent while she chattered into his ear, whispered incessantly like the wind. "She was bleeding like Jesus Christ on Good Friday, she was. From her hands and feet and side and head. Why—she even bled from her eyes. I swear. It was the weirdest thing you ever saw. She didn't seem terribly sick or anything. Didn't even seem to be in pain. It happened in church, they said." She crossed herself to ward off evil.

Suddenly his interest was aroused. "What happened in church?"

"Weren't you listening?"

"I was thinking. Tell me again."

"This little girl. She received the wounds of Christ. You

know, like those weird saints you read about. She just started bleeding after she took Holy Communion."

"Stigmata?" he asked excitedly.

She shrugged. "I guess that's what you call it. All I know is what Dr. Papajohn had me write in the report. He called it 'the psychophysical repercussions of ecstatic trance.' Said it was one for the medical books. Boy, I'll say!" She shivered in his reluctant arm. "It was scary." She hoped he would wrap his arm around her; but he remained motionless, his mind racing.

"What's her name?" he asked.

"What's whose name?"

"The little girl's, of course," he said impatiently.

"Oh, I don't remember. Lucia something. Some long Italian name. She was real pretty, though."

He roughly removed her head from his chest and rose from the bed.

"Hey," she protested. "What's the matter?"

"Nothing," he said, reaching for his pants.

"Why don't you stay overnight?" she asked pleadingly.

"Can't." He buckled his pants and lit another cigarette, striking a wooden match with his thumbnail.

"Why not?"

"That's my business." He blew out two quick gusts of smoke. "What time does your boss get in tomorrow morning?" he asked, beginning to knot his tie.

"Eight o'clock. Why?"

He made no reply. When he had donned his Panama hat he waved and winked at her. "See you in the morning."

The door closed behind him. She tugged the bed covers up to her chin, just below her pouting mouth. She didn't notice that the needle had reached the end of the Duke Ellington record. A tear trickled down her cheek as the needle scratched unheard.

9

❧ ❧

The stimulation of Dunlop's reporter instincts led him the next morning to the Fairmount Avenue office of Dr. John Papajohn, general practitioner.

The premises were as unpretentious as the good doctor's personality. He was a bachelor whose life was more or less confined to this two-story brick building in which he lived and worked. He used the ground floor as his office and the top floor as his residence. Each room was crammed with medical books and books on Roman history, Papajohn's passion. His crusty cigar-smoking exterior and raspy Bronx accent masked the soul of a scholar and, to some degree, of an esthete.

He was also a dedicated and skilled practitioner of the healing arts, able to treat bee stings and botulism with equal aptitude. It was not yet the era of specialists.

The house was set back behind a front yard where the doctor grew tomatoes. His shingle was hung behind a rusty storm door. Dunlop pressed the doorbell.

The front entrance was elevated two steps above ground level so the next thing he saw as the door swung open were Sophie's prominent breasts under the starched white uniform. He raised his eyes to her anxious face.

"Good morning, Al. Come in."

He removed his Panama and stepped on the straw welcome mat.

"I told him you wanted to see him," she said. "He was mad at first but then he said it was okay. He said I shouldn't tell the private business of patients outside the office. Oh—I was so mortified."

"But this thing was witnessed by at least five hundred people."

"He was mad anyhow. I'm such a blabbermouth." She took his hat and hung it on a clothes tree. "Come this way."

She led him into the outer office where there sat a reception desk under a big map of the Roman Empire and an inscription by Vergil: "Under whose auspices Rome shall extend her rule/ Over the earth and rise in spirit to Olympus."

"Have a seat," she said. "I'll tell him you're here." She entered the inner office with a worried look.

Dunlop sat in the waiting room alone. He browsed through an issue of *Time* with a picture of Bing Crosby on the cover. As he scanned the magazine he mentally composed his questions to the doctor. He sensed that he was on the threshold of a sensational story and the prospect excited him. He was in fact already forming preconceptions about the case, envisioning headlines and leads to which he would later slant the events to conform. His usual modus operandi.

The door opened. "He'll see you now," Sophie said.

Dr. Papajohn was a handsome man of Greek extraction. He had an athletic build and a cheerful disposition. Despite a vandyke, he looked more like a laborer than an erudite physician. His sparely furnished office reeked of cigar smoke.

The handshake was firm. Tobacco smells clung even to his person. "Have a seat, Mr. Dunlop."

He sat down.

The cigar box was out in a flash. "Care for a Havana?"

Dunlop selected one. "Don't mind if I do, thanks." As Papajohn lit the cigar for him he noticed that the doctor's hands were callused.

"Thanks for sparing me some of your time, Doctor," he said, after settling comfortably into the chair and expelling a gust of smoke. "I know how busy you are."

"Yes," Papajohn said curtly. He had been quietly sizing up the visitor, absorbing and storing details of dress, speech and mannerisms for later use in reaching the reasoned judgment he made about every person with whom he came into contact. He fancied himself, as we all do, a keen judge of character. And he was right. In agreement with Aristotle he regarded a man's character as bestowed by nature and thus immutable. So he puffed on the cigar and mentally thumbnailed Dunlop.

His interest of course was attracted by the amputation for which he had surmised a probable history: a war injury, he rightly guessed. This disability, he thought charitably, might account for the haunted look in his visitor's eyes. Or it might be insincerity.

Papajohn broke the conversational ice. "So you want to write a story about the little girl with the stigmata."

"Yes. If you don't mind."

Papajohn grunted. "You'd write it whether I minded or not."

Dunlop bowed in silent acknowledgment.

"Yeah," continued Papajohn. "That's why I agreed to see you. Wanted to make sure you got the facts straight."

"I'll try."

"You'll do more than try. I don't read your paper and I don't know your byline so I have no preconceived notion about your ability or integrity. But I do know that exaggeration is the first rule of journalism. I know from experience. My father, you see, was a newspaper editor in Rhodes until the Turks cut short his career. Where'd you lose the wing?"

"In a ditch in France."

"Thought so." He bit the cigar reflectively. "Well, at least you won't be shipped over there again when we finally go in to bail out the Frogs once more. You must have been just a kid."

"Nineteen. Old enough."

Papajohn grunted in agreement. "Ever consider wearing a prosthetic device?"

The visitor shook his head, deftly taking a notebook and pencil from his jacket pocket and resting them on his lap. "Nah. I manage okay."

Papajohn shrugged. "Just a physician's curiosity. I'm not trying to drum up business. Okay, ask your questions. I expect patients."

"Who is she and where does she live?"

Papajohn grimaced. "I feel a conflict here, I don't mind telling you, between loyalty to the idea of a free press and protecting the confidentiality of my patient. But I also know it won't take much for you to find out who she is without my help. Tell you what: let me get the family's permission first, okay?"

"Fair enough. How long will that take?"

"I'll do it today. Don't worry. You won't get scooped."

"It happened in Saint Bonaventure's, didn't it?"

"Yes. During mass."

"Could you describe the symptoms?" he asked, scribbling notes.

"She simply had wounds, wounds on the upper portions of her hands and feet, on her left side and at her temples. They weren't very deep but they were fresh and bleeding. There was also evidence that she had been bleeding from her eyes. Most remarkable."

"I believe your diagnosis was 'psychophysical repercussions of ecstatic trance'?"

"Fancy jargon for hysteria. What else could it have been? Hundreds of people witnessed it. The wounds appeared spontaneously. It was simply amazing."

"Did you treat the wounds?"

"It was a case for a head shrinker, not a sawbones," said Papajohn, squashing out the cigar. "The wounds seemed to be healing spontaneously too, right before my eyes. They weren't very serious to begin with."

"What causes this to happen?"

The doctor chuckled. "You'll have to consult a higher authority than me, Mr. Dunlop. These cases are rare but not unheard of. Surely you've read about Gemma Galgani and Theresa Neumann. While these cases all have been documented in the medical journals, no satisfactory natural explanation has ever been given."

"You mean you think it's supernatural?"

"I'm a scientist. Nothing's *super*natural. But many things are beyond our grasp. Our intellects, in case you haven't noticed, are rather limited. Breuer and Freud—two pretty fair thinkers, you'll have to admit—made attempts to explain and treat the phenomenon of 'conversion or transference neurosis.' Pardon my jargon again. Want me to spell that for you?"

"I can handle it."

" 'Conversion neurosis' is just another way of saying 'hysteria'—which tells you nothing, I know. Science is often a matter of licking labels on things. Pure phenomenology. The more we know the less we know, Hegel notwithstanding. Socrates was way ahead of him. Pardon the digressions. I'm getting a little highfalutin, I realize."

"Not at all, Doctor."

"I'm a frustrated lecturer."

Dunlop merely grunted. He was indeed impatient with the man's intellectual meandering but was too crafty a reporter to cut him short. He knew from long experience that he might find gems of information amid the slag. A wagging tongue was a reporter's best friend.

"Freud traced hysterical symptoms to bottled-up emotional energy," Papajohn continued. "Sexual energy, to be exact, with its origins in early psychic trauma. The symptoms could be anything, ranging from something simple like hives or a tic to what Lucia experienced—autohypnosis, catalepsy and the appearance of stigmata . . ."

Dunlop gloated inwardly. So her first name was Lucia. Then he recalled Sophie mentioning that name too.

Now oblivious to Dunlop's scratching pencil, caught up in his own discourse, Papajohn rambled on. "How does conversion occur? The Freudians like to use metaphors from electricity. Scientists are always reduced to employing literary devices to capture the butterfly of truth. There—didn't I tell you?"

Dunlop lay down his pencil to swat a fly from his forehead.

Papajohn continued: "The Freudians say that the wires connecting emotion-production with symptom-production somehow get crossed." He relit the cigar and puffed expansively. "Try to imagine a fuse box in the psyche, a defense mechanism that is triggered when the current of emotion flowing from the subconscious to the conscious mind exceeds a safe amount. What happens? You blow a fuse and break the circuit, so to speak. But the energy has to go somewhere so it becomes converted into hysterical symptoms. You following me?"

"Every step."

The doctor nodded. "So the patient gets twitches or spasms or tics or loss of voice or heartburn. The patient loses appetite or develops a taste for plaster or bleach; becomes constipated or feels the urge to defecate all the time; gets headaches, abdominal cramps, you name it."

"But that's a far cry from stigmata."

"Look—we know that we have a nervous system that operates independent of the will. But we don't have all the answers. We know that sometimes a conversion mechanism causes a demonstrable alteration of organic function. Autonomic imbalance, it's called. In other words, an emotional shock can cause anything from gooseflesh to vagotonia, a severe slowing of the pulse rate. We have discovered no accurate calibrator of individual passions. The same emotion that produces goose bumps in one person may produce bleeding wounds in another. If psychosomatic disturbances can cause a peptic ulcer, my friend, then why not the gaping wounds of the crucifixion?"

"But an ulcer takes time to develop."

"How do we know how long the stigmata had been developing? Perhaps since infancy. When they appear it may seem miraculous and spontaneous but they may have been festering for years in the body or the mind or wherever these things take place."

Dunlop's cigar had been smoldering in the ashtray on the doctor's desk. From time to time he put down his pencil and took a few drags. He did this now. Then he asked: "How are such symptoms treated?"

"Breuer used hypnosis and so did Freud for a while until he switched to free association. Hypnosis is a plausible treatment, especially if you believe that the symptoms are autohypnotic. The problem with mystic stigmatics is that they usually have no desire for treatment. They don't want to avoid the effects of sympathetic union with Christ and, who knows, maybe they're right. The thing that bolsters the spiritual explanations for these phenomena is how frequently successful treatment is achieved by yogis and Christian Scientists and visits to shrines, things of that sort."

"You don't actually think that what happened to Lucia in Saint Bonaventure's was a miracle?"

"I don't know," Papajohn said irritably. "It all seems miraculous to me. Miracles are mundane to a family doctor. Remember you're talking to a guy who regularly delivers babies."

Dunlop scribbled furiously.

Papajohn arched an eyebrow. "Did I say something particularly interesting?"

"Just a good quote." Duplop picked up the cigar and tapped it on the ashtray. "What was she like, this Lucia?"

"How did you know her name?"

The reporter flushed. "You mentioned it just now."

The doctor looked annoyed with himself, then shrugged it off. "She was quite pretty and seemed to have great dignity for one so young. She had presence, a certain aura about her."

"Would you say she was saintly?"

"Don't put words in my mouth. What's 'saintly' anyway? She seemed like an ordinary little girl except for this certain quality."

"A spiritual quality, would you say?"

"You might phrase it that way."

The reporter scribbled again. "Did she say anything?"

"She seemed to have very little recollection of the event. This is not surprising. She was in an ecstatic trance, a state of self-induced catalepsy. Just before the seizure, she said, she had been contemplating Christ's passion. It's the classic sequence."

"Was this her first seizure?"

"Not exactly. She told me she had received the stigmata two weeks before but the wounds had disappeared by morning. I questioned her mother and discovered that she had had her first menstruation that night. Freudians would have a field day. As a rule exterior stigmatization is preceded by what is called 'invisible stigmata,' strong pain in those places on the body where visible marks later appear. Sometimes they never appear. This is the kind of stigmatization historians tell us Theresa of Avila and Catherine of Siena had."

Making his impatience obvious, the doctor pushed back his shirt-sleeve and looked at his wristwatch. "Now it's getting late and I have work to do."

"Just a few more questions . . ."

"Save them."

"Did you take photographs of the wounds?"

"I instructed Miss Mariano to do so. They have not been developed yet."

"May I have a print?"

"Not on your life. They are part of the patient's private medical file."

"My paper would be willing to pay . . ."

The doctor's rugged features froze into a mask of contempt. "That is most insulting. I'll see you out."

Dunlop swallowed hard. Tact was not one of his strong points.

In the reception room Sophie followed their movements with wide-eyed wonder. Neither her boss nor her boyfriend looked very happy.

At the door Dunlop turned to the doctor and offered his hand. "Sorry for what I said."

Papajohn grasped the hand grudgingly.

"Thanks again," said the reporter. "You'll call me when you've spoken to the family?"

He nodded. "I'll ask them just as I promised."

Sophie watched Dunlop make a slight bow before donning his straw hat and making his exit. The look on his face made her feel uneasy.

10

I anticipate the loud protests of the Devil's Advocate: Catholic doctrine sees no intrinsic link between stigmatization and sanctity. Heathens and heretics alike have been seared by the bloody brands. The marks have appeared on the limbs of Jansenists and on the bodies of Moslem ascetics who meditate on the battle scars of the prophet Mohammed. Amen. I concede the point.

Then too, as Papajohn so ably explained, the wounds may spring from purely natural organic functions, the symptoms triggered by a malfunction of a psychic mechanism that causes sexual energy to go haywire. The learned doctor, by the way, has unfortunately passed away and cannot give testimony. (At least not in the lower courts.)

But neither are stigmata considered marks of disgrace. Otherwise Saint Francis of Assisi would head the list of the dishonored. In fact the Church makes no a priori decision on the question, allowing us to celebrate or not the stigmata of saints in the liturgy. No, I do not propose that these marks of violence taken by themselves brand my client as a candidate for sainthood. They compose only a fragment of the picture, a thread in the argument. But I'm weary of disputation. The coffee perks. The foreshortened landscape of an old man's night looms ahead. *Carpe noctem,* I say, inverting Horace. I have a story to tell.

Dr. Papajohn kept his word to Dunlop. He phoned Serafina Buonfiglio to inform her that a newspaper reporter wanted to interview Lucia. As the girl's doctor he advised against the interview, fearing that publicity might aggravate her condition. But he left the final decision up to Serafina and her daughter.

The woman was aghast at the prospect. She was thoroughly baffled by what had happened and didn't know whether to regard Lucia's strange affliction as infamy or honor. Though steeped in the superstitions of her ancestors, Serafina was not religious in the strict sense. Yet she feared intangible and invisible things.

"I don't want my child's name in the newspaper," Serafina whispered hoarsely into the mouthpiece of the phone mounted on the vestibule wall.

"I don't blame you, Mrs. Buonfiglio, and I won't tell him your name if you don't want me to. But, believe me, he'll eventually find out one way or the other." He was chewing on a cigar. "How is she?"

She looked dispirited, overwhelmed by events beyond her grasp. "She seems fine. The wounds—they almost all gone." After a pause she asked, "Doctor, is my daughter crazy? Is she a saint? Or do demons live inside her?"

Papajohn wore a harassed look. "Neither one, I think," he said into the phone. "She's a sensitive child, Mrs. Buonfiglio. Very sensitive. Her emotions are strong. I think she needs psychiatric care, if you ask me."

Serafina bit her lip. The strains of an aria came down the hallway from the kitchen where the radio was playing. She tuned in the Italian station every day for music and conversation to ease the boredom of housework. "You mean a head doctor, eh? So she *is* crazy."

"Mental problems are nothing to be ashamed of," he said in a scolding tone. "No more than influenza or diabetes. We are all mentally ill one time or another."

"But we don't have the money . . ."

"I could recommend a clinic. You think about it, okay?"

"Okay, Doctor."

"Keep me informed of any changes in your daughter's condition."

"I will."

"And don't get run down yourself."

"I'll try."

"How is Mario?"

"The same. He goes to the specialist again this week but . . ." She didn't finish the sentence. "There's a curse on this family."

"Nonsense."

"There must be."

"Courage, Mrs. Buonfiglio," he said hollowly. "Where is your daughter now?"

Her eyes darted to the stairway. "Upstairs resting. If she feels better should I send her back to school tomorrow?"

"I suppose so. But it'll be rough on her. Children can be as cruel as little Turks."

"She's gotta go back someday."

"Right. She may as well get the unpleasantness over with." He grimaced through gusts of cigar smoke. "Okay, I'll tell the newspaper reporter to get lost. I warn you though—he'll probably come poking around anyway. Remember, no law says you have to talk to him."

After they hung up Serafina went back to the kitchen. Through the static filtered the contralto of Diana Baldi singing "Pace, O Mio Dio." The windows above the sink faced west where the sun now sank in a blaze of glory sending orange spotlights plunging down through the clouds to light the landscape of the northeast Bronx. She was untouched by this lovely spectacle, lost in anxious reflection. A picture of FDR hung on the wall between the windows. The fading light made it seem as if his eyes were blinking. She washed a handful of potatoes in the sink. In less than an hour her hungry husband would be home.

She sat down at the table to peel the potatoes. A squadron of flies hummed around the food. She shooed them away. It angered her to think that people still had faith in a God of love, mystified her that she had spawned a daughter who she was sure would suffer for her goodness and empathy. Why had she not been able to instill in her the true lessons of life, of thwarting pain with a shield of suspicion. No. Her daughter invited suffering, bled with Christ. She knew it would all end badly.

She sliced the potatoes into small pieces for roasting. The bluebottles returned, whining over the white tubers. She swatted them with extra vehemence. She cursed in graphic language. Despite her daughter's piety Serafina cared little about sin and sacrilege or the fate of her immortal soul. For her the fires of hell already raged. She swept the potatoes off the edge of the table and into her aproned lap, gathered up the corners of the apron and carried the vegetables to the stove.

Upstairs in her monastic room Lucia lay sprawled on her bed. Her face was as hard and still as marble. Only an occasional eyeblink broke the illusion of chiseled immobility. She was thinking hard.

The stigmata had changed nothing. She still didn't know how to proceed as Our Lady's emissary. Mario's health steadily declined. And—what gnawed most at her faith—her mother's cynicism seemed to be deepening. She clutched her white rosary, the one with the ivory beads that her mother gave her four years ago at her first Holy Communion. Things had been better then. It was before they knew of Mario's illness, before Serafina's fragile faith had disintegrated. Lucia was confident that, whatever happened, Mario's untainted soul would be shielded. But what of her mother? She was guilty of what in the eyes of God was the vilest sin—despair.

Into what abyss would Serafina be plunged? Lucia's mental image of hell was a vivid picture of chasms and cliffs, of steam and flames, of winged and tailed creatures brandishing pitchforks. But these fanciful images only made tangible her quite precocious conception of hell as a spiritual state of mind, a box with no exit. The idea that a merciful God could create a hell posed no moral problem for her. She knew that God in His wisdom did not make the place directly but permitted it to exist. He made the real creator of hell when He fashioned Adam from the primeval slime. Serafina now was building her own crucible of despair. While Lucia might not have been able to express this train of thought in just such words, this was what she was thinking. And it saddened her.

Soon Serafina called upstairs. "Your father's home. Come to eat."

Ettore sat in an armchair, smoking a cigarette and reading the *Daily Mirror*. With furtive eyes he watched Lucia come down the stairs. After recent events he saw his daughter in a new light and simply didn't know what to make of her.

She went into the kitchen. Mario and Rosemary were already seated at the table, inhaling the fragrances of the meal. Rosemary sat at the edge of her chair, robust and hungry. Her brother's shoulders sagged with lack of interest.

Lucia greeted everyone brightly and sat down. She got sullen grunts in response. She crossed herself and mumbled a silent prayer.

"Ettore," yelled Serafina, carrying a steaming tureen of lentil soup. "*A mangiare.*"

Mario sniffed sourly as she ladled the soup into his bowl. "I hate lentils," he announced to no one's surprise.

"Eat," his mother commanded. "It's good for you."

"Lentils, lentils, we always eat lentils," grumbled Rosemary. "They're fattening."

"And cheap," said Ettore as he entered the kitchen and took his seat at the head of the table. "Pass the bread."

They ate in silence for a time. The second course was ham and potatoes. Stealthily Lucia glanced at Mario to see how he was eating. He nibbled at the ham.

"Drink your milk too," she urged him.

He looked up from his plate, warming to her smile. "Okay," he said, smiling thinly himself. He drank.

After Serafina served the salad she sat down again and shoveled food into her mouth without interest. Finally she said, "I spoke today to Dr. Papajohn."

Silence.

"He say a newspaper reporter came to his office asking questions about Lucia."

"What did he want to know?" asked Ettore.

"About those things," she stammered. "The wounds. You know."

Ettore frowned reflectively.

Serafina said, "I told him not to give him our name."

Ettore sliced a peach and soaked the slices in his tumbler of wine. "Good," he pronounced.

"But why?" protested Lucia. "Maybe I'd like to talk to the newspaperman."

"Don't be foolish," said Serafina.

"It's not foolish," she insisted. "Then I can carry out my mission. People who read the paper can hear the message of Mary."

Ettore raised his eyes skyward in exasperation.

Rosemary giggled.

"What's so funny?" snapped Serafina at the stepdaughter who was also her niece. She turned to Lucia. "Do you want the whole world to know how sick you are?"

Lucia looked hurt. "But I'm not sick. Who told you I was sick?"

"I don't need to be told. When you bleed from every pore."

"Christ bleeds through me. Oh, don't you see? I'm not sick."

"Do you want the world to know how cursed this family is? No. These are *le cose nostre*—nobody else's business. Let's keep them to ourselves."

Ettore wiped his mouth on a cloth napkin and grunted in agreement.

Lucia rose from the chair. "You don't understand."

"Sit down," Ettore ordered.

She sat.

He ate a wine-drenched peach. Chewing, he asked, "Did the doctor say anything else?"

"Yes," said Serafina, eyeing her daughter. "That she needs a psychiatrist."

"What's that?" asked Mario meekly.

Ettore frowned. "Never mind." The subject was almost taboo.

71

"That's a doctor for crazy people," said Rosemary. "Is anybody making coffee?"

"I'm not crazy," said Lucia.

Ettore began: "But we can't afford . . ."

"I'm not crazy," she repeated.

"If nobody's making coffee," said Rosemary, "I'll make coffee."

Serafina said, "The doctor told me he would find a clinic for her where we wouldn't have to pay."

"She's not crazy," said Mario angrily. "My sister is smart and she's not crazy at all." His eyes flashed hopefully at Lucia. "Are you?"

She shook her head.

"Basta," growled Serafina.

Ettore touched Mario's arm soothingly. "She's not bad. Just sick."

"Mental problems," said Serafina, backing up her husband. "That's what the doctor called it. He said it was nothing to be ashamed of."

"Then why can't I talk to the reporter?" asked Lucia.

"No more questions," said Ettore under beetle-brows. "Eat and shut up."

"Yes, Papa," she said, lowering her eyes to a forked leaf of lettuce.

Rosemary reluctantly got up to brew the coffee.

After drying the dishes Lucia went out to the porch for some fresh air. Mario was there rocking in a wicker chair and gazing at the muddy bay water. It was a muggy night and the tide was low and fetid, miasmic as the boy's gloomy mood.

"Hey, Buddy," she said. "Want some company?" She sat at his feet on the wood floor, leaning her back against the porch front, peeling a banana. "Want half?"

He shook his head. He hardly ever accepted offers of food but she never gave up trying. They sat in tacit communion. She bit into the banana and smiled at the scrawny boy who was dwarfed by the big rocker creaking under his ghostly weight. She smiled to mask the agony she felt, watching the minute movements of his fine fragile features.

"I'm not crazy," she finally said.

72

His eyes softened. "I know."

They lapsed back into silence. They seemed to have a mutual understanding that needed no words, a contract that was written in flesh, marrow and blood. Her smile faded. She struggled to dam back tears.

He came over and touched her cheek. "It's okay," he said, bright with wisdom. "Somehow, it's okay now." He kissed her.

She laughed through her tears and hugged his brittle bones. She kissed him on the forehead, kissed him fervently, this pawned soul whom God lent her as a brother.

11

❦ ❦

The imperatives of my role as narrator, I'm afraid, over-
power my priestly reticence. I lead you into the marital
bedroom.

The children all have gone to sleep. Ettore sits in his paja-
mas on the edge of the bed and gazes sadly at the face of the
moon riding over the bay. This voyeuristic cleric now sees the
wife sitting before her vanity, brushing raven hair stranded
with gray. She is dressed in bra and panties. I flinch at her
slack cellulitic flesh. The rustle of the hairbrush is slow and
rhythmic.

"What now?" he asked.

The brush whispered in her hair. And she made no reply.

"I don't like the idea of a newspaper reporter who stick his
nose in our biz-a-neese." He glowered at the jeering moon.

She grunted agreement and attacked a stubborn knot in
her hair. It was obvious to her that Ettore wanted to talk and
unwind but she refused to gratify him. She had in fact made
almost an art of grudging him, the man whose carnality she
regarded as the root of her trouble. She tied up her jungle of
hair with a scarf for the night and said, "Go to sleep."

He turned to her with a small and haunted look. Then he
turned away again. "I'm not sleepy."

She shrugged, picking a harvest of hair from the bristles
of the brush.

"I work like a horse all day and I'm not even sleepy." He

reclined moodily on the propped pillow, his face hound-sad. His brawny chest rose and fell under the striped pajama top. "I'm afraid for the kid. I'm afraid for her."

His eyes followed his wife's form as she ducked behind a closet door to remove her underclothes and put on a cotton nightgown. She taunted him with her silent modesty and implied reproach. He wished he could stir her to some violent feeling, even anger or disgust. Any emotion was preferable to this fixed apathy, any tinder to raise a spark. As his body tingled his anger rose.

He studied her face as she got into bed. The eyes were vacant and lusterless. The mouth was a defiant line. A breeze came through the open window and the night rattled with low eerie sounds that seemed to urge him on. He looked down at his large capable hands that clasped and unclasped as if under their own power. With all his strength and health he felt powerless and frustrated inside.

"Take a glass of wine," she suggested. "It'll help you sleep."

He was silent and motionless for a long time. Then he turned to her, riveting her vacant face with his eyes. "*Siamo maledetti*," he said. "We are cursed."

She avoided his gaze, looking instead out the window at the winking necklace of light from the Whitestone Bridge reflected in the bay. "Yes," she said.

He was mildly surprised at her ready acceptance of this idea. And frightened too. He had said it merely to test the waters. He realized that he had wanted her to protest against it, to raise arguments in refutation. Her agreement plunged him more deeply into gloom.

"I'll get you the wine," she offered, starting to get out of bed.

He placed a hand on her wrist. "No. I don't want any."

She shrugged. "Suit you-self." She picked his hand off her wrist as if it were a crab. She was afraid that her offer to fetch him a glass of wine might have been misinterpreted as a gesture of affection or even—heaven forbid—something stronger and more elemental, rather than what it was: a convenient way to snuff the wick of his sleeplessness.

At length he said, "Jesus is punishing us. She bleeds for our sins."

She scoffed. "For a man of the world, so-called, you are simple and gullible."

"She is born of sin. Mario too. That's why he's sick."

"If the Lord is so just why does he make children suffer, eh?"

He shrugged his muscular shoulders. "That's just the way things are."

"How do you know these things? You never go to church."

"My heart tells me." He lit a Lucky Strike and watched the plumes of smoke rise to the ceiling. Her silent agreement again had upset him.

She coughed in annoyance. "Do you have to smoke in bed? You burn us up one day."

"I'll put it out in a minute."

"My mother used to say, you smoke your soul away."

"So what?" he said bitterly.

"Besides," she continued with a sour expression, "the smoke, it gives me nausea."

He was sullen, but he softened as he looked at her. He squashed out the cigarette.

She rewarded him with a small smile taken from her meager supply of affectionate gestures. "Thanks. Maybe you should be like King George and give up cigarettes for the war effort."

"Humph. Tell you what—I give up polo ponies instead. Besides, he didn't give them up. He just rationed them."

"Okay. I don't read the papers as close as you do."

"And my country is not at war anyhow."

"Italy is at war."

"You forget—I'm an American citizen. America is not at war."

"Not yet anyway."

Ettore was heating up like a tea kettle now as he always did when politics entered the conversation. "And you forget another thing—my native country is not Italy but Sicily. There's a big difference, you know."

She made a face as if to say, Here he climbs the soapbox again.

But he continued the oration, a fanciful Cicero prosecuting Verres. "No matter who wins the war you can count on one thing: Sicily will be plundered. By that pig Churchill or that rooster Hitler. What's the difference?"

She frowned at the prospect of a long speech. "Okay, go to sleep."

"The Greeks raped Sicily, the Romans raped Sicily, the Saracens, the Normans, the Spaniards . . ."

She plumped the pillow and turned her back on him.

Abruptly he discontinued the lecture and looked at her through narrowed eyes. "Anyhow," he said, drawling the words, "smoking is one of my few pleasures."

She pretended not to catch the significance of this remark. "Besides talking," she said evasively. "You look like Al Capone when you smoke."

"How nice you insult me. Before or after he got syphilis?"

She scowled. "Don't talk dirty to me."

"You brought him up," he protested.

Silence reigned again while they both sulked. The chirping of crickets mocked him.

"I put out the light," she said.

Darkness engulfed the room. He tossed and turned like a man in a hair shirt. Her body was rigid and cool. She winced as his knee jabbed her hip like a hot poker. But she kept her body still. His hand crept to her full and malleable breast.

She groaned, not from passion. "*Lasciami*," she said in a cold and imperious tone. "Go to sleep." She removed his hand.

Without protest he turned his back on her and was quiet.

She sighed with relief and chased the phantom of sleep, a state—the kin of death—where she was most content. She did not hear her husband softly crying.

"We're cursed," he muttered to himself. And the brick-layer cried himself to sleep.

12

❧ ❧

nd there was one herd of many swine feeding on the
mountain; and they besought him that he would suffer
them to enter into them. And he suffered them.' "

The nun paused in the scriptural recitation and tried to
catch Lucia's dodging eye. She resumed, " 'Then went the devils out of the man and entered into the swine; and the herd ran
violently down a steep place into the lake and were choked.' "

With a thunderclapping sound the nun shut the leather-
bound book. The words still resounded in Lucia's head. She
knew the purpose of Sister Mary Rachel's lecture on devil-pos-
session was a cruel thrust at herself and it worked. Her cheeks
burned with shame.

Her classmates, who vividly remembered the stigmatic seizure, stole glances at her under the revolutions of the ceiling
fan. Despite her fiery cheeks Lucia struggled to keep her dignity. She held her head high and gazed steadily back at the
implacable nun.

"Now think about the Devil, children," she said, prowling
the classroom and brandishing the yardstick, tapping it on her
open palm. "Think hard about him."

The infernal June weather was conducive to such meditation. The nun's ivory face, jutting out from the tight black wimple, shone under a light coating of perspiration. Finally she
paused in front of Irma Lichtenstein's desk. "Who is Satan?"
she asked the plump girl.

Irma rose unsteadily to her feet. "He's . . . he's a man with horns. And he's got a long tail and hoofs like a horse."

"Wrong," said the nun, bringing the yardstick down hard on Irma's desktop. She flinched.

"I know, Sister. I know," said Joey Fazio from the next aisle, waving his hand furiously. "Call on me, call on me."

The nun glared at the boy. "Fazio, don't you dare speak unless you're spoken to. Stand up, young man."

He stood up, stuffing his shirttail back into his trousers. Unruly bangs of hair hung over his right eye. His breathing was labored.

"Who is Satan, then?" asked the nun. "And this better be right."

"He's a big boa constrictor," said the boy, puffing up with pride.

Suddenly the nun whacked him on the bottom with the yardstick.

"Ow," he yelled, his voice elevated to a falsetto. He rubbed his behind as the nun silently walked away. She stood before her desk and scanned the sea of young faces in the classroom. They seemed to her like a school of staring fish, mute frightened creatures over whom she had great if not absolute power. There was a catch in her throat, a shortening of breath as she watched their faces.

"Mary Joyce," she called out.

A gangly girl whose face was so freckled that her features were hardly discernible rose to her feet. She did not seem frightened by the teacher. "Yes, Sister."

"Do you want to try giving an answer?"

"Satan is a fallen angel," she said confidently. "He was thrown out of heaven by God."

"Right," said the nun. "He is not a man but an angel. He is not a snake but an evil spirit. Good, Mary. You may be seated."

A few hands shot up like flags in the classroom.

"Yes, Claude," said the nun.

A mulatto boy with fine puckish features stood up. "But if Satan is a spirit, Sister, how come he smells bad?"

"He is pictured that way in art and literature. He smells of

79

sulfur from hell. He is a powerful spirit who can assume material forms. Sometimes human forms. He took the form of a serpent when he tempted Eve in the Garden of Eden." Here she looked directly and maliciously at Lucia. "But he doesn't always take ugly forms. He's too clever for that. He doesn't always enter the bodies of pigs and snakes and like creatures. Sometimes he inhabits the body of a handsome and polite gentleman. In fact, he can take just about any form—even that of a pretty little girl."

Lucia's scarlet cheeks betrayed her mortification. She felt the eyes of every classmate on her.

The nun continued the lecture. "People can be possessed by Satan or his devils. This is an article of faith. When it happens an exorcist must be called in to drive them out just as Christ did in the verses from Saint Luke that I just read to you."

A smile stole over Sister Mary Rachel's face, a face as coldly beautiful as marble. The girl's obvious distress gave her pleasure, a feeling her conscious mind camouflaged with an attitude of righteousness. The smile soon faded. "Satan is powerful, children, the most powerful pure spirit next to God. He can perform wonders too. Evil miracles."

She paced the room, collecting words as barbs for an assault. The only sound in the room was the creak of floorboards under her weight. "He uses heretics and heathens as his pawns, his instruments of evil." She stopped by the classroom door where stood a terrestrial globe. She rotated it in an idle manner. "Satan strides the world." She spun the globe faster. "He entered the bodies of fanatical Moslems who fought like demons against the Christian Crusaders. In France he controlled heretics called Jansenists. In godless Russia today he has possessed the dictator Stalin. He comes to earth at all times and in all places." She stopped spinning the green metal sphere. "Even here and now in the Bronx."

Lucia sank in her chair. She stood outside herself and wondered whether there was truth in the nun's veiled accusations. Her sense of her own innocence was pure but fragile, like a flower. It lacked the nourishment of self-confidence. She had much faith in God but little in herself. She was very dispirited.

Instead of spreading the word of Our Lady she had earned a reputation for evil.

". . . Satan, the Prince of Evil, Belial, Lucifer—he goes by many names and titles, takes many guises. He is Beelzebub, the Lord of the Flies. Like God, he is omnipresent." The nun paused as her eyes swept over the surroundings. "He is right here in this classroom." The children looked uneasily over their shoulders. Only Lucia stared straight ahead, steeling herself to resist the nun's attack. She felt tears brimming in her eyes but fought them off. If Saint Stephen could face the stones of the Hebrews surely she could withstand the barbs of this unholy nun. But the stares of her classmates stung more than anything else. While Lucia was in many ways an extraordinary child she still had the fragile feelings of an eleven-year-old for whom the taunts of other children have a sharp bite.

Still lecturing in a monotone, Sister Mary Rachel circled Lucia's desk. The girl heard the drone of her voice but somehow blocked out the individual words and their meaning. Blood throbbed at her temples. She sensed the nun's nearness, smelled her pungent soapy odor, but stopped listening. She knew it was wicked not to pay attention to her teacher but she couldn't bear to listen anymore. She tried to concentrate instead on plotting ways to carry out her mission.

"Did you hear what I said, young lady?" the nun asked irritably.

It suddenly dawned on Lucia that Sister Mary Rachel was addressing her. Flushing, she rose to her feet. "I'm sorry, Sister. Would you please repeat the question?"

"Were you daydreaming, Miss Buonfiglio, or perhaps contemplating some new dramatic performance?"

"I don't understand."

The nun's lip curled. "Don't you now? I asked you what the name 'Lucifer' meant."

Lucia was well-versed in catechism. "It means 'light-bearer' in Latin. He was an angel, son of the morning, who was thrown out of heaven."

"Why?"

"Because he refused to serve God."

"Was he alone driven from God's presence?"

"No. Many other spirits were thrown into hell along with him."

"Yes. Many then and many since. They return to plague us."

At these words the three o'clock bell rang. A rustle of papers and creaking of furniture was heard. Then the children froze at a stern glance from the teacher. After a long pause she said, "You are dismissed."

Lucia sighed in relief.

The children gathered in little knots here and there in the schoolyard. On one side of the quadrangle a half-court basketball game was in progress. Although some time remained before July Fourth, strings of small firecrackers chattered in the surrounding streets. As summer vacation approached a sense of imminent freedom intoxicated the students. Lucia alone seemed to feel sad and sober, piloting through the noisy clusters of kids.

As she passed, a group of four girl classmates formed a buzzing huddle. Finally one of them called out, "Hey, Lucy, wait a minute, will you?"

Lucia stopped and smiled shyly. "Hi, Betty."

The girls approached her in a group. Their facial expressions blended wonder and deviltry. Betty O'Brien, the obvious ringleader, stepped forward. She was a very pretty girl with small well-sculpted features on a perfectly formed oval face. She had blond cornsilk hair. Lucia had always admired her looks.

"Is something the matter?" Lucia asked.

"We want to ask you a question, okay?" said Betty.

"Sure."

"We heard that Mussolini is your uncle. Is that true?"

"Of course not."

"Can we ask you another question?"

"Yes."

Betty's large hazel eyes widened. "Did it hurt?"

"Did what hurt?"

"You know. The wounds. The bleeding."

"No, it didn't hurt. I didn't even feel it."

"Gee, how come?" asked Irma Lichtenstein, peering over Betty's shoulder.

Lucia shrugged. "I don't really know. I guess it's one of God's secrets." She tried to be polite but she sensed the prospect of an unpleasant encounter. Her innate goodness didn't blind her to the potential for cruelty in people, especially youngsters. So she was on her guard.

"I bleed too," said Betty haughtily. "You know where. Do you bleed there?"

This remark shocked the other girls and made them giggle behind their hands; they sounded like chimes in the wind.

Lucy's damask cheeks grew even redder. "That's not your business, Betty."

"Why? I told you."

"I didn't ask you to."

"Okay, don't get mad."

"I'm not mad."

Betty now wore an impish smile. "I bet you'll get pee-ohed if I ask another question."

Lucia's patience was not infinite. She grimaced and said, "I'm sure you'll ask it anyhow. Go ahead and get it over with."

"Okay." Betty's satiny lips pursed. "When you fell on the floor in church that day, were you sleeping with Satan?"

"No," replied Lucia through clenched teeth.

"Yes, you were. I could tell you were. You were doing it."

"How could you even think of such a thing?"

"Sister Mary Rachel said you were possessed by the Devil."

"She did not!"

"She hinted at it."

Lucia's extreme mortification left her tongue-tied. Even worse, the accusations mysteriously gave her gooseflesh and made her nipples tingle. Abruptly she turned to leave.

"Wait."

Something in Betty's tone acted like a magnet. "I didn't mean what I said. It was only a test. Please don't go."

Lucia was frozen in her tracks. She didn't know why she hesitated. She knew in her heart that the girls were toying with her, using her troubles for their amusement. But she couldn't help herself. She turned and faced them.

Betty's expression was deadpan, perhaps even a little sympathetic. The girls behind her looked expectant; there was a gleam of mischief in their eyes that Lucia mistook for friendliness.

"We have a little present for you," announced Betty.

Lucia remained silent while her feelings rocked between skepticism and hope.

Betty snapped her fingers and Irma came forward carrying a small brown box tied with a bright blue bow. The other girls poked her from behind, making her stumble forward. The box was thrust toward Lucia.

Her faith in human nature was as hardy as a dandelion. Given an inch of soil in which to grow, it sprang up among the strangling weeds. "Oh, thank you," she gushed, taking the box from the girl's chubby hands.

They gathered around her as she unwrapped it, removed the lid with fluttering hands. Her scream pierced the dank June air.

The girls had scattered like a flock of murmuring pigeons. Lucia sat weeping on the concrete ground, her shoulders bobbing as she hugged her knees. A Good Humor truck passed with bells chiming. In the nearby grass lay a dead garter snake, its mouth daubed with nail polish to simulate blood.

He walked under shade trees toward the school, his eyes narrowing speculatively at every adolescent girl who came into view. From time to time he consulted the photo he carried in his right-hand pocket. So far each candidate definitely wasn't she. Beads of perspiration formed like tiny pearls on his brow.

Then he spied her walking toward him, carrying a ragged book bag. The severely cropped hair identified her immediately and conclusively. A smile of triumph spread over his jaunty features.

He stopped her. "Lucia?"

Her eyes, red from weeping, widened at the stranger's approach. "Yes."

"Let's have a chat, okay?"

"About what? Who are you?"

He smiled at her. "I hope to be your friend. Name's Dunlop. *Bronx Home News.*"

"Oh. The reporter." Silently she studied him: he looked kind and rather romantic. She was unaccustomed to tweed jackets. The amputation somehow added a debonair touch. "I'm not supposed to talk to you," she said.

"And why not?"

"My family doesn't want any publicity."

His face betrayed no disappointment under the fixed smile. "Do you like ice cream sodas?"

"Who doesn't?"

"Chocolate or vanilla?"

"Black and white."

He offered her the crooked elbow of his surviving limb.

She sipped contentedly through a straw. After what she had been through that day she found it hard to resist his friendly invitation. Her desire for a sympathetic ear rather than thirst for a soda was what really had led her to Goldstein's candy store on Westchester Avenue. But the soda was welcome too. The straw sputtered as the liquid descended to the bottom of the glass.

"Another?" he asked.

"Oh, no. I couldn't," she protested.

From her position seated on a stool behind the counter old Mrs. Goldstein removed the empty glass and swabbed the countertop with a rank washcloth. She was a dour woman with frizzy gray hair and a nose as pitted as a pickle. She eyed Lucia and Dunlop with suspicion.

"Why not?" he insisted.

"No, thank you," she repeated firmly.

He marveled at the authority conveyed in that small voice. He was captivated by her, by her precocious dignity and poise. In fact she was perfect. He could not have invented a more suitable Bernadette. All she lacked was the halo.

He seemed rather perfect to her too. After all the discussion of rebel angels he seemed her personal Uriel. After the serpent prank he seemed especially archangelic. But her contentment was marred by guilt. Her parents had forbidden her to give the interview, presenting a moral dilemma to the scrupulous child. On the one hand her natural mother would disapprove of her actions. But she was convinced that her supernatural mother would ratify any effort to publicize the vision. Indeed, weren't the evangelists sort of news reporters? "Gospel" meant "good news." Yet it pained her to disobey her parents. Finally she decided to tell him everything; starting with the vision.

Dunlop fiddled with a soda straw. "Will you show me where it happened?" he asked.

Her features betrayed inner turmoil. "Are you Catholic?" she asked.

He was tempted to lie but decided not to risk it. Something told him that her antennae were highly sensitive to falsehood. "No. Protestant."

"What kind?"

"Episcopalian."

"Do Episcopalians believe in Mary?"

"Of course." Here he might have strayed a little from the truth. Since he was not a practicing Episcopalian he didn't know the correct answer so he guessed.

"Do you believe I saw her?" she asked urgently. "Do you believe it's possible?"

He thought to himself, My, what an intrepid little interrogator! "Lucia," he began, filling his voice with warmth and familiarity, "I've seen many wonderful and strange things in my life. I fought in a war. As a newspaper reporter I once even attended a voodoo ceremony. I'm not a skeptic, if you know what I mean. As Shakespeare said, 'There are many more things in heaven and earth, Horatio, than are dreamt of in your philosophy.'" With a smug smile he finished drinking his soda.

Lucia was impressed by this oration but not entirely satisfied. "You didn't answer my question," she pointed out.

He gazed into her clear blue eyes. "Of course I believe."

Except for a few finishing touches spring had completed its annual renovation of the park. The apple blossoms, already past their prime, shivered in the light wind. The lawns were deep green, the soil moist and black. Everything teemed with life. Lucia and Dunlop silently walked by this cyclorama where raged unseen some insect Philippi and somewhere grew a herbal love that perhaps would produce a messiah fern. These dramas unfolded as they neared the site of a miracle.

"This is the tree," she said. "You see—my brother's initials are carved in it."

"You first saw her where, exactly?"

She pointed at a nearby clearing to the north. "There. A few yards away. I had stooped right about here to pick up the injured bird."

Without ostentation he drew out his notebook. She had not formally agreed to the interview and he was afraid of scaring her off so he decided to return the notebook to his pocket. He would write the story from memory as he often did. In any case his practice of journalism was based more on imagination than fact. "What did she look like?" he asked, trying to make the question sound idle.

After hesitating she told him the whole story, including as many details as she could remember. The words were torrential, poured out in a spasm of relief. She had been so starved for credence. At last she had an ally in her fight—a powerful one at that. Her enthusiasm overcame any scruples she felt. As she spoke birds babbled encouragement from the surrounding trees.

"Now tell me about the wounds," he said gently. "The stigmata."

She launched a second monologue. As she spoke his eyes roamed the park. Perhaps the apparition would return.

"May I see your hands?" he asked after a time.

She held them out to his inspection. "There's nothing there anymore."

"No. Not a trace." He rubbed his chin reflectively. "And your feet and side?"

"Gone too."

"Will you have them again?"

"I don't know."

Now his eyes surveyed the green prolific park. A faint wind rose in the late afternoon. He leaned against the tree in which Mario had carved his initials and shaded his eyes against the slanting rays of the sun. On the street behind the wrought-iron fence sedans and coupes roared by in flurries of dust. He waited until it was quiet.

"Is she here now?" he asked.

"Who?"

"Your lady, of course. Can you see her out there, floating toward us?"

"Not at all."

His aquiline face, dappled by the shade tree, betrayed disappointment. "Are you sure?"

"Of course I'm sure," she said irritably.

He restrained himself from saying something more. No use pressing his luck. "Okay, little lady. Just as you say, just as you say."

She had been gazing out over the clearing where the beautiful vision had first appeared a few weeks ago. Or was it eons? Now she turned her candid eyes on the smiling interviewer, who in reaction to her direct gaze ruffled his curly hair and winked irrelevantly.

"Do you believe I saw God's Mother?" she asked again.

"Little lady," he protested with a wounded look, "didn't I already tell you so?" He squatted down and chucked her under the chin. "I know you wouldn't make up such a thing. I believe in you."

"Then you'll help me?" she asked fervently.

"Sure."

"I have a job to do. I have to make people listen to the message—the message of the thornless rose."

"Okay. Leave it to me."

She smiled.

"Soon your 'thornless rose' will be a household word."

"What's that mean?"

"It will be on everybody's lips. The power of the press, little lady."

Solemnly she crossed herself. "It's God's will."

He rose from the squatting position. "Can I walk you home?"

She suddenly looked troubled. Pangs of guilt touched her

as she imagined her mother's reaction to this interview. "Oh, no, it's just a short distance." She frowned. "What time is it?" He looked at his wristwatch. "Nearly four-thirty." She cupped her mouth in horror. "Oh, I'm late. I have to take care of my brother."

"Hurry then." He jerked his finger westward. "I go this way—the subway."

" 'Bye," she said hastily.

"Whoa. Can I have your phone number?"

"It's listed. My father's first name is Ettore. E-T-T-O-R-E."

"Righto, little lady," he said with a wave. "I'll be in touch."

They hurried off in different directions.

Lucia's distress over being late was not as strong as her joy. She finally had a comrade. She skipped and whistled a song. Once she turned to look back. Shielding her eyes from the sun she gazed at the diminishing form of her new friend—her angel with one wing.

13

❦ ❦

He cradled the receiver on his shoulder and dialed. With the ease of a veteran reporter he blocked out the city room babble and listened to the rings on the other end of the line.

"Hello," came Sophie's hesitant voice.

"Did you get them?"

"Yes."

"Great. I'll send a messenger."

"When?"

"Right now. Tonight." His voice was brittle, curt. "You'll be there, won't you?"

"I'll lose my job for this," she whined. "He'll fire me when he finds out. He'll fire me for sure."

"Don't be melodramatic. Give the messenger an hour. Are you listening?"

"Then what will I do—when he fires me? Will you take care of me? Fat chance."

"Now, now, Sophie, everything will be all right. It's a sensational story. Tell you what: I'll take you to the Copa with the bonus money."

This promise pacified her. "Really, Al?"

"Sure. I'm no ingrate."

"When will you take me?"

"When I get the money. Good night now. I have to write."

"You'll come over later?" she asked, plaintive again.

"I'll be much too tired. Sweet dreams."

"Oh, Al, please . . ."

He hung up on her and frowned at the phone in its cradle. It annoyed him to have to mollify her, to sugarcoat his words when he felt like telling the cow to drop dead. But she still had her uses.

He swiveled the chair to face the typewriter. He stared at the blank sheet of copy paper in the carriage and a smile soon appeared in the folds of his face. As he concentrated he ran his tongue along his upper lip. The fingers of his solo hand alighted on the keys. In the upper left-hand corner of the page he typed in caps the slug:

MIRACLE—FOR TUES

Then in a febrile, almost trancelike state he began to write.

In less than an hour the article was finished. He leaned back in the chair with a satisfied air and read over the copy quickly, with an uncritical eye. As he read, the messenger arrived with the photos.

He felt a breathless anticipation as he fanned them out over the desk. In all there were five prints; the camera's eye had captured Lucia in all her mysterious glory. The feet, the hands, the wounded rib cage, all were there in black and white. The centerpiece of the collection was a close-up of her face as she wept blood. Dunlop chortled with pleasure. What a spread for the picture page! He gathered up the photos and copy, attached them with a paper clip and marched erect as a disabled tin soldier into the managing editor's office.

He entered the house by the back screen door which Mattie always left open as part of an unwritten pact with her prodigal husband. Mosquitoes whined around his ears. He cursed softly and swatted the air. With a stealth of movement that was by now second nature he crossed the screened-in porch and entered the kitchen.

By moonlight he navigated to the refrigerator and got out a bottle of beer and a wedge of Muenster. He found the table, sat and ate and drank in the tranquil darkness serenaded by the distant sound of his wife's snores. He felt the usual sense of quietism after writing a particularly satisfying article. Satiety for Albert Dunlop came after the pouring of shopworn words on cheap paper and in expectation of reading his own byline in the next day's first edition. He was a hack of easy virtue, content with the cheap perfume of provincial triumph.

He fell ravenously on the cheese, washing it down with beer. He ate vigilantly as an animal, constantly looking over his shoulder toward the bedroom of the rented ranch-style house he occupied in uneasy alliance with the woman whose snores now rumbled in his ears. Genuine peace of mind was an alien state to him. He drained the beer and decided to have another to help him sleep.

He toyed mentally with the feature story he had just written, trying to foresee the play it would get in the first edition. He guessed that they would use a page one tracer above the main headline which most likely would concern some aspect of the war in Europe. Already his mind was flickering over the possibilities for follow-ups, ways to keep the story alive in the public imagination, methods of spicing the yarn with controversy. Perhaps it would lead to another press club award, two of which already hung on the walls of his cedar-paneled den. The beer felt warm in his stomach.

He gazed contemptuously at the bag of bones in the twin bed beside his. He turned down the sheet, put on earmuffs and lay down naked in a bath of moonlight. Behind his eyelids he immediately saw rockets of color, fireworks of the mind. These images soon dissolved into the picture of a rose, a thornless rose.

He tossed and turned. Sleep played the coquette. Then he fell into the Gothic nocturne of his fears. When he awoke to the dream he found himself in the trenches.

Lucia slept soundly, rocked by the hand of an angel.

This seems a good place to conclude the first part of my narrative apologia. I'm not sure why except perhaps that my muse is an instinctual Aristotelian and, yes, I'm fully aware of the paradox inherent in that label. In other words the thing needs a beginning, middle and end and, dear tribunes, we've come to the end of the beginning. Up to now you have read in these scribblings an original version of the parchment of events that launched my client on the path to sainthood. From here on the story is partly a matter of a public record which bears about as much resemblance to reality as a carnival mirror. I will seek to set it straight. Besides, the odors emanating from Catherine's kitchen tell me that dinner is almost ready and my sister's stew is justly renowned.

14

✦✦ ✦✦

For the remissorial record here is the verbatim text of the first article that appeared in the *Bronx Home News:*

THE MIRACLE OF PELHAM BAY PARK
BRONX GIRL HAS "VISION,"
BLOODY STIGMATIC WOUNDS
APPEAR ON HANDS, FEET

BY ALBERT DUNLOP

Did a miracle occur in Pelham Bay Park last month? Does the Bronx have its very own Saint Gemma Galgani?

These intriguing questions are prompted by the case of Lucia Buonfiglio, a pretty and devoutly religious 11-year-old girl who exhibited the wounds of a stigmatic (see photo above and on pic page 24) before more than 500 witnesses during mass last week at Saint Bonaventure's Roman Catholic Church, 2251 Westchester Av.

The girl suffered the stigmatic seizure not long after she had a purported "vision" of the Blessed Mother one May morning in Pelham Bay Park.

(May is the month designated by Roman Catholics for special devotion to Mary, Mother of Jesus.)

Dr. John Papajohn of 522 Fairmount Av. treated Miss Buonfiglio immediately after the stigmatic attack. He described the phenomenon as "psychophysical repercussions of ecstatic trance," the medical term for hysterical reaction. The doctor said the attack was "simply amazing" and would not rule out a supernatural cause. Asked how the stigmatic attack occurred, Dr. Papajohn said: "You'll have to consult a higher authority than me."

Referring to other stigmatics in recent history, Saint Gemma Galgani and Theresa Neumann, Dr. Papajohn added: "While these cases all have been documented in the medical journals, no satisfactory natural explanation has ever been given."

In Saint Bonaventure's school Miss Buonfiglio has a reputation for sanctity. In an exclusive interview this reporter found her to be an attractive, bright and sincere youngster.

She no longer has any signs of the wounds which, according to Papajohn, had "healed spontaneously before my very eyes."

She led this reporter to the site of the alleged vision in a bucolic grove in the park. She reported that the apparition had identified herself as "the thornless rose"—a traditional appellation of the Virgin Mary—and had commissioned her to bring faith to the people of the community.

"She told me to ask people to believe," said Miss Buonfiglio. "I have a job to do. I must make people hear the message of the thornless rose."

The article had dropped like a bombshell on the neighborhood when it first appeared in print one humid morning in June. Dr. Papajohn had gone to Westchester Avenue to pick up a copy of the *Times* in the stationery store under the el. He was lured by the prospect of reading the frightening news of the day, of Japanese bombers thundering over Chungking, of the fall to the Luftwaffe eagles of Crete—the place where Icarus had soared—of the brother-against-brother clash of Frenchmen in Syria. But his eye was caught by a copy of the *Home News* emblazoned with the familiar photo of Lucia weeping blood. Fuming, he hurriedly grabbed a copy, threw a nickel on the stack of tabloids and rushed back to the office to deal with Miss Mariano.

Sister Mary Rachel had been dawdling over breakfast in the large kitchen of the convent. As she held out her coffee cup to the pour of a deferential novice she saw the newspaper story. The article of course infuriated her. Now that the haughty girl was a public figure of sorts, she also prompted some secret lurking fear in the nun. She left the table and went upstairs to pack her bags for a vacation with her mother in Massachusetts.

Basil Two-Times's mother read the article aloud to him in their dark three-room apartment on a treeless street under the el. The boy listened intently, gazing wonderingly at the cracked plaster walls. Among the thousands of readers were the forgotten of the community—the young polio victim who lived on Saint Raymond Avenue; the fish store owner whose mind had snapped when her son fell from a tree and broke his neck; the faithful and apostate and those in need of miracles. They read with avid eyes the tale of Lucia's vision.

A certain auxiliary bishop of the New York Archdiocese, however, read the story with jaundiced eyes and great alarm. I shall return to him later in the narrative.

Lucia was setting the dinner table—actually a large bridge table placed in the driveway under the musty grape arbor where the Buonfiglios liked to take their meals on summer nights. The long day was in glorious decline and the western sky over the garage was brushed with rose strokes. She whistled happily. *Pasta e fagioli* was her favorite dish. "The Aldrich Family" was on the radio that night and all was relatively well in her life. She had not yet read the newspaper.

Ettore had bought a copy of the evening paper on the way home from work. He entered the kitchen to find Serafina cursing softly to herself. She had burned the bread. She saw his ashen face. "What'sa matter?"

He handed over the paper and sat down to pull off his work boots. With a blank expression she read the article. At first she was speechless.

A boot thudded to the floor. "She disobey us," he said.

"Yeah." She frowned. "How awful she look in those pitcha."

"I'm gonna take the strap to her."

"Don't be too quick. Let's think about it."

The other boot fell echoingly. Ettore wore a pained expression, mingling anger with fear and awe at what his daughter had become—the central figure in a newspaper story. This was no longer just a family matter which he could handle with stern words and a licking. It had spilled over into that hostile realm—the outside world—where his child escaped the bridle of paternal control and became . . . What? A character with a halo? An object of ridicule? Certainly, a thing beyond his grasp.

Serafina's mind raced in another direction. She glimpsed the possibility of profit.

Ettore sat wilting physically and emotionally in the humid air. He was baffled by his wife's silence. "What do we do now?"

"Maybe nothing," she said. "Maybe we just wait and see."

"What are you up to? What goes through that head?"

She took a knife and began to scrape the burnt edges off the bread, applying to the task a fierceness and gravity that showed in her hard face. "Who knows?" she said cryptically. "This could be a good thing for us."

"How?"

Serafina sat down and swatted away the flies. "Use you' brain for once. Who's got the most money in the world?"

"The Jews?"

"No, you stupid. Even more than them. The Cat'lic Church, that's who."

"So?"

"So how do they get the money? The people pay money to the saints. They put it in the collection plate on Sunday or in those little boxes when they light candles or buy indulgences. They collect a lot of money that way—from people who want something from God or a saint, something like a new boyfriend or a good job. They know you get nothing for nothing in this world. You gotta pay. Why do you think the statues of the saints always have their hands out?"

"What does all this have to do with us?"

"Many will think that Lucia is a saint."

His laughter had a derisive ring. "No saint came from our unholy union."

His mockery failed to discourage her. For all her dark pessimism Serafina had a streak of opportunism in her nature, a desperate flair for scooping up nuggets of good fortune in the dross of circumstance. As it turned out her intuition had a prophetic quality. Serafina had a vision too. But her madonna, like the ancient Mediterranean idols, had a black face.

"Maybe," she said, "we could ask the Church for a percentage of the profit. Maybe we don't have to share at all."

"*Dio mio,* what a crazy idea." His eyes flashed with anger. "No, I won't take profit from my child's sickness. I won't disgrace her in such a way."

"Think of Mario, you fool. Think of your poor son. With the money we could get specialists for him. Do you want him to die because of your scruples?"

He scowled. "Gimme a piece of bread."

She handed him bread. "Here."

His teeth tore at it angrily as he thought. "When do we eat?"

"Soon. Lucia's setting the table outside."

"Lemme think about it."

She shrugged, smiling inwardly. She knew she had won the argument.

"I gotta have a talk with her," he said with a reflective air.

"Sure." She ladled the pasta into a serving dish. "Wait till after dinner."

He jabbed at the newspaper. "Has she read this?"

"Who knows? She don't tell me nothing. Open the screen door for me, eh?"

Lucia's slender form was in the doorway. "Read what?" she asked.

Ettore and Serafina looked at each other.

"The *Bronx Home News,*" Serafina finally said. "We talk about it later."

Lucia stood haloed by twilight in the doorway. Her tawny face showed excitement. "Oh, please let me see it."

"You know what it is?" Ettore asked sternly.

She looked ashamed. "I think so."

"We told you not to talk to him."

Her eyes scanned the floorboards. "Yes."

"You were very bad to disobey."

"I know." Her pleading eyes sought his. "But I didn't mean to disobey. I didn't know what else to do. Sometimes children have to displease their parents. Even Christ was naughty when He was twelve. Remember the story: He worried His mother sick when He was missing in Jerusalem. She found Him lecturing the rabbis in the temple."

"And now you lecture me?" asked Ettore. "Do you compare yourself to Christ?"

"Oh, no," she stammered. "I'm sorry."

Serafina smiled thinly. "She must be about her Father's business."

Lucia looked at her but said nothing. She had detected the irony in her mother's tone and it puzzled her. She was burning to see the newspaper article. "May I see it?" she asked again, risking her father's wrath.

Silently he handed the paper over.

She was stunned. To see herself under the spell of the angel of ecstasy was both a horror and a humbling revelation. Was this her face, cheeks covered with gore, pale eyes focused on the fifth dimension? She quickly read the article. It seemed both fair and accurate. With trembling hands she opened the newspaper to the picture page and found the grisly diptych of photos.

She felt depressed. The whole affair somehow seemed so cheap. Yet she realized this article was no more sensationalist than the Church's ancient glorification of the cross and the martyr's palm. Undoubtedly this was God's way of bringing the message to the people. Who was she to question it?

"I . . . I look so horrible," she said.

Ettore felt a stab of pity. Why couldn't his daughter be like ordinary little girls with their heads filled with thoughts of pretty dresses and furry animals? Why was her life like a passion play?

Serafina stood in the doorway with the steaming plate of food. "A mangiare," she said caustically. "Even saints gotta eat."

As the family gathered around the outdoor dinner table Lucia watched the day dissolve into dusk in a patch of sky over the fig tree where birds glided in flight patterns. Would the Holy Mother now be pleased with her? Would her mission now bear the fruit of faith? On the threshold of fame—or infamy— she felt strangely sad. It was as if she foresaw her future trials.

Her father lit the Chinese lantern; her mother served the food; Rosemary chattered shopgirl talk, while Mario sank into some private reverie.

Under a ghostly pale moon Lucia silently said grace.

I frowned at my lathered face and scolded myself with the wave of a shaving brush. Mark Twain had been right to call it "a good walk spoiled." Why was I so unimaginative that I followed the example of every priest who ever sang Sanctus through his nose and played golf on Saturday mornings? The prospect of chasing a pitted white ball over the greens of Split Rock-Pelham in the company of a simpering seminarian was now very repugnant. But, in a moment of weakness, I had made the date with Tomlin and it was too late to back down.

I turned on the tap water and burbled away the traces of shaving soap from my pink flesh. I was in a generally grumpy mood. It was the day after Dunlop's article had appeared and I had slept poorly because of it. What impact would this notoriety have on the poor kid's life? It made me uneasy.

After mass I met Tomlin at the entrance to the golf course. The sight of him in his fruity knickers made me still more desolate. Besides, it was too muggy a day to be lugging golf bags (we were both too cheap to hire caddies). Ah, well. I could deduct it from my allotted time in purgatory.

The third hole was a 450-yard affair doglegging left. Tomlin selected a number two driver and stepped up to the tee. He had decided to drive straight down the fairway rather than risk landing in the rough. I grunted in mental agreement. The better part of valor, given the powder puff quality of his drive. Gene Sarazen had little to fear. The closest Tomlin came to a golfer's form was a striking physical resemblance to Babe Didrikson.

Savoring such uncharitable thoughts, I rested my clubs against the trunk of an elm and sat on the ground. I needed a breather. I looked up at the sky. The horizon was filled with big dark clouds made mauve by the sun. Distant sections of sky blinked and rumbled, announcing the advance of a thunderstorm from the east.

Tomlin swatted at the ball. He shielded his eyes from the

hazy sun and gazed after it as it dribbled down the fairway. He turned to me with a sheepish smile. "Phooey," he said.

I rose, wiping the seat of my Bermudas. "Not exactly a power drive," I said with a rakish air.

Tomlin bridled at criticism. "Let's see you do better," he challenged with a pout.

I looked up at the threatening skies. "Maybe we'd better head for the clubhouse," I suggested. "Looks like a thunderstorm brewing."

"Oh, shoot," he said, stamping his foot. "It'll probably miss us by miles. You're just afraid I'll beat you for once."

Not likely, I thought, glancing at the scorecard. After two holes I was already up five strokes. I shrugged, rattled a driver from the bag and stepped up to the tee. Squinting through practice strokes, I decided to try to beat the dogleg by clearing the rough. Tomlin watched me with a grudging expression that turned to delight as I lofted the ball into the tall grass.

Beetle-browed, I slogged down the fairway.

The grumble of the skies grew louder as grass blades swayed in the rising wind. As we moved silently over the course my thoughts turned again to the young stigmatic and some strange and ancient foreboding stirred in me. Maybe it was just the moodiness that haunted moments directly before a storm when nature seems to whisper secrets. Her face came to my mind, polished like cowrie and daubed with blood, just as it appeared in the paper.

I reached the ball in the grass and hit it back on the fairway, placing it right near Tomlin's. He stood there, crowing, "I've gained a stroke."

"Wait until we finish the hole before you count strokes," I admonished, tugging on the brim of my news-boy cap and stalking off. He moued, as if to say that he hadn't meant to anger me.

It took us both eight strokes to reach the green on a par five hole. No rain fell yet but the darkened skies now seethed and glittered with turbulence. Tomlin stood twenty feet from the flag, putter in hand.

"Let's call it a day," I urged, looking at the menacing heavens.

"Not on your life," he replied, lining up the long putt.

Ribbons of lightning suddenly festooned the sky. It started to rain. I became alarmed. "Tomlin," I shouted.

"Don't be a sugarplum," he scolded, tongue extended in concentration over the shot.

All at once the metal club in his hands glowed for a split second. He screamed in pain and dropped it. I rushed to his side, grabbed him by the crook of the elbow and dragged him over to the shelter of a group of trees. I remembered hearing that the best place to be outdoors in a thunderstorm was under a small tree in woods thick with taller trees. I sat him down under a young oak, steadied his frail shoulders and examined his face. His eyes were open but he was obviously dazed.

"You okay?"

He nodded dumbly. "I think so. What the hell happened?"

"Shouldn't touch metal objects during an electrical storm," I explained, shouting over the patter of rain. "Your golf club was a lightning rod." I squinted at him. "How do you feel?"

"Okay, I guess. Sorta numb. Stiff."

I patted his shoulder. "You'll be all right. Just recharged your battery a little."

"Close call."

I chuckled. "Maybe the Lord was trying to tell you something."

"Like what, wise guy?"

"To show more respect for a man of the cloth like myself."

15

✦✦✦ ✦✦✦

Ah, the membrane of an old man's memory—what a quaintly presbyopic thing! I have already forgotten what I had for dinner last night yet I have a vivid picture of the shrine that the cultists of Lucia Buonfiglio erected in a glade of Pelham Bay Park in the summer of 1941.

The statue was carved by a Sicilian mason out of white stone. A brocaded blue cloak clung to her shòulders and rosaries, scapulars and holy pictures garlanded her neck. Red roses were strewn on the wooden platform that served as an altar. A smile of sweet tolerance was sculpted on the Virgin's polished face.

On a certain Saturday in July her smile fell on a large gathering of cultists, most of whom sat in folding chairs before the roped-off alfresco altar. The crowd, exuding the musk of religious fervor, rattled in noisy expectation. Lupino, the blind man, looking like a weathered troll, sat in the front row, leaning on his cane. His scrambled egg eyes were fixed on the invisible blue sky. The widow McManus, once plump and apple-cheeked and now hollowed out by cancer, sat next to him. Appollonia Sansevero, sitting in the third row, formed a pyramid with her moist hands and prayed for a husband. Off to the left side sat Patricia Sadowski clutching an Irish sweepstakes ticket.

Wheelchairs flattened blades of grass. A lunatic woman wearing a white gown and the powder and rouge of a harlot roamed the site chanting, "I am the Blessed Mother. I am the incarnation of the Virgin Mary." Swarms of busybodies and curiosity-seekers swelled the crowd. It was a Pantagruelian scene in the great tradition of our popish ways. At any moment one expected to see cartwheeling medieval acrobats.

Observing the scene, unnoticed himself, was its author. He leaned against a gnarled old elm and wore an expression of amusement. With his remaining hand he shucked peanuts and popped them into his mouth. Soon he was joined by Willie Blake, who chewed a blade of grass and fiddled with his camera.

"Got a mess of crowd candids," the photographer said. "What now? She gonna show up?"

"Hope so," said Dunlop.

Blake pushed his hat back and surveyed the crowd. "Boy, what a bunch of loony tunes these Roman candles are." He smirked. "I saw this one gal, she was writhing in her chair like a nympho. They really expect the skies to open up, don't they?"

Dunlop merely grunted in reply.

Blake reloaded the camera, making small talk as he worked. He was a tiny man with a mouselike face and Napoleonic air. The camera was for him an instrument of aggression, something he used to compensate for his puniness. Dunlop disliked the photographer but tolerated him for the sake of a smooth working relationship.

The lunatic woman glided by. "God has called me to bring faith to man," she intoned.

Blake snapped her picture. Then he shook his head theatrically. "What a bag 'a walnuts."

"Did you get the mother and father?" Dunlop asked.

"Yep. Big as life."

"Good. Too bad the little brother isn't here."

"Yah, too bad."

A man walked by hawking gory photos of Lucia blown up from the newspaper. "Pitchas of the saint," he shouted, using the title prematurely. "Only two bits."

"When's she coming?" asked Blake, brandishing the camera. "Maybe I can get a piece of that action."

"No freelancing on company time," said Dunlop joking.

"Where's it written I can't play a parlay?"

Dunlop smiled thinly, looking at Blake with veiled eyes.

"Nowhere, I guess." He scanned the crowd, the beast that had sprung from the soil of Pelham Bay Park to spoor the site of the vision. He made notes. The feature editor expected a page one spread from this pilgrimage.

It was the feast day of Mary, the whore of Magdala, who had dried the feet of Jesus with her silky tresses. And they had come from miles around to tread the steps of the Blessed Mother, perhaps to see the vision themselves. The movement had grown steadily in the days following the first article by the evangelist Dunlop. A week later at the site a man from Passaic had thrown down his crutches and walked. And then the fever mounted. It spread like brushfire throughout the five boroughs, even to sections of Long Island, New Jersey and Connecticut. A child from East Harlem was reported to have regained her sight. The tumor of an old woman was said to have vanished. Rumors multiplied of charismatic cures and floating visions unmatched since Fatima or Lourdes. Dunlop fanned the flames with story after story about the "miracles." Rival newspapers trotted out quotes from various doctors and psychiatrists alleging that the cured pilgrims had had psychosomatic ailments. "Studies have shown," the *Daily Mirror* said, quoting a local physician, "that positive patient attitudes can effect cures." Still the pilgrims flocked to the shrine.

But Lucia was stagestruck and stayed away.

"I can't go," she told her mother, who had since become friendly with Dunlop and was urging her daughter to make an appearance at the shrine.

"Why not?" Serafina asked in the Buonfiglio kitchen one day, cajolingly, concealing the fact of a $25 offer from the reporter if she persuaded her daughter to come. "You supposed to be winning souls to God's Mother, no?"

Letting this argument sink in, she kneaded pasta dough on the kitchen table and watched the girl's glum expression out of the corner of her eye.

"Yes," Lucia sighed in a resigned tone.

"And what about Mario? You have to pray for his cure?"

Lucia's face brightened. Fervently she asked, "Do you believe now, Mamma?"

"Sure," Serafina said, lying.

Tears of joy came to the child's eyes. "Oh, good. Yes, I'll go to the shrine."

The date of her appearance thus was set for the feast day of Mary Magdalene, prototype of the penitent sinner. Dunlop wrote a story heralding the event and attracting the great crowd that now thronged the park and that included no members of the clergy (except, of course, for me, in mufti, trying to look inconspicuous in sunglasses and Bermuda shorts).

Dunlop looked nervous. He glanced at his wristwatch. Then he walked over to where Lucia's parents were sitting. "Where is she?" he asked the woman. "She's late."

"She went to church to pray first. She's always praying. Don't worry, she'll be here soon."

"Keep your pants on," said Ettore.

"Is Mario coming too?"

"That wasn't part of the deal," barked Ettore.

Serafina shushed her husband. "He's not feeling well," she told Dunlop. "Stayed home with his big sister."

"Okay, we'll save him for next time."

Ettore seethed to hear his family being carved up by this faker. But he suffered silently under his wife's yoke.

"What kind of prayers is she saying in church?" Dunlop asked.

Serafina shrugged. "She pray for guidance."

Dunlop scribbled a one-handed note. "That's a good touch, I guess." He looked anxiously at the murmuring crowd. "But I wish she'd get here. Her public is getting restless."

Candlelight played on the tendrils of Lucia's hair and shone in her eyes. She knelt before the main altar, gazing at the resplendent tabernacle. The planes and hollows of her face were rendered in sfumato by the light. She was absorbed in prayer.

She wore a Sunday dress of yellow satin with two enamel cherries fastened to the waistband. She trembled. How did Our Lady expect her to behave? What would she do and say before all those people? She had followed the newspaper accounts of the cult's activities with wonder and some repugnance at the circus atmosphere. She could hardly believe that she herself was the source of this strange thing. Where was her humility? Our Lady, not she, was the matrix of it all. She was only a tool in her hands. She must never forget that, she thought, bowing her shorn head.

She was alone in the church. It was so quiet she could even hear the wax melting and sizzling in the votive cups. She was practiced in the art of prayer so she steeped herself in meditation and soon tapped some secret source of courage. Now she was ready to go to the park.

The pilgrims kept vigil under a hot sun. But the patience of many was wearing thin. A few cultists sang hymns, others mumbled rosaries. Dunlop muttered obscenities. "If she doesn't get here soon . . ."

The infidel's prayer was answered. She came across the football field, her slight figure dwarfed by the fleecy trellis of clouds. Pride and diffidence somehow were blended in her gait. There was a catch in Dunlop's throat. He jabbed Blake in the ribs. "Here she comes now."

Like the wind rustling through the trees the knowledge of her arrival passed through the gathering. A murmur of anticipation rose and fell. Then silence.

She approached the shrine. Despite the sultriness of the day, the face on which all eyes were fastened was marble cool. She looked straight ahead until she reached the foot of the altar where she genuflected, made the sign of the cross and rose. She turned to face the crowd.

"Good morning, friends," she said.

Simple words. But they seemed to have a profound effect on the gathering. Devotees dropped to their knees. Some returned the greeting. Still others shouted hallelujahs. The lunatic woman fell in the aisle and did a version of Saint Vitus's dance.

Ettore felt mortified. He clasped and unclasped his hands, trying to control himself, to cool his emotions. Serafina was a pillar of salt.

Lucia's cheeks now were aflame. A wind was rising, the trees swaying slightly. Her embarrassment at the crowd's idolatry made her temporarily mute. "Please," she finally managed to utter. "Get up, all of you. And sit down. I have just a few things to say. Thank you kindly for coming. I won't take long."

"Plead hep mee-eh," came the muffled cry of a harelipped young woman in a black dress. The fuse was lit.

The crowd exploded, clamoring for her attention, baring wounds of soul and body. They surged forward, straining at the rope that cordoned off the altar.

Ettore was about to go to his daughter's aid when she raised her arms in a surprisingly imperious gesture and tamed the crowd-beast. "Be still," she shouted.

Silence and order descended.

"I saw Our Lady—the thornless rose," she said, her eyes sweeping over the crowd. "I saw her right here where you have put the statue. She looked beautiful and she was real—round and human. Not like a ghost or anything but like a pretty young mother from the neighborhood. God and His love are just as real."

Total silence enveloped them. They listened with parted lips, frozen by her eloquence. Later accounts have distorted the picture. Truly, she was so graceful an orator that mere quotation does little justice to the impact she made. Sincerity—lately a devalued quality—crowned her speech. Her naturalness and unaffected wisdom enchanted her listeners, magnetized them as could no amount of empty sermonizing by the patriarchs of my gaseous profession. Here for once was a whole-souled preacher. For this youngster the reality of the Virgin Mary was as material as the earth beneath their feet, as vivid as the spittle in the apparition's mouth which she described to me at our first encounter. No, quotation cannot convey the power of the moment. Nonetheless, I quote:

"Oh, friends and neighbors, I wish you could have seen what I saw. It would have filled you with hope and a sense of peace. I saw the sky open up. I glimpsed something—something endless. Something tender and forever good."

Such words tumbled from the mouth of a mere girl.

"Her beauty would make you faint," she continued. "But

she wasn't see-through like a spirit. She didn't come down in a bubble like Billie Burke. She was solid like you and me. Try to see her through me—her stand-in. I don't know why I was picked for this job. A few minutes ago I had no idea what I was going to say to you. But Our Lady speaks through me." Her face grew radiant. "Have faith, good people. That's the message I bring. Remember—eternity is real too. Feed faith like a fire. It makes your burdens light, removes your fear. And don't be ashamed of faith. Wear it proudly like the breastplate of the Bible. And the enemy will run away. Now let us pray."

She faced the altar and knelt. The crowd too dropped to its knees. " 'Hail Mary, full of grace.' "

The cultists joined in: " 'The Lord is with thee. Blessed art thou among women and blessed is the fruit of thy womb, Jesus. Holy Mary, Mother of God, pray for us sinners now and at the hour of our death, Amen.' "

Until now the crowd had been under her thumb. Now it grew restless again. Some scrambled up from their knees and renewed their entreaties. "Give me sight," begged Lupino, arms outstretched. "Make Our Lady appear," demanded an old woman. The rouged madwoman resumed her chants and the hawkers of holy objects repeated their litanies.

Lucia became alarmed. The people were getting out of hand and disrespectful. She was afraid that the Virgin would be displeased with her performance, that she hadn't conveyed the message persuasively enough. The crowd's boisterousness also disturbed her sense of decorum. She felt she must do something to curb their behavior. She tried to look stern as she surveyed the gathering. "Please be quiet," she said. "Thank you all for coming but I think we should all go home now. It's getting late and . . ."

The crowd ignored her. "Give us a miracle," someone shouted like a music hall patron. "We want a miracle."

"The Lord works miracles," said Lucia. "Not me."

"This girl is a fraud," shouted the demented woman, pointing her scarlet talon in accusation. "I am the Blessed Mother."

The crowd surged forward. In an instant they had surrounded Lucia and were clutching at her clothing.

Ettore leapt to his feet and hurled himself into the crowd, muscling people out of the way. But his daughter was too deeply embedded in the bramble of human limbs for him to reach her. "Let me through, you animals," he shouted. "Get out of my way."

Blake stood on the periphery of the disturbance excitedly taking photos. Dunlop leaned nonchalantly against the oak tree.

In his rage Ettore—strong as an ox under ordinary circumstances—summoned up superhuman strength. He knocked people down like scarecrows. The altar was littered with bodies when he finally reached her.

On the ground near a massacre of trampled dandelions lay the tattered yellow dress. He scooped her up in his arms, shielding her nakedness. Her lithesome body trembled with sobbing.

Serafina rushed up to them. "She okay?"

His anger boiled over like lava. "No thanks to you, witch."

Suddenly Blake approached and snapped a photo of them. Then he tipped his hat. "Thanks, folks."

Ettore's eyes flared murderously. "Gimme that film. She got no clothes."

"Not on your life, buddy. Freedom of the press, you know."

That was all Ettore needed to ignite his Sicilian temper. He released his daughter and lunged at the photographer. Shivering in her underpants, Lucia ran into her mother's arms.

Tart odors arose from the laden earth. A choir of vespering birds perched on the makeshift altar. It was about four-thirty, a long time from sundown, but the day was oddly done. An air of finality overhung the park site littered now with broken folding chairs and other debris, including a demolished camera.

A wren alighted from the altar and swooped down to peck speculatively at a bright enamel cherry. The bird then fled in the shadow of an approaching figure.

He stood alone before the outdoor shrine, his eyes glazed with recollection, mouth slack. He was oblivious to the chattering birds. One earlier event of the day was etched in his memory. He had witnessed many astonishing things in this place today. He had seen a painted lady writhing on the ground and foaming at the mouth. He had seen people yelling and screaming and pushing each other like lunatics. He had even seen a newspaper photographer get a mouthful of teeth knocked out.

But all these events were effaced by one sight that burned in his memory. Over and over on his feast day of the whore of Magdala Basil Two-Times remembered the sight of Lucia's unclothed flesh.

16

❧❧ ❧❧

Learned tribunes, I beg your indulgence for the quaver in my hand as I introduce Bishop Lawrence McArdle, former auxiliary to the primate of the Archdiocese of New York. I assure you that the tremor in my composition is not a product of my senility. Although the poor man has long since donned the leaden cloak designed by Signor Alighieri for hypocrites I still quail like a curate at his name. If I only had Boccaccio's gift for defrocking friars I could do some justice to this portrait.

He was handsome and vain, the good Bishop McArdle, though artful at concealing his narcissism behind the domino of irony and intellectual charm. His voice—aired weekly on a radio program of folksy homiletics—rang clear as a bell in the Alps. Had he less physical grace he would have served as a vulgar model of prelate as popinjay; but the gaudy robes of the episcopacy were tailored to his lean frame. In looks he personified a common genetic anomaly. He was the son of a peasant (potato farmer) with the chisled features of an aristocrat. He still bore vestiges of the romantic aviator, the career he followed before an airborne brush with death led him to the priesthood.

These qualities primed him for the role of archdiocesan public relations man and ex officio ambassador to the secular political community. Indeed, he looked more natural hoisting a cocktail than holding aloft the sacred host. In his hands the inlaid crosier fit like a dandy's cane.

Above all he was the embodiment of Aristotle's dictum that man is a political animal. His courtship of the powers-that-be had been so successful that in July 1941 he could at whim pick up the phone and reach Al Smith, Herbert Lehman or Fiorello La Guardia.

This, then, was the man who sat frowning behind a Directoire desk on which he irritably flung down a copy of the *Bronx Home News*. He pushed a button on the intercom.

"Who's the pastor of Saint Bonaventure's in the Bronx?" he growled into the machine.

"Don't know offhand, Your Excellency," said the voice of his male secretary. "I'll look it up immediately."

"And get him on the phone."

"Right away."

The man sitting opposite the bishop fidgeted in the chair. "I get at least ten calls a day about it. What should I tell them?"

"That the cult does not have Church sanction, of course." He shook his head. "This comes at a very awkward time."

"The girl has a large following, Bishop. Exceedingly large. And it's growing every day."

Having spoken, Father Eugenio Acosta knitted his pudgy hands together in his lap and awaited his superior's reaction. The Jesuit, rotund and oily, made few unnecessary movements.

McArdle grumbled. "This kind of thing only gives ammunition to our enemies." He prowled the wood-paneled room. "Men like Niebuhr are snickering at us as it is."

Father Acosta watched him silently through hooded eyes.

"Stigmata indeed," the bishop huffed. "Visions of Our Lady. We must nip this thing in the bud."

Acosta appraised the ex-aviator with an air of detachment and even an edge of superiority. The Spanish priest had a wintry character under the sunny and complacent exterior. Down deep, he didn't think much of McArdle's mental gifts. He had the cunning subaltern's contempt for a figurehead boss.

"At the same time, Bishop," Acosta said mildly, "we would be ill-advised to disregard the devotion that this child inspires among the laity. She is becoming quite popular."

McArdle struck a musing pose by the bay windows overlooking Madison Avenue. He tucked a pastille under his tongue. "I guess you're right. We'll have to proceed with some delicacy." He shuddered. "Just what we needed: a gaudy masochist in the diocese. And a well-publicized one at that. Just as I was on the brink of convincing certain influential people that we had entered the twentieth century."

The intercom buzzed. The call to the pastor had been put through and he was waiting nervously on the line.

"You talk to him," McArdle instructed Acosta, wrinkling his small nose with the disdain of a lazy Siamese cat. "Set up an appointment, eh? You know how to handle these things."

Acosta smiled knowingly and reached for the phone. "Leave it to me," he said.

And so an agent of the Chancery in the form of this fat Jesuit entered Lucia's life. He first visited my pastor who—displaying the usual moral courage of his kind—passed the buck to me, her confessor and confidant.

Acosta took a courtly continental approach: he invited me to lunch at a midtown Spanish restaurant. For a curate from the sticks of the Bronx the prospect was as exotic as a trek to Timbuktu. I donned my double-breasted suit of black gabardine and patted cologne behind my protuberant ears.

The restaurant captain and waiters cooed like a flock of doves around the Jesuit's table. He was obviously a regular and favored customer. I later learned that place—El Sol de Valencia, I think it was called—was owned by Acosta's uncle, a heavy contributor to the Falangist cause. Had I known this at the time I might have choked on my *calamares*. But I didn't know and they were delicious, as I recall.

Over Moroccan coffee he broached the subject obliquely. He began with a soliloquy on the status of Mother Church in the modern world, on the need to reconcile the advances in science and psychology with the immutable doctrines of Christ and His gatekeepers, and on the perils of the unfortunate image abroad of the Catholic community as a collection of primitive idolators presided over by "shamans in soutanes," as he phrased it. He launched then into a brisk attack on godless Communism and concluded the oration with a long discourse on the administrative clergyman's favorite topic—money.

"You see," he said in a confidential tone, "the good bishop is just now embarking on a major fund-raising campaign. It's a delicate undertaking, to put it mildly."

"I can well imagine," I said timidly.

He peeled a pear as he continued. "It just wouldn't do, you know, to have the whole project scuttled. It wouldn't do at all." He popped a section of fruit into a perfectly round mouth that seemed to me a wonderfully supple implement, a marvel of orality in which food, words and the Lord knows what else were raffinated. I was enthralled by this mouth.

"Don't you agree?" he asked, puncturing my reverie.

"Oh, yes indeed," I answered, not quite knowing to what he was referring.

"Any scandal," he said, "any tinge of controversy might scare off some contributors."

"Yes," I said, puzzling over what was to come next.

"I'm told you have a friendship with this girl," he said after dabbing his lips with a cloth napkin.

"Not exactly a friendship. I'm her confessor."

"And don't you see her outside the box?"

"Occasionally."

"She trusts you, confides in you?"

"To a degree, I think. Although I can't fathom why."

"You have influence over her?"

"I don't know. Why do you ask?"

Acosta produced a cardboard box of Turkish cigarettes. "Smoke?"

I shook my head.

Plumes of smoke curled upward. "Bishop McArdle would be happy to see this whole 'vision' nonsense evaporate. You understand."

"I do?"

"Perhaps we could get the child psychiatric care."

"I'm not sure she requires it."

"Do you think you could talk to her? The bishop would be most grateful."

I was in an awkward position. My vow of obedience, though not invoked, hovered over the conversation. I was also painfully aware that incurring the bishop's displeasure might not brighten my future. As visions of a transfer to a leper colony formed in my brain, I asked, "Talk to her about what?"

He leaned forward confidentially. "You could reason with her. Get the truth out of her. We want you to persuade her to publicly renounce her story."

"I don't think you understand, Father Acosta. This kid is no publicity hound. And I don't think she's as malleable as most eleven-year-olds."

"She's mentally disturbed, then."

"Maybe. But we can't merely discount the stigmata."

"Hysteria, pure and simple."

"I think that's probable. But you don't know her. Her faith in this thing is as steady as a rock. She's a remarkable little girl."

He sat back in the chair and appraised me. "I see. You seem quite taken with her."

I flushed. "I don't know if I'd put it that way, exactly." I groped for words. "I admire her. Yes—she's only a child but I must say I admire her. And I don't think I could shake her from her story. Whatever happened in Pelham Bay Park that day, Lucia truly believes she had a vision."

"But you'll try, won't you?"

"May I be permitted a small question?"

"Sure. More coffee?"

I nodded. As he poured I said, "Shouldn't we leave open the possibility that this so-called vision has . . . well, has some *basis?*"

I'll never forget his expression then. It was more vacant, more devoid of emotion, art or significance than any I have ever seen; it was a blank canvas.

"Sugar?" he asked, not deigning to answer the question.

"Please," I said, doing my best to muffle the sound of my conscience. The pact was sealed.

17

I took the first opportunity that came my way. It was a sultry day and the tar in the streets bubbled in the sun. I took a busload of kids to Wilson's Woods pool just over the line in Westchester County. Among them were Lucia and her brother Mario.

The bus, an old four-cylinder job, rattled down Boston Road, hitting every bump and pothole so that the strains of the children's communal singing had the cracked quality of a worn phonograph record. Still they were undaunted, working lustily on the railroad and knocking the full ninety-nine bottles of beer off the wall.

I sat moodily behind the driver and squirmed in the caned seat, mentally composing my speech to her. I stole glances back at where she sat. She glowed with pleasure as she sang along with the other children, her arm firmly clasped around her brother's shoulder. When she caught my eye I stared quickly at the oaken floorboards.

We arrived at the pool, set among shade trees, and the bus disgorged its squealing freight. Soon they were splashing and frisking in the green water, lambent where the sun shone through the netted canopy of trees.

Lucia and Mario were apart from the main group, pariahs of their odd history. She supported him around the middle and taught him the rudiments of swimming. The odor of chlorine filled the summer air.

I basked like a lizard at poolside, dunking my ruddy feet and watching them play.

Joey Fazio surfaced, a glistening baby whale bubbling with urgency. "Come on in, Fadder. The water's great." Then he submarined again, spraying me unmercifully. I stifled a cuss-word and shivered in my Hawaiian shorts. The boy put charity to the test. I surrendered, though, and dove into the water.

When the sun was low and the froth of the children's en-thusiasm skimmed off by hours of play, they sat drying off in the grass. I bought them all lemon ices at the concession stand and chose a spot near Lucia to sit and eat mine.

She smiled radiantly at me. "We had such a good time, Father Fogarty. We can't thank you enough."

I smiled back. "My pleasure."

She wore a modest one-piece bathing suit of white, pat-terned with yellow daisies. Her brown body had the fleeting beauty of her tender age. Before God, I won't lie: she stoked a small but unquenchable fire. I could not avert my eyes from the down that feathered her golden thigh. Gladly will I pay my debt in purgatory for this quickened moment. At least I won't burn in hell for the greater sin of deceit.

I spoke haltingly. "Lucia . . ."

"Yes, Father? You want to talk to me about something, don't you? I noticed the way you've been looking at me all day."

"Yes, I do want to talk to you."

She touched her brother's cheek. "Go over there, Mario." She pointed to a huddle of boys sprawled in the grass. "Go play with those kids."

He started to protest, then checked himself. He left si-lently.

I gazed after him. "How is he?" To ask about a doomed person's health always sounded hollow.

A pale smile. "A little better, I think. The doctor says the sickness is 'stable.' He's in God's hands, isn't he?"

"Yes." She had this remarkable way of making me feel like an acolyte.

Lucia stretched like a languorous kitten and looked all around her, inhaling the sweetness of the surroundings. "Isn't this great? We sure beat the heat today."

Hair fringed her underarms. My eye involuntarily traced the graceful line that ran from her outstretched arm to her pectoral muscle. I looked down at the grass and cleared my throat. "Lucia," I repeated.

"I know, Father. You want to talk to me about Our Lady. About the shrine and the cult and things."

"That's right."

"Okay." She looked at me in expectation.

"Don't you think it's gone far enough?"

She fluttered her lashes. "You mean when they went crazy and tore my clothes off? The poor people. They didn't mean it, really. I guess they're so desperate for her love that they can't help themselves."

"You know, Lucia, the publicity was very bad for the Church."

She looked horrified. "I'm so sorry."

"It makes us Catholics look like . . . like superstitious lunatics."

She wrinkled her brow and thought for a while. "I don't know what to do about it. If only Our Lady would give me more guidance." She questioned me with her eyes. "Could you advise me, Father?"

"The news even reached a bishop downtown. He was very upset about it. He sent a representative to speak to me."

"What does he want me to do?" Her gaze was direct, trusting.

I looked away. The late sun glowed through the trees. Roses perfumed the hedges surrounding the pool. "You could . . . well, *they* want you to deny the vision." Like Pilate I had passed the buck.

Her mouth fell open. "But how can I?"

In sheepish confusion now, I fumbled for words. "Lucia, you can't be positive. I mean, isn't it possible that what you thought was a vision was really something else? Couldn't you see your way clear to . . ."

"I know I saw her," she said firmly. "And she gave me a job to do."

"Surely you can serve God and His Mother in a more private way."

"I wish I could. I used to. But she chose me for a mission. I don't know why." Her face showed anguish. "Oh, why did it have to be me?"

I couldn't endure anymore. "Now, child, don't worry. It'll be all right."

"Does the bishop want me to lie?"

"Of course not."

"That's what it sounds like."

"He just wants you to try to look at this thing in another way."

"But there is no other way. Our Lady gave me clear instructions."

"They might put you through certain tests."

"Who?"

"The archdiocese."

"What kind of tests?"

"I don't know. Mental tests, psychological tests. They would rather just drop the whole matter."

"Okay, I'll go through the tests. I want to obey the Church." Sad-eyed, she studied my face. "I thought at least you would believe me."

"I believe in your sincerity."

She sighed. "That's not enough."

"I'm sorry, Lucia. It's the best I can do."

She gave me absolution with a smile. "Yeah," she said. Then, impulsively, she tousled my red hair.

Suddenly Mario had returned. "They won't play with me," he said.

She looked up at him with sympathy and took his hand.

I rose from the grass, wiping the seat of my shorts. "Time to head back." I bustled around the pool, corralling the reluctant chicks.

The declining sun led the bus in our southwestering homeward trip. It blazed through the speckled windshield, obscuring the approach of Westchester Avenue. The children were unnaturally quiet and the mood was calm, almost soporific.

I could focus neither my thoughts nor my feelings. My scalp still tingled where her fingers had touched my hair.

18

※※ ※※

W oe be unto the pastors that destroy and scatter the sheep of my pastures, saith the Lord."

Mea maxima culpa. There is a tradition of apotheosis that I follow too closely for comfort. Nero kicked Poppaea to death, then declared her a goddess. Romulus was deified by the very senators who slew him. Perhaps I was not Judas. But I was Pilate and Thomas rolled into one. I had little faith and I washed my hands of the matter. I failed her.

I beat my breast, tribunes. Forgive me for the sacrilege of equating our ways with pagan practices. After all, we are not like the benighted Greeks and Romans, are we? We make fine distinctions. We merely borrow from their languages.

We distinguish "latria"—the supreme adoration we render to God alone—from "dulia"—reverence for the saints—and "hyperdulia"—reverence for the saint of saints, His Mother. By such rhetorical hairsplitting do we put distance between ourselves and the idolators.

Now let me atone. Let me resume the narrative argument that Lucia Buonfiglio stands in the sight of God.

Father Acosta took the news with frosty silence. My inability to persuade Lucia to renounce the vision did not seem to surprise him. But it was an annoyance.

He shrugged over a plate of bluepoint oysters. "Then I suppose she may have to run the gauntlet."

I peered at his pudgy inscrutable face. "What do you mean by that?"

The deft mouth vacuumed an oyster. "Doctors, psychiatrists. Perhaps a full-fledged episcopal inquiry. Of course, we would rather avoid such a thing."

I toyed with my fork. "Perhaps it would be for the best. Clear the air."

Now the mouth pursed with disdain for my mental powers. "Muddy it, rather. But don't worry, we'll break her."

"You'll what?" I said with obvious surprise.

He smiled at my apparent naïveté. "Don't tell me you believe her story?"

My heart sank with guilt at my disloyalty. He was right. I didn't believe her. "Will they send an apostolic delegation?" I asked.

"I hope it won't be necessary. Let's first try to dispose of the matter on a local level."

"I know the physician who examined her stigmata. He's a good man."

"Papajohn?" Acosta shook his head firmly. "Can't use him. He's Greek Orthodox."

"I thought he was Uniate."

"Maybe. But we prefer *Roman* Catholics. We can get somebody highly qualified to examine her, don't you worry. A former classmate of mine in Madrid is now practicing in New York. Studied under Breuer. He's a Knight of Malta too. Perfect candidate for the job."

His smugness got my dander up. His soul seemed as black as his cassock. Even from my own glasshouse of moral cowardice I decided to hurl a few pebbles his way. "I hope that your *experts* would keep in mind that even the word *medicine* itself is taken from the lexicon of magic and miracles. Derives from *Medea*, you know, the princess of sorcery."

I made a tent of my hands. This bit of pedantry, used as an indirect word of support for Lucia, eased my conscience a little. But it had no perceptible impact on my listener.

"So?" he said.

"The ancients often made no distinction between doctor and priest."

"Neither do savages in Africa or heathen Indians. We know better nowadays, don't we?"

"I wonder. I'm surprised at you, Father. I thought the works of Comte were on the Index."

"Just because I don't believe in witchcraft doesn't make me a positivist."

I paused. "Do you believe in miracles?"

"There is much that is still unknown about nature."

"That's an evasion of my question." I wouldn't let him wriggle off the hook. Nor myself. This debate, I now know, was a way of externalizing my own internal *contredanse*.

" 'A miracle,' " he recited, " 'is an extraordinary event, perceptible to the senses, produced by God in a religious context as a sign of the supernatural.' "

"Bravo," I said, slapping my palms in mock applause. "I can see you were a diligent seminarian."

After interrupting the discussion to confer with the sommelier, he skillfully picked up the thread. "A man cannot move a mountain, Father Fogarty."

"Can God?"

"In his way, yes."

"Can he sidestep nature and make man move a mountain?"

"He wouldn't."

"And what about faith?"

"What about it?"

"Did you get faith in the seminary too, along with sophistry?"

"Did you?" he asked with curling lip.

I stared grimly at the tablecloth.

With consummate grace he poured a ruby-red burgundy. "Try this wine from the mountains of the Côte d'Or. It's splendid."

My fingers groped for the glass.

And so the ordinary episcopal authority launched a "preliminary official inquiry" into the case of Lucia Buonfiglio. Witchhunters disguised as clergymen combed the neighborhood for witnesses to the girl's stigmatic experience or to alleged miraculous cures at the shrine. Meanwhile an ecclesiastical letter was sent to the parishes condemning the cult of worship spawned by Lucia's vision. The letter—which reminded the congregations of the decrees of Urban VIII prohibiting public worship before beatification—was read aloud from pulpits and thus fell on the burning ears of the girl whose simple faith caused all the ruckus in the first place.

Lucia bowed her head. She felt the eyes of her fellow parishioners boring through her. The chanting of high mass lent solemnity to her shame, underscored it like a cymbal at a symphony. *Ite, missa est.*

She rushed down the steps of Saint Bonaventure's, eager to escape the scrutiny of the congregation. Why did she feel like those sinful women she had read about in the Bible? She was not like Magdalene. She had done nothing wrong. Why did she feel so stained and naked? Clutching the missal to her pounding heart, she ran down the street, bemusing the Sunday strollers. She ran headlong, losing herself in a sense of shame.

The next thing she knew she was sitting on a rock and looking at the sky filled with the puffy chariots of clouds over City Island. The bay sprawled before her, gray and stagnant. A gliding gull was suspended in motion over the craggy and forbidding shoreline.

She was numb, beyond weeping. She mustered up a prayer for guidance. It rose toward the unfathomable where it dissipated or found its way into the endless ledger.

Prayer had had its usual sedative effect on Lucia. She started for home.

A stray dog bounded out of the underbrush, barking and baring jagged teeth. Lucia froze. Then she squatted and petted the animal and soon the dog was whimpering. Lucia read its sudden docility as a good omen.

Monday was washday. Lucia, helping Serafina with the family laundry, was upstairs hanging clothes on the backyard line when Father Acosta rang the doorbell.

Serafina swung open the door. Her face registered surprise at the sight of the Roman collar. "I thought it was the iceman," she said before inviting him in.

She treated the unfamiliar priest with a mixture of deference and suspicion. She offered coffee. He accepted, settling his gelatinous flesh into a parlor chair. "I guess you wanna see my daughter about something," she said bluntly.

Acosta nodded politely.

"Loo-chee," she yelled upstairs. She wiped her hands nervously on her apron, still eying the priest with suspicion. "I'll make the coffee." She went into the kitchen.

The girl stood motionless at the foot of the stairs. Her heart drummed at the sight of the strange priest in the sitting room.

"Hello, my child," he said unctuously.

She curtsied as her first-grade teacher had taught her. "Hello, Father."

He nodded. "My name is Father Acosta. Come—sit down."

She sat opposite him. Even her deep reverence for the priesthood couldn't erase the instinctive dislike that the Jesuit inspired in her. It was the first time in her life that she had taken an instant dislike to anyone, much less a priest, and it startled her. Did this mean that she had fallen from grace? She searched the face of this fat man in black robes for some sign of goodness, some shadow of the Holy Ghost. Yet she found in his piggish eyes and artificial manner nothing but guile. Surely it must have been her own eyes that betrayed her. After all, he was a man of God. Lucia's powers of intuition warred against her native innocence. She was a lamb with a fox's nose.

"Can I do something for you, Father?" she said, straight from the shoulder.

"Yes," he said, equally direct. "You can do something for me by doing yourself a favor."

"I don't understand."

"I heard you were a bright little girl."

She avoided his eyes.

"I have no doubt that you are," he continued, "and devout as well."

"Thank you, Father."

"I don't know why, then, you would want to make up such fantastic stories."

Her candid face showed that she felt both hurt and puzzled.

"Stories?"

"Please, young lady. Don't pretend you don't know what I'm talking about. It ill becomes you."

"I know you must be talking about the vision. But I'm telling the truth. I saw her."

He breathed a heavy sigh. "You're making it difficult for yourself, my child."

"I can't help it if Our Lady gave me this job to do."

"Do you realize that your persistence in this is hurting the Church?"

She looked forlorn, a mere child before the throne of Peter, a girl pitted against the majesty of the mystical body. How could she hurt the Church? "That's impossible," she protested. "I'm only following her orders. I wish more than you that I hadn't been picked for this. I don't know why I was. I'm really not worthy. But what can I do about it?"

"You make us all look ridiculous in the eyes of the world," he said.

"What can I do about it?" she repeated imploringly.

"Deny it. Deny the vision."

"That would be lying. You don't want me to lie, do you?"

His face turned crimson. He was losing his accustomed composure. "You're a stubborn little girl."

Serafina, her face set like concrete, had returned carrying a tray with a coffee pot and cups and Stella D'Oro cookies. She put them down on the coffee table. "What'sa matter, Father? What she do?"

"Nothing, Mamma," said Lucia. "I did nothing wrong."

The Jesuit had regained his equanimity. "Forgive me, signora. Your daughter is correct. She's done nothing wrong. It's obvious that she really believes in this vision. It's not her fault if she is subject to delusionary episodes."

"What's that mean?" asked Serafina.

"She imagines things."

"I didn't imagine it," said Lucia. "She was real, I tell you."

"Maybe we should talk about this in private," Serafina suggested. "Go to your room, Lucia."

"Better she stays," he said. "Two lumps, please."

Serafina poured. "But she's only a child . . ."

"Without her cooperation," he said, "we can do nothing."

126

"What must be done?" asked Serafina.

"We could arrange to have her see a psychiatrist."

Serafina looked downcast. "We have little money."

"Don't worry about that," he said in a soothing voice. "The archdiocese would take care of everything."

Serafina's ears perked up. She sensed an opportunity for bargaining. "Ah, we are an unfortunate family, Father Acosta. You don't know how much troubles we have."

Acosta smiled. At last he was on familiar ground. At haggling he was as skillful as a Syrian. "I can well imagine, signora," he said, his voice laced with sympathy. "Times are hard."

"Especially for us Italians, eh?" She eyed him in a comradely way. "Here they think we all love Mussolini and should get on the next boat back. You're Italian, aren't you?"

"No, Spanish."

"Still—you understand." She squared her shoulders. "I think Francisco Franco is a great man."

"Indeed."

Lucia was growing impatient with this conversation. She easily detected the underlying cynicism and it saddened her. But she was too docile to interrupt.

"More?" Serafina asked, lifting the coffee pot.

The Jesuit nodded.

As she poured, Serafina continued in a lamenting tone. "The only one around here who cares about us is Vito Marcantonio, God bless him. They say he's a Communist but I don't believe it. Fiorello, for my money, he's no good. Anyway he's a Jew and a Protestant. He tries to be everything. A typical politician."

Acosta was making grunts of assent as he nibbled on a cookie.

"Me?" continued Serafina. "I'm no interested in politics. My husband, though, he worry his head about it all the time. What good it does? He should worry more about his family." She assumed a confidential tone. "You hear about my boy, Mario?"

"No."

"He's very sick. Cooley's anemia. Ever hear of it?"

"Ah, yes. It strikes people of Mediterranean blood. I remember a cousin of mine in Valencia who was afflicted with the disease."

"Thank God the union pays most of the specialist's bills," Serafina said, crossing herself.

"I know a doctor downtown who specializes in these illnesses. He comes from the island of Cyprus. He's an expert in racial blood disease. The best there is."

"Do you think he would see Mario?" Serafina asked.

Acosta looked doubtful. "He's very busy and outlandishly expensive."

An awkward silence followed. Lucia squirmed in her chair. Was it possible that her mother and the priest were bargaining over Buddy's fate? It couldn't be.

The Jesuit finished his coffee. "But I promise you, signora, I'll see what I can do."

"Thank you, Father."

"Of course it may depend on certain things."

"I understand."

"I'm sure you do." His smile conveyed that a tacit agreement had been reached between them. "And now, signora, I must leave."

They all stood up. The girl waited demurely off to the side while Serafina saw him to the door. "What about my daughter?" she asked in a whisper.

"I'll give you a day or two to consider things. I hope you will use your powers of persuasion. If she is not swayed by a priest maybe a parent will have more influence with her."

Serafina nodded with determination.

He looked at her hard. "You understand now—if she doesn't renounce her story she will have to face severe tests. Physical and mental. It will not be a pleasant experience."

"I'll talk to her."

"Good." From the foyer he said goodbye to Lucia.

Before shutting the door Serafina said, "You won't forget about this doctor?"

The sun was high, casting shadows on his fleshy face. He gave her the ghost of a nod and walked off.

As her mother returned to the sitting room Lucia was standing at the window silently watching the penguinlike priest waddle down the street. She heard Serafina say, "Lucia, I want to talk to you."

19

Lucia fidgeted under Serafina's gaze. She steeled herself for the inevitable bout of wills, saddened that she and her mother were so often at odds. In her untried adolescence she considered herself no match for the stony Sicilian woman who sat across from her in the curtained parlor. But she underestimated herself.

"The wash," she said anxiously. "I have to go upstairs to finish the wash."

"You can do it later."

The girl nodded and waited, hands folded, pale as cut lilies in her lap.

Serafina sat ramrod straight. Her beaked nose and wavy hair plumaged with streaks of gray lent her an imposing aquiline appearance. She said, "You love your brother, don't you?"

"Of course, Mamma. But I didn't like that priest."

Serafina sniffed the air. "Me neither. So what? He may be able to help us. That's the important thing."

Lucia's concern showed on her freckled face. "I never met a priest like him before. He didn't seem holy at all. He didn't even seem like a weak man who tries hard to be good but fails."

"You gotta learn something, young lady," admonished Serafina. "Not all priests are good."

"I guess not."

"No matter. The question is, will you cooperate with him?"

"I can't deny the truth. That would be a sin."

"You gotta learn how to compromise. He can help Mario."

The girl glanced uneasily at the staircase. Her brother was napping in his room upstairs. "I just can't say that I didn't see her, Mamma."

"You joost a little girl. Still wet behind the ears. How do you know what you see? How do you know what's true or false in such a complicated world? Maybe you don't see what you think you see in the park. You think you're too smart, that's your trouble."

These words stung but Lucia stuck to her guns. "I can't prove what I saw. But a person knows certain things in the heart. I saw her."

Serafina's dark eyes narrowed. "So you don't love your brother."

"That's not fair."

"You let him die."

Tears sprang to Lucia's eyes. She went to Serafina and clutched her hand. "Please try to understand me, Mamma."

Serafina's body stiffened.

Lucia searched the woman's eyes. Under layers of defensiveness and bitterness she glimpsed a haunted look. Suddenly she felt profound pity for her earthly mother. "I know your pain. I feel it too. But I promise you he won't die."

Serafina laughed derisively. "You really think you can make miracles, don't you?"

Her laughter grew louder until Lucia looked worriedly at the stairs. "Please, Mamma. He'll hear."

"Okay, what if you have to lie for Mario? Is that too much to ask? I would kill for him. And you won't even lie?"

"Don't talk that way."

"Why not? Saints kill too. Like Saint Joan or Saint George."

"I'm not a saint, Mamma. I never said I was a saint."

"What are you, then? A magician? A witch?"

"Mamma, please . . ."

The woman's voice now conveyed genuine awe. "An ordinary little girl—you are not. It's hard to believe you' my flesh and blood. I think you' so strange."

This confession wounded the girl. "I'm . . . I'm not strange."

"What kind of thing are you?" She placed her hands on her belly. "Did you really live in this womb? Was your navel really tied to me? Or did an angel deliver you?"

Lucia blushed hotly.

"Nah," Serafina said with an empty look. "Angels are not accomplices in sin."

Lucia's cheeks were streaming with tears, like a flower in the rain. Her mother's words had filled her with confusion and a mysterious shame. "I love you," she said. Though it sounded irrelevant, it was the only phrase she could find.

"Then obey me," was the implacable woman's reply.

"I will do what I can."

"I'm you' mother. You do what I say, whatever it is."

Lucia was silent. Sadly, she could pay only partial allegiance to this worldly mother. She loved her, it was true. But her full loyalty was pledged elsewhere. "I can only promise to try," she finally said.

"Okay, think it over. Are you so sure you saw the Blessed Mother? You know how the mind can play tricks. Maybe you need to see a doctor. What harm can it do?"

Lucia mulled this over, then shrugged. "No harm, I guess."

Serafina saw a glimmer of hope.

"But nobody's going to make me say I didn't see her," Lucia added hastily. "Nobody."

Serafina was crafty enough not to press the point. She squinted with satisfaction. "Joost keep an open mind, that's all I ask. Would God want you to doom your own brother? Look at it this way: maybe the Lord above planned all these things as a way to save Mario."

"Somehow I don't see this Father Acosta as a helper of the Lord."

Serafina shrugged. "It's his job. He's a priest, isn't he?"

"What kind of priest uses a sick little boy as . . . as bait."

"A bad priest."

"If I don't do what he wants, then he'll let Mario die. Is that it?"

For a few seconds Serafina sat stiffly in the chair, gripping the arms tightly. She dueled with an old enemy—the impulse to show her emotions. Her face was impassive but her body was unsteady. Though her features may have been carved from granite her breast heaved like human flesh. "He will probably die no matter what we do. This doctor from Cyprus may not be a miracle worker like you."

The voice at the top of the stairs speared them. "Will it hurt?" asked the boy, rubbing his eyes. "Will it hurt when I die?"

Serafina and Lucia exchanged looks of mutual horror and ineffable remorse.

The next day Lucia was sent by her mother to buy produce from the fruit and vegetable truck that stopped on their block three mornings a week during the summer. Under a canvas canopy in the back of the vehicle were arrayed many crates of fresh provisions harvested from the nearby Bronx and Long Island truck farms. The Buonfiglios did not have to buy many things from Mr. Carbone, the portly and cheerful peddler. Serafina may have had a blue heart but she also had a green thumb and cultivated a thriving garden on the plot of land adjoining the house, a boon to the family budget. Beside the grape arbor, she had planted fig, cherry and peach trees, tomatoes, herbs, squash and cucumbers to fill both the summer table and the Mason jars that lined the cellar shelves. And the red riot of roses that gallivanted around the driveway showed a taste for beauty in this sour and outwardly practical gardener.

Lucia's errand, then, involved buying only a few items such as peas, corn and watermelon, to supplement the family crop.

The truck stopped in at the usual place, right at the middle of the block in front of Mrs. Carney's clapboard bungalow. Carbone summoned his customers with three sharp toots of the horn and a peddler's song. "Whoa, peachie, swee' cohrnn. Watermel-own, watermel-own. Fresh tomater, fresh potater. Ahrahn-jiz . . ."

At the conclusion he hopped from the van, quickly snapped open a brown paper bag to take orders from the flock of housewives that had already swooped down on his truck. Among the women stood Lucia, clutching a change purse and shopping list, waiting her turn.

Carbone, a bewhiskered Neapolitan who had a fondness

for Lucia which he often displayed by sneaking free strawberries into her shopping bag, greeted her warmly. She merely nodded politely, causing him to frown.

She was preoccupied. Branded into her mind was the memory of Mario's pathetic question the day before. Afterward she had done her best to persuade him that he was not going to die but the effort was undermined by the words he had overheard and the shakiness of her own faith in his future.

"You won't die, Buddy, believe me," she had said, smoothing the bangs of hair on his forehead.

"Yes, I will," he answered evenly. "I heard Mamma say so."

"She said you *may* die. And you certainly will someday, when God calls you. But it won't be for a long long time."

"I don't believe you. You're just trying to make me feel better."

"No. I mean it."

Hope flashed in his haunted brown eyes. "What can you do about it? How do you know I'm not going to die?"

The question fired her emotions. How? Her certainty about so many things had lately been shaken. Her once strong faith now tottered. Yet she managed to scrape together the raw material of conviction, unsteady as it was.

"Trust me," she said with firm affection.

The boy smiled thinly, happy to clutch this slender lifeline. "Okay, Lou. Even if I have to die, I'll trust you."

Carbone's booming voice interrupted these recollections. "You next, young lady." He squinted at her with concern. "What'll it be?"

She batted her vacant eyes to life and began to recite the list. As he filled her order Carbone kept up a jovial banter with the housewives who were still waiting their turns. The women hooded their eyes and pursed their lips at his repeated references to the juiciness and plumpness of his provisions. In deference to Lucia the peddler paraded his naughtiness in the sheep's clothing of innocent salesmanship. His background naturally inhibited his making openly off-color remarks in the presence of an eleven-year-old girl. And back-door banter was more fun anyhow.

Lucia was not fooled and blushed repeatedly at his obvious burlesqueries. She was relieved to pay the bill and start for home. As she stooped to put the packages into her string bag she felt a tap on her shoulder.

"Howdy, little lady," said the fastidiously dressed man.

All eyes revolved toward him. The women, acutely aware of Lucia's celebrity, were titillated by the presence of this mysterious man with the jacket sleeve tucked into his pocket. They wondered what role he played in Lucia's unorthodox life.

Carbone was suspicious. "Who's this guy?" he asked Lucia, gruffly protective.

She favored Dunlop with a wan smile. "It's okay," she assured the peddler. "He's a friend."

The reporter looked at them all in an expansive way. "Lovely day, isn't it?" He turned to Lucia. "Walk you home?"

She wondered whether her mother's new compact with Father Acosta now broke Serafina's alliance with the reporter and whether she therefore would object again to her sharing Dunlop's company. But, after a moment, she said, "Sure." For once her curiosity was stronger than her scruples.

Under the glare of her neighbors and the peddler, they started down the street. They walked in silence. The sun poured gold on the shade trees, lending the green leaves a look of tarnished treasures. The sidewalk teemed with the traffic of insects. Gaudy summer mocked her brother's illness and Lucia's own preoccupation with immaterial things.

"So, little lady," he said. "How's tricks?"

She resisted a temptation to make more than a perfunctory reply and said, "Okay, thank you." Her gaze rested on his pixyish features. His smile made her feel oddly uneasy.

"Where do you live?" he asked.

She nodded at the two-story brick house near the dead end. "Over there."

His glance swept east over the waterfront and the boats plowing through the calm bay. "Nice neighborhood. Real nice. Hardly know you were in New York."

She pointed across the waters. "That's City Island over there. Sometimes Daddy takes us over for clams on the half-shell. I love 'em. Just with lemon, not tartar sauce." She made a face. "I hate tartar sauce." She looked at him again. "How about you?"

"What?"

"Do you like tartar sauce?"

He was surprised by this glimpse of her childlike side. He often forgot how really young this exceptional girl was. "Can't say as I do, little lady. Can't say as I do."

They approached a bus stop sign shaped in those days like a giant lollipop and he suggested that they sit for a while on the bench provided for waiting passengers.

"I have to get home," she protested.

He clutched her wrist, gently restraining her. "Just a minute or two," he said with an appealing rise of his eyebrows. "I promise I won't keep you long."

She shrugged, sat down and watched the clouds drifting across the sky. She picked up a fistful of gravel from the ground near her sneakered feet and tossed the pebbles toward the curb. He chitchatted for a while as her impatience mounted. She knew he had something to get off his chest and wished he would just come out with it. But she was too shy to suggest this. Silently she tossed the pebbles and waited with the infinite patience of one for whom hurting others' feelings hurt herself.

Finally he announced, "I want to write another story about you."

She looked quizzical. "There's nothing new to write, is there?"

"That's my question to you."

Her puzzlement grew. "I don't get it, Mr. Dunlop."

"Well, you see, my editor's been pressing me to come up with a new angle," he said with an amiable smile. "Something flashy for page one, you know. Ad renewals are coming up and he needs a quick circulation booster. But all this business talk is probably way above your pretty head."

It was.

"Suffice to say, little lady," he continued, "your partner Al Dunlop needs a word or two for the typesetter."

Now she was thoroughly confused. "Huh?"

A frown ended the forced sunniness of his expression. "Come on, little lady, don't play dumb."

She was mortified to apparently have angered him. "I'm sorry. I honestly don't understand."

He was mollified. "Okay, I'll spell it out in plainer English: I'll just write that you had another vision, something spectacular for John Q's nickel. You just back up whatever I write. I'll make it worth your while."

Lucia's face dropped. Could her ears have deceived her? "But . . . but I didn't have another vision." She smiled tentatively, hoping that the response settled the matter. But the annoyance he showed dashed the hope.

"Sure you did, kiddo. Tell your mother I have some silk stockings for her. From Japan via Macao, off the black market." He eyed her from head to foot. "A pair or two for you also," he added, swollen with an air of generosity. "You're getting to the age where you'll want them too."

The full significance of his words finally came home, making her mute. After this stunned silence, she said chokingly, "No. I won't do it."

His lips curled in scorn. With his lonesome hand he produced a package of Luckies from his hip pocket and, with the practiced ease of a circus performer, one-handedly flipped a cigarette into his mouth. "I get it," he said after extinguishing the lighter. "You want me to up the ante."

His slang eluded her. Baffled, she remained silent.

"You're just like your old lady," he said. "You guineas drive a hard bargain."

Now he might as well have been speaking Sanskrit.

"Okay, tell you what." Full of tricks, he blew a couple of smoke rings. "There's twenty bucks in it for you. That'll buy plenty of candles in church . . . hey, where ya going?"

Suffused with hot shame, she had sprung from the bench and bolted toward the house. She felt pursued by serpents and demons, running toward the haven of the brick stoop that her father had built with his own hands.

Dunlop remained sitting on the bus stop bench, blowing smoke rings, outwardly calm but secretly cursing her.

She finally found refuge in her room upstairs. She had run puffing and panting into the kitchen, relieved that her mother was off somewhere performing a chore. She had deposited the shopping bag on the wooden table and stealthily mounted the stairs to solitude.

The room was as Spartan as a priory. The surroundings were filled not with photos of movie stars and school pennants but with the grim adornments of Christian iconography: a crucifix brooded over the bed; a church calendar bearing a portrait of the Sacred Heart was tacked up near the dresser on which stood a plaster statue of Saint Lucy. The only sign that the room belonged to a child and not an ascetic was a doll in flamenco costume propped on the bed. This anomalous touch was added after Ettore had knocked over milk bottles with a baseball at a church bazaar, giving it, too—though obliquely—a religious connection.

Lucia flung herself on the bed, her eyes stinging with tears. She cried quietly for a few minutes, then stopped. She should have denounced him, she thought. But she shrank from confrontation. She could muster no protest stronger than flight. How bad people were! With what few qualms did they lie, bribe and blaspheme! It shocked her to think that her own mother had been in league with the man. She vowed then and there to have nothing more to do with him. After all, she concluded, the Blessed Mother had no need of any help from an unscrupulous man like him. She reflected that maybe these recent trials had been preordained to tutor her in the darker lessons of human nature.

Occupied with such thoughts, she rose from the bed and went to the window overlooking the bay. She watched a group of familiar neighborhood children use a monkey wrench to open a fire hydrant. Soon the geyser spouted and they frisked with pleasure, laughing with the kind of abandon that she hardly ever felt anymore. Fresh tears salted her eyes as she furtively watched their glistening bodies under the hydrant water. What was rare for her, she almost felt resentment. She watched the children, noisy and playful as seals, and wished with all her might that she could be like them.

20

❧❧ ❧❧

Dunlop nodded curtly in reply to the greeting of the obsequious elevator operator, a pale little Irishman of doubtful masculinity who had been employed by the *Home News* for over twenty-five years and used the peripheral though daily association with minor writers like his present passenger to make himself feel important. Thus he was disappointed in Dunlop's only perfunctory response and regretted having missed the opportunity to quip as usual that his day so far had had "its ups and downs." Dunlop, engrossed in mental composition, noticed nothing.

The elevator doors parted at the third floor lobby and he floated off on this cloud of abstraction past the receptionist and into the noisy news room. He ignored the sardonic greetings of his colleagues and called a copy boy to fetch him a container of coffee. He lit what was the twentieth cigarette of the still young day and mused over the typewriter keys. Albert Dunlop, reporter of facts and events, was lost in the brown study that preceded the art of creative writing. Finally, after three swigs of very sweet coffee and another cigarette, he set his five fingers on the keys.

The results of his composition lay the next morning like a writ of heresy on top of Bishop McArdle's ornate desk. The prelate paced the inner office like a caged panther. Finally he lifted his baleful blue eyes to the approaching form of Father Acosta.

The Spanish priest wore his customary mask of impassivity. The small black eyes darted with light disdain. "Yes, Bishop," he said in a sycophantic tone.

McArdle flung a manicured hand toward the desk. "You saw this?"

Acosta nodded and waited.

The bishop's handsome face was creased with concern. "It's getting serious now. She's entered the realm of politics. The archbishop called me about it this morning."

"Indeed," said Acosta, tilting his oiled head. He feigned ignorance although his network of office spies had already informed him of the call.

The bishop looked grim. "You have failed, Father Acosta, to put a lid on this affair. I'm disappointed in you."

Acosta shrugged. "I tried my best, Bishop. I can't work miracles."

McArdle laughed. "Perhaps you lack the sanctity."

"No doubt," he replied, lowering his eyes in a parody of humility.

The prelate sat down behind his imposing desk, routinely riffling papers and signing documents as he continued the conversation. "Even though it's silly and improbable, this newspaper account might provoke an international incident."

"Surely . . ." Acosta drawled.

"I'm quite serious," McArdle snapped. "Do you realize that the story was picked up by the Associated Press and put on the international wire? It's making headlines all over Europe."

Acosta hadn't been aware of this and felt a pang of self-criticism at the failure to keep abreast. It bruised his ego to know that his hierarchical superior (though clear mental inferior) had learned something the Jesuit didn't know.

"That a fact?" he said with concealed scorn.

"Yes." He interrupted the paper-shuffling to tuck a pastille under his tongue. "You know how the laity hungers after sensationalism. The nostalgia for Lourdes and Fatima is still strong."

The bishop finally nodded to a chair. Acosta sat eagerly.

"How true," said the Jesuit after making himself comfortable. "They want loaves and fishes and burning bushes and all that." Abruptly McArdle glared, then squinted. Their mutual cynicism had come out into the open. "They do at that." He paused. "So she claims to have had a second vision, eh?"

"At least according to this reporter," Acosta cautioned, folding pudgy hands in his lap. "I've checked up on him. He has a reputation for embellishing the facts."

McArdle rose, locked his hands behind his back and circled the desk with an abstracted air. Acosta watched, musing that the man used poses and gestures to substitute for real thought. A smile curled his lips.

The bishop touched the newspaper on the desk. "Why didn't she at least stay away from politics? Even Gemma Galgani had the sense to do that. Stick to religious matters."

"Perhaps she models herself after Saint Joan."

A cruel glint shone from the prelate's eyes. "Is she prepared to meet a similar fate?"

Acosta shrugged.

McArdle picked up the newspaper and read aloud: " 'The child told this reporter that the Virgin Mary had commanded her to urge her countrymen to exert pressure on their political leaders to enter the war against the Axis powers.' What nonsense! Our Lady of Jingoism."

"Surely no one will take this tripe seriously."

"I'm not so sure about that. Remember the Lateran Treaty. We still owe a great debt to that clown."

Acosta, who harbored Falangist sympathies, bridled at this description of Mussolini. He dropped his servile pose for a minute to venture this acid comment: "That clown, as you call him, and his colleague in Germany, are halfway to world conquest."

The ex-aviator grimaced. "Yes," he admitted. For all his vanity and unscrupulousness the bishop had no taste for the cruder examples of global Fascism then in ascendancy. He leaned more to the silk-scarf strain of this political orientation. Like the brahmins of Germany, he regarded Hitler as a parvenu, a vulgar postcard peddler.

"Back to the matter at hand," McArdle said.

At this signal Acosta resumed the veil of servility, leaning forward to listen.

"Perhaps we should haul her in before a court of inquiry," McArdle suggested. "It would be fairly easy to discredit her story."

"With all due respect, Bishop, let's not act hastily. Let me first try less drastic measures. I'll call her in for a personal interview. Here at the Chancery. I'm fairly certain that in these imposing surrounding she can be persuaded to mend her ways."

I lift my metaphoric quill from description of this hypocritical scene. The behavior of these priests reminded me of a quote from the Curé of Ars: "Sometimes the ancient serpent lodges in hands joined in prayer." That the fate of this good child lay in those same hands still nauseates my abused and ancient stomach. But so it was.

Before continuing the narrative I feel that I should provide (particularly to the lay reader) a little background to help explain how it happened that a young girl from the Bronx could have an impact, however small, on international politics. Even the worthy tribunes might need a reminder that Vatican coins bore the mottoes: "Money is the root of all evil" and "It is better to give than to receive." Yet one could trace numbered bank accounts in the Crédit Suisse de Genève to agents of a vast financial empire presided over by a man who occupied a nineteen-room apartment on the top floor of a palace overlooking St. Peter's Square. Do I make myself clear?

Let's turn the clock back even more years to the Feast Day of Lourdes in 1929. On this rainy day in February an avowed atheist entered the Lateran Palace, was ushered into the room where Charlemagne had been the guest of Leo III, picked up a gold pen that had been blessed by Pope Pius XI, and signed a treaty. This atheist—a man who often touched his private parts in public as a gesture to ward off *malocchio* (the evil eye)— was Benito Mussolini.

The Lateran Treaty provided a great windfall to the Vatican, some $90 million in indemnity for the land that the Kingdom of Italy had confiscated from the papacy in 1870. From this day forward Mussolini was hailed if not as a saint at least as a national hero by the Princes of the Church. Il Duce ordered the crucifix to be placed back in the classroom and outlawed Freemasonry. Even twelve years later in 1941, after Eugenio Pacelli had ascended the throne of Peter and relations between the dictator and the Church had cooled, it was still not wise or politic to criticize Mussolini. This was Lucia's sin, as alleged in Dunlop's article. How was it possible for the Virgin Mary to raise her blue banner against the man who had bestowed on Holy Mother Church the charismatic gift of corporate tax abatements? Of course it didn't matter that the attack on the Italian dictator actually had been launched by the liar Dunlop.

I should also like to remind both my clerical and lay readers of the character of McArdle's superior, the Archbishop of New York, a person with easy access to the sanctuaries of Wall Street. Early in his career the archbishop distinguished himself by service in Rome as the first American assistant to the papal secretariat of state. He cemented relations with one Cardinal Pacelli and an influential Italian layman whom I shall call the "Count." When, after the signing of the Lateran Treaty, the Vatican found itself with this bundle of cash to invest, the archbishop was selected as the official American agent for a Vatican office known as the Special Administration—a financial bureau. In other words he was made the Vatican's Wall Street broker. The Count also had a major role to play in Vatican money matters and his name appeared among the boards of directors of many Italian companies in which pontifical funds were invested. He was named governor of Vatican City, among other papal jobs. Such was the man's influence in the temporal realm of Church affairs that Italian cynics had dubbed him the "Lay Pope."

Given this background, it is natural to conjecture that any criticism of a Church benefactor like Mussolini, particularly by a pretender to divine inspiration, would be met with strong disapproval by such men. After all, what dictator Mussolini giveth, he might taketh away.

Forgive the digression. I merely wanted to show what my innocent protégée was up against. Her depiction by that scoundrel Dunlop as an enemy of the Black Shirts, as a *Jungfrau* who heard voices exhorting her to political action, put her in jeopardy. Her situation did not improve when in the next few days the growing cult of her devotees eagerly took up the banner of anti-Fascism.

They gathered on these sultry nights by the shrine in the breezy park. To the bubbling brew of mysticism (supersitition, if you like) was added the spice of chauvinism. Some worshippers carried placards caricaturing the Axis leaders as demons with forked tails. Here and there fistfights erupted with Fascist sympathizers, some of whom had come by subway from Yorkville in Manhattan. The American flag was placed beside the crucifix. And the press avidly recorded it all.

Lucia, who was formed more in the mold of the Little Flower of Lisieux than Joan of Arc, was puzzled and disturbed by these events. She stayed away from the shrine, even though she was revered by the cultists and the stories about her had assumed the glow of legend. There was, for example, the report of how no mud clung to her clothes when she once knelt at the shrine during a rainstorm. There was a long list of miraculous cures: the stonemason who regained sight in his damaged right eye; the child whose withered right hand was restored to normality; the widow who threw off the symptoms of paralysis of the spine and walked again. Naturally scientists dismissed these phenomena as psychosomatic cures, but many of the laity were undaunted in their belief. They saw no distinction between a miracle and what the phenomenologists of science called "mind over matter." And they flocked to the shrine, armed with insignia both religious and patriotic.

Lucia remained aloof from it all. She was ashamed of the parish letters read from the pulpit condemning the cult of worship and loath to offend ecclesiastic authority. She was outraged by the lies printed in the *Home News* and deeply disturbed by the chauvinist and fanatic tenor of the cult movement. The memory of the time that the worshippers tore off her clothes still burned in her mind. Yet she had a lurking feeling that these events might somehow fit into the Blessed Mother's inscrutable plan for kindling faith.

Such thoughts occupied Lucia as she sat in the kitchen one

day watching her mother prepare flour for baking bread. Serafina performed this task in the ritual old-country way, having made her own yeast sponge and left it to rise overnight. She now passed flour through a sieve. Her hair was wrapped in a kerchief and white smudges powdered her cheeks, hands and dimpled arms. An Italian news program was on the radio that sat on the window ledge and the announcer was describing the latest defeats suffered by the Italian Army in North Africa. The woman listened with a cynical smile.

"Look what's happened to the new Caesar," she said. "The British, they whip him good. The *stupidone*, all he can conquer is tiny Albania. Benedetto Croce hit the nail on the head: Hitler, he's a devil. But Mussolini? He's joost a clown." She poured water into the flour and smiled sourly.

Lucia knew next to nothing about world politics. But it made her sad to think about all those boys dying: Italians, Greeks, British, Albanians, whatever lands they came from. Surely the Blessed Mother hated war too. What kind of world was it where newspapers published lies, and clowns and devils led young men to early graves? She had always known in an abstract way that evil existed in the world. But now for the first time she was smelling its foul breath. And it was difficult to reconcile with God's goodness. She longed to discuss these matters with her mother but she knew it was useless. Serafina lately had increased the pressure on her to renounce the vision and barter for Buddy's recovery, especially since the injection of politics into the cult issue. Lucia feared raising the subject again.

As Serafina blended the yeast and flour and began to form the dough she too was thinking of these things, although from a different perspective. She was wondering how the political implications of the affair would be greeted by Acosta and his superiors and how the cult's tawdrier side might be used to persuade her daughter to disavow it all.

"So," she began with a sideways glance at Lucia, "the Lady asked you to bring America into the war, eh?" Her laughter filled the kitchen.

Lucia frowned. "I told you, Mamma. He made it all up."

The woman added salt, then folded and kneaded the

dough, slapping it against the floured countertop. "Sure, blame it on Dunlop."

"He's bad, Mamma. He's a liar." Her eyes narrowed in rare disapproval. "And you take money from him."

Serafina was stung. "Not anymore. Not since that day at the shrine when the people attacked you. I have nothing to do with him anymore."

Lucia smiled broadly. "I'm glad. He's not a nice man."

"You said it," exclaimed Serafina, grunting over her work, venting her emotions by slapping and kneading the dough.

"What kind of bread you making, Mamma?"

"Garlic bread. *Caccia nanza.*"

"Yummy."

"We'll eat it for a snack this afternoon, with a glass of wine. Okay?"

"Sure," said Lucia delightedly. Such moments of intimacy between herself and her mother were rare. She was savoring it. "But we have to save some for dinner."

"Don't worry. I make four loaves."

Serafina was softening her up like the dough in her hands.

"Can I help?" asked Lucia.

"Okay. You slice the garlic."

"Be glad to," she said, running off to fetch garlic from the vegetable basket.

"Eight cloves," said Serafina, "and slice 'em thin."

Two hours later the loaves emerged from the oven, piping hot and fragrant with spices. Lucia was filled with a rare sense of well-being as she sat with her mother at the kitchen table to sample the results of their cooperative effort. For the time being she even forgot that a park called Pelham Bay existed. In this warm world of food and shared pleasure she took refuge from her recent cares. She ate the bread with ferocious pleasure. "Dee-licious," she said.

Serafina poured two glasses of amber-colored wine. "Try this stuff. Your father's foreman brought it back from Calabria."

"Homemade?" she asked, accepting the tumbler.

"What else? Drink up, you a big girl now. You a woman already."

Lucia blushed, but drank. An amber mustache formed above her lip. She ate the bread. "What kind of spice is this?"

"*Rosmarino.*"

"Rosemary? Like my sister's name?"

"Yes. You like it?"

"Uh-huh."

"Your father loves this bread too."

"I know. Why don't you make it more often?"

She shrugged and cut another slice for herself. "Who has the time?"

Lucia grew thoughtful. As she nibbled she wondered why Serafina didn't show more affection toward Ettore. The thought often had occurred to her that some secret breach divided her parents and she would do anything to reconcile them. But she always had been too reticent to mention it. Suddenly she summoned up the courage to ask, "Mamma, do you love Daddy?"

Serafina's brows knitted in severity. "What a foolish question!"

"But . . ."

"The wine must have gone to your head."

"No, it hasn't," she protested. But in a way, it was true. The wine had given her the boldness to broach the subject.

"Love is for young people," Serafina said tartly.

"That's not so, Mamma. Love is for everybody."

"That's enough," she commanded. "You' not old enough to discuss such things."

"But you said I was already a woman."

"That's enough, I said."

Lucia lowered her eyes. "Yes, Mamma." It was uncharacteristic of her so to overstep the bounds of familial propriety. Yet she was in an odd way glad that she had mentioned it for she guessed that it might do some good in the long run.

Serafina changed the subject. "Do you think about our talk the other day?"

"What do you mean?"

"About Mario and the specialist? About this vision business."

"Yes. I've thought about it."

"Well?"

"I don't know," she said anxiously. "I'm still thinking about it."

"Now—with this political stuff—it becomes a real circus. You better tell them to call it off."

"Please, Mamma . . ."

"Okay. I don't push you." She began to clear the table. "Remember the promise. Your mind is open."

"Yes," she answered with an air of gloom. "My mind is open." But it was already clear to her that she could never renounce the vision. She saw what she saw. Her brother's fate was in the hands of God.

Serafina seemed abstracted now as she stacked dishes in the sink. Had Lucia's questions stoked unpleasant memories and long-buried passions? Certainly something was smoldering beneath the sullen exterior.

While drying the dishes Lucia furtively watched her mother but couldn't figure out her mood. What had started out as a very pleasant afternoon was ending up on an odd and disturbing note. She wondered if she would ever succeed in getting Serafina to come out of her shell of cynicism. With God's help, she thought, she someday would.

When they had finished doing the dishes Serafina took the remaining three loaves of bread and stored them in the unlit oven to keep them warm for Ettore.

21

᯽᯽᯽ ᯽᯽᯽

She came dressed in her school jumper and white blouse, clutching her father's hand. Ettore was asked to wait in the reception area as the girl was ushered into Acosta's carpeted office. Her wide eyes swept over the elegant surroundings. She was struck by how much the Chancery reminded her of movie versions of a rich man's library with its dark woods, heavy Gothic-style and Italianate furniture and leather-bound books. The room was softly illuminated by shaded wall sconces, the first such light fixtures she had ever seen. Her revolving eyes soon fastened on the portly form of the disliked priest.

Here I am compelled to quote Lucretius. *Tantum religio potuit suadere malorum* (So many evils could religion prompt). This clergyman and his all too numerous counterparts would make a blackbird of the Holy Ghost.

It was a few days after Dunlop's latest fiction had been published and Acosta, as planned, had called Lucia to Madison Avenue to intimidate her by the grandeur of the setting and the force of his personality into recanting the story about the vision. He was determined to avoid the expense, trouble and possible bad publicity attached to calling the girl before a formal panel.

She stood stiffly before his desk. The din of traffic came through the window from the street below. It was an awkward moment as the priest said nothing, appraising her with his black eyes. He had confidence in the power of psychological terror tactics to disarm and unnerve his adolescent adversary. His plan included periods of intimidating silence.

"Be seated," he finally said.

She sank into a preposterously large oak chair upholstered in red velvet and waited for him to speak. He was silent again, allowing the majesty of the surroundings to take hold. He knew that he would have to proceed gingerly. His instincts told him that a core of strength lay beneath her timid exterior and he was always mindful that the girl had become something of a folk heroine as her fame spread and tales of cures, mythical or real, reached the ears of those whose faith was—like most virulent organisms—simple and strong. He examined her appearance closely: the demure clothing, the severely cropped hair and polished china complexion; when it came to her candid blue eyes he dropped his glance to the desktop.

"Now then," he said, trying to sound amiable. "How are you, young lady?"

Her innate friendliness surfaced. "Just fine, Father," she said with a sudden bright smile. "How are you?"

He mumbled in reply. The signs of her indomitable kindness gave him a momentary pang. A wince marred the bland inscrutability of his fleshy features and somewhere under the cartilaginous layers that had formed over his heart there stirred a fleeting memory from his boyhood in Andalusia. The sight of this artless girl kindled an ember from his own age of innocence when he first heard the call to the banner of his compatriot Saint Ignatius Loyola, when he burned to save souls. He felt a stab of regret. Then his face resumed its glacial expression. "Young lady," he said, "do you realize what you're doing?"

"I'm sorry, Father. I don't understand."

He rose from the chair and looked sternly down at her. "Indeed you don't. This meddling in politics—you don't realize the effect it might have."

"It's not my fault," she protested. "I didn't have another vision and I didn't say that I did. Mr. Dunlop made it all up."

He paced the room to let another vacuum of silence work

its power. He stopped and stood under an oil painting that depicted the apparition of the Virgin to Saint Bernard, a copy of a work by Filippo Lippi. He pointed to a crucifix hanging on the opposite wall. "Do you lie in the shadow of the cross?" he asked.

"I never lie," she said undaunted.

"Never?" he said mockingly. "Have you never lied in your life?"

She gave the question serious thought. "I suppose once or twice," she finally said. "When I was very little."

"My, my. You *are* a saint."

She blushed. "No, Father."

"But you accuse Mr. Dunlop of lying."

"I only say that what he wrote wasn't true. I don't accuse anybody of anything."

"That's the same as lying, isn't it?"

"Maybe he thought he was telling the truth. Maybe somebody told *him* a lie. Or maybe he just made a mistake. It's not for me to judge."

Her indomitable charity irked him. After an interval he said, "Be that as it may, this cult of yours is getting out of hand."

She said, "Forgive me for contradicting you, Father, but it's not *my* cult."

"Whose is it, then?"

"I don't know. I have no control over those people and what they do. I don't really like what's happening. But what can I do about it?"

"Put a stop to it."

She knew what he was driving at but still asked, "How?"

"You know how. Do you realize that the news of your so-called apparition has reached the ears of the Holy Father?"

Now her heart pounded. Visions swam in her mind of the hawk-nosed prelate in white skullcap and robes whom she had seen in newsreels blessing the multitudes in Saint Peter's Square. It staggered her to think that so unimaginably lofty and holy a personage had heard of her or anything about her.

"N-no," she stammered. "I didn't realize."

"Yes. Through a wire service known as the Associated Press. And the news, dear child, is bound to have displeased him."

"Omigod."

Acosta paused again to let the enormity of all this sink in.

"I didn't mean to cause any trouble," she said, on the brink of tears.

"Of course not," he said readily, sensing a crack in her defenses. "You can still set things right."

"I know—" she said, inspired by an idea. "I'll call another newspaper and tell them that the story wasn't true about Our Lady telling me to make the United States go to war and all that."

"You will have to do more," he said sternly.

"I can't."

"Consider it very carefully, young lady. You must renounce this vision nonsense altogether."

"Renounce?"

"Recant. Take it back. Admit it never happened."

"But it *did* happen."

"Do you realize what a bad effect your stubbornness is having? Are you happy to anger His Holiness, to give a black eye to the Church, perhaps to cause her to lose money that she uses to clothe the poor and feed the hungry? Would Our Lady want all that to happen? I ask you, would she?"

Lucia, looking very small in the big chair, sank down in dejection, overwhelmed by the magnitude of the accusations and awed by the importance of the issues at stake. She was assailed by doubt. Was she by sticking to her guns not only jeopardizing her brother's life but also mocking the throne of Peter and impeding the Lord's good temporal work? Isn't it possible that she had imagined everything? The burden of these questions was too much for her to bear alone. Silently, under the veiled gaze of the fat priest, under the somber watchful portraits of saints and martyrs, she prayed.

A long time passed before she said, "I can't. I just can't." The words were uttered in a resolute tone. She had searched her soul and that was that. She vowed to herself to give the same answer to her mother. She was deeply sorry to offend the

Pope, terribly unhappy that the Church on earth might suffer, and finally inconsolably sad if she contributed to her brother's death. But what could she do? She had prayed and the answer had come. No ambiguities clouded the oracles of her heart. Lucky she, the art of prayer never failed her.

Acosta's cheeks bloomed with anger. "Then you're sticking to your ridiculous story?"

"I have to." Although he always tried to keep a cool exterior she could see that he was upset. Secretly she didn't really care.

"How dare you," he challenged, pointing to the painting of the monk and the Virgin above him, "put yourself in the same category as saints such as he?"

"I don't," she said. "But the Blessed Mother did."

"How dare you?" he repeated.

She lowered her eyes but would not give in.

"How would you like to face a panel of inquiry? How would you like to have to tell your absurd story to doctors and psychiatrists and very learned priests?"

"If it would help me do the job Our Lady gave me, then I'll face them."

The reply silenced him for a moment. It stung his pride to think that he was losing a battle of wits and will with an eleven-year-old girl. It infuriated him. He had used the panel as an idle threat for he also didn't relish the prospect of a formal hearing. He much preferred handling such matters informally and privately. Furthermore, the girl and her candor posed an unspoken reproach to his Byzantine ways and padlocked heart. While he wouldn't fully admit it to himself, this unnerved him. He vowed to crush her spirit, one way or another.

He recovered his composure. Then he said, "I must compliment you, my dear. Despite the unsavory qualities of the cult, you have inspired great faith in the people and that's a good thing."

"It wasn't my doing. It was Our Lady's."

He paid little attention to her response. A plan was forming in his mind. He chose his words carefully. "The Church must beware of false prophets, fakers, people like that. You understand, don't you?"

"Yes."

"I'm sorry if I was a little harsh with you."

"That's okay, Father."

"We'd like to be on your side. We really would."

"Well—that would be wonderful."

He went over to his desk and sat down again, watching her closely and smiling benignly. He folded his hands and said, "Perhaps the Church could give sanction to the cult, sponsor your cause. There might be a way."

"How?" she asked, eyes bright with hope.

"The traditional way. We need something tangible to go on. You know—a *sign*."

"A *sign*?"

"Yes. Like the flowering rosebush of Saint Bernadette. Or a spring of water. Some visible mark of Our Lady's presence."

"But what if I can't do it?"

A touch of cruelty now colored the smile. "Surely the Virgin Mary will produce something for you. She wouldn't abandon such a close friend, now, would she?"

She looked worried. "She never promised anything." Her eyes suddenly sparkled. "What about the stigmata? Weren't they signs?"

"Psychiatrists have natural explanations for them. They'd probably say you needed a *rest*, my dear."

Lucia caught the significance of this remark. They would say she was crazy and maybe lock her up in a mental institution. She was afraid.

There was a long silence. "Okay then," he finally said with an air of concluding the interview. "I think we understand each other now."

"I guess so, Father."

"Good afternoon then."

"Good afternoon." She rose, pale and forlorn. She stopped at the door. "Father?"

"Yes."

She paused. She often asked priests to give her a formal blessing and from force of habit was about to make the same request of Father Acosta. But she couldn't bring herself to ask him. "Nothing," she said quickly to cover her embarrassment. "Good afternoon."

He smiled at the door she had shut behind her, pleased with the idea that had struck him. When she failed to produce the sign the cult would lose interest, even turn against her. Soon the whole affair would be forgotten. But first he had to find a way to publicize the *sign* angle. He picked up the telephone.

"Outside line, please." As he waited for the operator to make the connection his thoughts strayed to the pebbly shores of Málaga and the pearly dreams of his youth. He muttered to himself. Then he got the dial tone.

"*Bronx Home News,*" came the nasal voice of an operator.

"Mr. Dunlop, please," he said gazing at the Mudejar crucifix hanging on the wall. He averted his eyes.

22

❧❧ ❧❧

The story appeared the next day, quoting an anonymous "Chancery source." I did a slow burn as I read it. More poison from the deceitful pen of Albert Dunlop. Surely Lucia wouldn't have promised to produce a sign, as the article alleged. It just wasn't like her. I felt like chopping off the reporter's other arm but the skunk would probably type the lies with his toes. I pictured him armless and legless like the snake he was. I wondered if this new angle came from his own fevered imagination or if he had had some help this time in the creative process. Who was the "Chancery source"? I had a sneaking suspicion.

This put Lucia in a bad spot indeed. It wasn't hard to follow Acosta's reasoning: the article would stir up the rabble, make them clamor for a burning bush or some such pyrotechnic and divert attention from the political side of the cult. Moreover, Lucia's failure to produce a sign would discredit her. In a way I also hoped the plan would work. It would liberate her from these fanatics and spare her the ordeal of facing an inquisition. But my hope was short-lived, as I will soon relate.

On the very day that the article appeared, a sealed communiqué addressed to the archbishop arrived at the Chancery offices on Madison Avenue. It was from Rome or, to be exact, from that diamond-shaped, seventeen-square-mile sovereign nation that flies a flag showing two vertical stripes of yellow and white and the papal tiara over two crossed keys. The author of the letter was the archbishop's old Vatican crony—the Count. Even Acosta's spies could not find out the precise contents of the communiqué but it soon became clear that it concerned the cult of Lucia Buonfiglio.

Bishop McArdle spent the morning closeted with the "Boss." When he later emerged through the oak doors his face was grim and white. It wasn't long before Acosta's feet stood on the bishop's hand-woven Anatolian.

"There's no choice now," said McArdle.

"No choice?"

"She must face a hearing."

Acosta frowned. "I see."

"Attend to the arrangements."

"Yes, Bishop." Acosta was too circumspect to ask any questions about the letter from the Vatican even though he itched to know more details. In any case it was clear that the archbishop (who, by the way, was then angling for a red hat) had ordered the hearing in the hope of defusing the situation once and for all. He could only speculate whether the decision originated with the archbishop or came from an even higher authority. He himself doubted the wisdom of the action, fearing that the publicity might make matters worse. And what if (by some veritable miracle) the girl survived the attempt to discredit her? The burden rested on the Jesuit's rounded shoulders.

"I'll take care of everything," he promised as he reached the door. It had a hollow sound.

The court of inquiry would be held on the "ordinary" (church jargon for "local") level. The girl would be examined by a panel of so-called experts, including a physicist, neurologist, internist, canonical attorney and—most important kangaroo of all—psychiatrist. Witnesses to the stigmatic attack and other events would be examined. Character witnesses would be called. A general show of thoroughness and objectivity would be made. But the linchpin of the strategy was the threat to Lucia of committal to a mental asylum. The threat would be posed repeatedly to her and particularly to her parents, whom Acosta deemed more susceptible to influence. In some secret den of his bartered conscience he now viewed the case as a personal challenge rather than just another of his sometimes unsavory ecclesiastic chores. Since the day of the private interview with the girl in his office a subtle but profound change in his attitude had taken place. He now saw her as not merely a political and bureaucratic nuisance but as an affront to his essential self. For the first time in many years he had had trouble sleeping. More and more his thoughts had been turning to the past, to his youth and early priesthood. Was it possible that cynicism had not completely blighted his character? If so it was unfortunate for Lucia. For the conflict turned the darker and stronger side of his nature into a snarling and formidable enemy. If she didn't renounce her story he was hell-bent to find a way to have her declared insane, immoral or both.

Lucia was informed by letter of her first scheduled appearance before the panel—August 11. She was, of course, under no legal obligation to comply, but what did this matter to one so devout? She had less than a week to prepare herself. Now she was in a double-bind. Not only was she under pressure to produce a miraculous sign but she also had to defend herself before a forbidding panel of investigators. Yet she took the news with stoicism, her fears tempered by relief. In a way she welcomed the chance to clear the air and spread the message of Mary. She also welcomed the news that I had been appointed her "advocate."

"Advocate? What's that mean?" she asked me as we sat in the rectory garden amid tea roses and marigolds. I had asked her over to discuss things.

"It's sort of like your lawyer."

"Am I on trial or something?"

"Not exactly," I said, shifting uneasily on the stone bench. "But the Church has certain rules of procedure."

Her frown of concern dissolved into a smile. "I'm glad you're in my corner," she said.

I reddened. "I'm not exactly Clarence Darrow."

"Who?"

"Never mind. I'll do the best I can, Lucia. I hope your

confidence is justified. I'm not sure it will make much difference, though."

She looked puzzled.

I patted her hand. "Don't worry," I said without conviction.

After she left I remained in the garden for a long time, staring at a tea rose basking in the hot sun of August, proud as a courtesan in its pink petalage. I listened morosely to the twittering of birds and pondered.

I later sat before a stack of books on the desk in my bedroom, boning up for my reluctant role as advocate. I cracked the encyclopedia and read:

"Miracles occurring in connection with a claim of supernatural revelation serve as a divine signature to the truth of that claim. But miracles function as signs also in other ways. They not only confirm supernaturally revealed truths but represent these truths. Thus the Resurrection of Christ is not only a guarantee of His teaching but a symbol of His redemptive victory over the spiritual death of sin and an exemplar of the resurrection promised to the faithful."

I longed for a Devil Dog. I continued reading: "Miracles are also in themselves direct manifestations of one or more divine attributes; e.g., a miraculous cure bespeaks God's compassion. And miracles may testify to the sanctity of a man, as do the miracles accepted as evidence in processes of beatification and canonization."

Oh, how the Devil can quote scripture, I thought. I opened another book. Aquinas was in clear contradiction with this bit of wisdom. He wrote that visions and other graces were not in themselves sanctifying, and that no nexus existed between them and the merit of the recipient. Well, maybe this wasn't strictly a contradiction. But it showed how shifts in emphasis could muddy the picture. I had to remind myself that I was not proposing Lucia for sainthood, only trying to defend her from the fangs of the ecclesiastic wolf pack. My ardor for defending her faltered before the realization that those selfsame wolves were my occupational superiors and had the power to banish me to a slum parish or even an uncivilized outpost if I took one false step. Unfortunately my vocation was never marked by missionary zeal and my flesh rebelled at the prospect of self-denial. Religious altruism was never a strong suit of this ordained minister. Fainthearted indeed was the poor girl's public defender.

And if this conflict of interest weren't enough, another potentially more serious one nagged at my stunted conscience: how to reconcile my role as Lucia's confessor with that of advocate? What if certain confidences divulged in the sacramental shadows loomed important in the daylight of the inquiry? It was a tricky situation, to say the least.

I resumed studying, now taking up the likely procedure of the inquiry. She would be questioned by all the experts and individually examined by the internist and psychiatrist. Full medical and psychological reports would be prepared and sent to the archbishop. Witnesses to various "miracles" and her stigmatic attack would be questioned. Character witnesses, friends and family would be quizzed. There was no exact prescription for the sequence of these procedures; that depended in this case on whoever was running the show (Acosta—I would have bet the collection box). As advocate—begging the tribunes' pardons—I was just a figurehead. Lucia had no rights of due process. Mother Church, of course, as the font of all wisdom and justice, made no bows to democratic rules. Had I any guts then, I would have had a gut feeling that Acosta was determined to railroad my client into the booby hatch. And I was, at bottom, powerless to do anything about it. Or was I?

The other tack the inquisitors might take would be to accuse Lucia or her family of staging the whole affair for profit. Such charlatanism was rather common in episodes of purported visions and miracles. I feared my protégée was on shaky ground here, not because she herself had been tainted but because I suspected her mother had accepted "considerations" from Dunlop. And Mario's illness made the family vulnerable to bribery of a much more insidious kind.

From my vantage, then, it looked pretty bleak for Lucia. The only possible leverage she had was the force of public opinion and Acosta had cleverly defused the advantage by planting the story about the supernatural sign. Now the burden was on Lucia. Now the multitudes would be disappointed if they didn't get to see the Red Sea rolled back. Perhaps they would turn against her. I stared darkly at the pile of reference books on my dusty rolltop desk. Soon I was downstairs raiding the rectory icebox for a midmorning snack.

The panelists went straight to work investigating the first item on their schedule: Lucia's stigmatic attack. They took depositions from Dr. Papajohn, Sophie Mariano and many of the witnesses to the seizure in church. The process was not like a trial where testimony was heard in the subject's presence, but more like a fact-finding mission. We therefore had no opportunity to correct the distorted picture rendered by certain witnesses.

"She's nothing but a trickster and a troublemaker," said Sister Mary Rachel, summoned from vacation to appear at the Chancery for questioning.

"Why do you say that?" asked Acosta, serving as canonical lawyer. The other panelists leaned forward and peered at the sullen nun.

"I ought to know," she said. "I'm her teacher. I observe her in action every day. She is clever, but vain and deceitful. She disrupts the class with her blasphemous pretensions to sanctity. I have often had to punish her." She folded her arms smugly.

"For what, precisely?"

She furrowed her brow, then said with satisfaction, "Pride. She is guilty of the sin of pride."

"Yes," said Acosta impatiently, "but what form does this take?"

"She thinks she's superior to her classmates. She shows up for school at whatever time suits her. She boasts about visions. She lies. Believe me, Father, this is not the kind of girl the Lord would single out as a pawn in the propagation of faith." She lowered her eyes and added, "With all due respect."

"You saw the stigmatic attack, did you not?"

"Yes, I saw it."

"Would you kindly describe what you saw?"

"She did an obscene little dance—in church, God forgive

her—and began writhing on the floor like . . . well, like some Arabian belly dancer."

"But she was bleeding, was she not?" asked the psychiatrist, a gnarled little Frenchman named Andrieu.

"I guess she was bleeding a little. Hysteria."

"We have testimony that she bled profusely," Andrieu responded. "From the limbs, even the eyes."

"As I said," she replied dourly, "I noticed some bleeding. I can't really say how much."

The grandfatherly psychiatrist toyed with a pince-nez. "You don't like her, do you?" he said directly.

"No," the nun replied in just as straightforward a manner. "I think she's bad."

"Bad?" he repeated, smiling. "That's such a vague word. How do you mean it, exactly? Do you mean bad like 'troublesome' or 'naughty'?"

Her nostrils flared. "I don't think it's a vague word, sir. I mean bad as in 'evil.' She's a brazen young thing."

Andrieu thought he glimpsed more than defiance in the nun's shining eyes. "You feel so strongly on the matter. From all we have heard she's rather a nice little girl. Perhaps intense and perhaps even disturbed. But evil?"

"Maybe the good sister knows her better than most," Acosta said as the three remaining panelists mumbled vaguely.

"Maybe," said Andrieu musingly and without conviction. He turned his gaze back to the witness. The psychiatrist's whetted instincts impelled him to explore the motivation behind the nun's strong dislike. He watched her cold blue eyes gleam with a kind of hatred that he had encountered often in his clinical experience, a hatred that was the bastard of pleasure. He realized that this was not the proper place or method in which to psychoanalyze the nun but he couldn't resist the impulse to tinker with her psyche a little. "When did you first come to the conclusion that the girl was bad, Sister?"

"From the moment I laid eyes on her," she snapped.

"Really?"

"Sure. I could tell. Never trusted her with that sweet voice and slender body. Oh, she pretended to be pure and demure, all right. But I could see beneath the saintly disguise."

"What could you see?"

She shifted her weight uneasily in the chair. "That she was hot-blooded and bad, that's what."

"Hot-blooded?"

"Like all Sicilians." Regretting this remark, she lapsed into a sullen silence.

"Like Santa Lucia?" asked Father Morrissey with a small smile. "She was Sicilian."

The nun glared at the Jesuit physicist who had asked the question. She was adamant. "The girl is bad, I tell you."

The smile vanished from Morrissey's florid Irish face.

Nervously Acosta broke in. "I think that will be all, Sister. Thank you for your testimony."

"You mean that's all?" she asked.

"That's all," Acosta answered.

And so the nun left the hearing room, her face showing frustration. As she stumbled out of the Chancery she heard ringing in her head a strange high song of remorse, a shrill dirge of prodigal understanding.

The sun flooded Madison Avenue as Sister Mary Rachel reached the street. The internal song whined in her ears like a trapped bee. The stony peaks of Saint Patrick's Cathedral reared in the west and on impulse she walked a block and entered its portals. But in the echoing vaults she found no sanctuary from the harsh imputing sound, no sign of vindication from the surrounding waxworks of saints and seraphs. She knelt in the first pew facing the main altar. And soon her sobbing drowned out the merciless drone of her conscience.

Sister Mary Rachel, a dazed look on her face, had passed without recognizing me in the antechamber of the hearing room. I shrugged and turned the doorknob. I was the next person scheduled to appear before the panel in this preliminary hearing.

I nodded to the panelists and sat in the chair indicated by Acosta. The inquisitors smiled benignly. Morrissey's beet-red face was familiar to me from photos of him in a Jesuit magazine that I occasionally thumbed through; Andrieu's patriarchal face was unknown to me, as were the bland countenances of Dr. Mark Klewski and Dr. William O'Hare, the internist and neurologist who rounded out the panel. I appeared this day not strictly as Lucia's advocate but as a popular curate of Saint Bonaventure's and character witness, of sorts. Obviously, juggling roles was not anathema in a Church court setting. I soon launched into a defense of Lucia that was not as forcible as the one I now in my dotage would muster. In those days I still courted the good will of my betters. I cited her devotion as a daily communicant, her loyalty to her sick brother, her indomitable cheerfulness, her obvious loathing to hurt others. But I could not say that I believed in the vision, only in her subjective sincerity.

"But I must add," I said with some fervor, "I'll never forget the details she gave me of the vision, her references to the 'thornless rose' and 'girdle of Saint Thomas.' These were touches, if not beyond her intellectual capacity, at least beyond her experience and knowledge."

Acosta was unconvinced. "We know that she's very bright."

"Bright, yes," I said. "But not sophisticated. Not versed in Church lore."

"She might have picked it up somewhere," Acosta said, with justification, I had to admit, for the same thought had crossed my own mind. I was silent.

"Do you know the girl's parents?" Andrieu asked.

"Not well," I said.

"Do you have any knowledge of their attitude toward her mystical experiences, if that's what they were?"

"I don't."

Acosta seized this line of questioning. "What about the mother?"

"What about her?" I asked.

"There is reason to believe that she is using the poor disturbed girl for monetary gain."

"I know nothing of this." Cravenly I had stifled the impulse to point out that Acosta's description of her as "the poor disturbed girl" showed his prejudice in the case.

"In fact," Acosta continued, "there is reason to conjecture that the mother herself might have cooked up the whole story with the reporter Dunlop for their mutual gain."

"That's not true," I said firmly.

"How do you know?"

"I'm sorry, Father Acosta, but I can't explore this area any further."

"And why not?" he asked testily.

"I am the girl's confessor."

"Ah, so there is something to it," he said with a note of triumph.

I flared into anger. "As a priest yourself you must know that my silence on the question indicates nothing one way or the other."

He fell into a chastened silence.

I continued: "As for making pacts with unscrupulous reporters, I wouldn't cast stones." I swallowed hard. I had gone too far. I had no proof for this veiled accusation and, besides, Acosta had the power to make life miserable for me.

Acosta reddened slightly but otherwise remained cool.

"Why don't you ask the reporter in person?" I suggested.

"We asked him to come," said Morrissey, "but he refused. As you know, we have no secular subpoena power. His appearance would have to have been voluntary."

Lucky stiff, I thought.

"Do you have any opinion of the girl's mental state?" Andrieu asked.

"I'm not a psychiatrist," I said. "But I believe she's perfectly sane, if that's what you're driving at."

"What do you know of her sexual attitudes?" he asked.

I flushed. "That area, too, is proscribed to me."

"Oh, of course," Andrieu said apologetically. He looked at his colleagues. "I think it's important to know whether we're dealing with a girl here or with a woman."

"That's one of the reasons," said the internist Dr. Klewski, "we must first make her undergo a full physical."

"It will be done at her first appearance," said Acosta.

I cringed to think of her in the talons of these condors.

Soon I was allowed to leave the hearing room, having been admonished to return with Lucia three days later. In the vestibule I ran into Dr. Papajohn, the next witness. He promised to give me a full report of his own testimony later.

Papajohn's attitude in the hearing room was relaxed and somewhat sardonic. He slouched comfortably in the hard chair and without asking permission to smoke, lit up a fat Havana. His clear conscience and erudition gave him a casual poise. He started his testimony by recounting the clinical details of his examination of Lucia after the stigmatic seizure.

"She showed," he said, "all the classic symptoms of an ecstatic, the lowering of vital heat, faint heartbeat as if near death—the usual thing."

"Do you specialize in neurology, Doctor?" asked O'Hare, the neurologist.

He sent gusts of smoke aloft in the high-ceilinged room. "I'm a GP," he replied.

"Had you ever seen a stigmatic before?" asked Andrieu.

"Not in the flesh," replied Papajohn.

The psychiatrist gave him a blank look.

"Only in medical journals," Papajohn explained. "I've studied the literature, both medical and nonmedical. Neumann. Galgani. Padre Pio. Even Saint Francis."

"Aren't most stigmatics female?" asked Andrieu.

Papajohn shrugged. "The ones I just mentioned are fifty-fifty."

"But in general?"

"I believe so."

"Is it not true that females are more masochistic? More hysterical, to put it bluntly?"

A caustic smile played on his lips. "Look, I'm no expert on females. I'm a bachelor."

Morrissey laughed. "Like most of us in this room," he said.

"What, if you know, is the difference between an ecstatic and a hysteric?" asked Andrieu.

Papajohn removed the cigar from the clamp of his teeth and stroked his vandyke. "Isn't that Dr. O'Hare's bailiwick? Why don't you ask him?"

The neurologist cleared his throat. "Yes, indeed," he said. "It's a simple distinction, really. After the so-called mystical experience or a series of them, if that's the case, the general health of the hysteric will fail. But the health of the genuine ecstatic will improve. She will, in fact, glow with health."

"What is the general state of the Buonfiglio child's health?" asked Klewski.

"Except for the stigmata," said Papajohn, "she was in tip-top health. Of course I haven't examined her since."

"She seems rather wan to me," said Acosta.

Klewski said, "The facts will be determined in three short days. When we examine her."

The panelists nodded in agreement. Papajohn spouted smoke and gazed with scorn at them. They seemed to him a bunch of pseudoscientific dabblers eager to sink their hooks into the poor girl, vivisect her like a helpless white mouse. She was in their eyes not a charitable and gifted youngster but a textbook case of aberration to be poked and prodded and finally pronounced unbalanced. He held the cigar in the vise of his stained teeth and glowered at them. But he said nothing. It was none of his business.

As the panelists continued to ask him perfunctory questions Papajohn's eyes wandered the hearing room. He admired the craftsmanship of the ornately carved woodwork in the beamed ceiling, the scrollwork in the granite fireplace, the stained-glass windows, the somber tones of the massive oil paintings. His eyes finally rested on a beautiful copy of the Madonna in the style of Raphael mounted on the wall directly above Acosta's chair. The oval face of the Renaissance girl was tilted gracefully, the eyes half-shut in a liquid gaze, a pool of buttery light in which the artist's amber-dipped brush had captured the haunting look of compassion and regret that mirrored her future vigil at the foot of the cross.

23

On the day before her scheduled appearance at the Chancery Lucia made every attempt to settle her fluttering stomach. Determined to act as if everything were normal, she ventured outdoors after her chores to join the neighborhood girls in a game of skip rope: "One, two, three, a-nation, I received my Confirmation, on the day of Decoration, one, two, three, a-nation."

Her feet constantly got tangled in the rope and the butterflies in her belly became only more agitated by the jumping so she had to stop. She endured the taunts of her playmates for this inept display and sat on the sidelines, content to watch. She sat on the hard curbstone and admired Linda Gardner's skipping—so haughty and skillful. Lucia smiled at her in an openhearted way. Her pleasure in the accomplishments of others usually was untainted by the brush of envy.

"One, two, three, a-nation, I received my Confirmation, on the day of Decoration, one, two, three, a-nation."

Much as she wanted to fit in with the kids, she felt terribly alienated from them. There was a gap in her childhood that she knew would never be bridged. With a sketchy wave to her playmates she drifted off. Soon she found herself on the soft skirt of the bay. She sat on a boulder and hurled rocks into the water, watching the ripples form. The day was achingly beautiful with sparkling air and lightly fleeced skies. The shoreline was tatted with pink mimosas swaying in the mild breeze. Here she squandered more than an hour, fretting specifically about the inquiry and especially about the sign she had been commanded to produce as proof of her claim. Frowning, she listened to the bloop of the rocks that she tossed into the water.

She returned home late that afternoon and saw her father's Buick parked under the grape arbor. What was he doing home so early? Her heart pounded as she rushed up the driveway to the back door.

Her parents were in the kitchen. Their faces confirmed her worst fears.

"Where is he?" she asked.

Red-eyed, Serafina looked up. "Fordham Hospital."

"I'll take the bus."

"No," said Ettore. "Visiting hours are from seven till nine. I drive you then."

Lucia was impatient to be at her brother's side. "Can't I go now?"

Ettore shook his head. "They won't let you in. Wait. We go together, okay?"

She sat down heavily. "What's wrong with him? Is he real bad?"

Serafina's heavy sigh conveyed total hopelessness, as if she were tired of caring. "Who knows? They have to take out his spleen."

"Won't that help?" she asked.

"He may die anyhow," Ettore said evenly.

"When will they operate?"

"Day after tomorrow," said Ettore. "They have to take a lotta tests first."

"Can he live okay without the spleen?"

Ettore shrugged. "I'm not a doctor. They say he has a chance. But they didn't sound so confident, you know?"

They all stared into the distance, like eyeless busts in the temples of Syracuse.

Lucia did not eat a morsel of dinner. She was settled in the back seat of the second-hand Buick even before her parents had emerged from the house. They drove up Pelham Parkway into the blaze of the setting sun. The road was flanked by islands of green thronged by old folks in deck chairs, kids playing catch, sprinting dogs and hand-holding lovers. The Buonfiglios' eyes were fastened on the monotonous ribbon of asphalt that led to Fordham Hospital. The car passed the entrance to the Bronx Zoo where tired children emerged holding clusters of balloons. The Buonfiglios neither heard nor saw.

They got out of the elevator and asked a nurse for directions to his room.

He was sleeping peacefully.

They approached the bed and sat in folding chairs, careful not to waken him. Their eyes fastened on his still face, sallow but serene over the luminous white of the hospital sheet. There were no tubes in his arms or nose, none of the usual hospital repair shop gear. He might have been at home in his own bed, dreaming of Christmas. Lucia watched his lightly fluttering eyelashes and gently heaving chest and found it hard to believe that he was on the brink of death.

She then asked herself why—if she trusted God—was she so reluctant to let him pass over to that painless dimension so surely foreshadowed in sleep, a place at once familiar and impenetrable? Like most of us who profess to glimpse the mystery, she found no answer. Except that she would miss him very much.

Soon his body stirred, his eyelids trembled and he was awake. At first he didn't recognize the three figures hovering at the bedside. As they came into focus he smiled.

"Hiya, Buddy," said Lucia. The parents were grim and silent.

"Hi, Lou," he said huskily.

Serafina's eyes shone with dammed-up tears. Ettore's lower lip trembled as he tried to smile.

"How do you feel?" asked Lucia.

The boy nodded vaguely.

"You eat good?" Serafina asked with artificial severity.

Mario shook his head. "Not hungry."

"You gotta eat," scolded Ettore.

"Not hungry," he repeated. "I drank some orange juice."

Lucia had lain her hand on his. Skin and bones. "Would you like anything?" she asked. "A book, maybe?"

He nodded. "*Treasure Island,* remember? The book Sean Collins showed me."

She said, "Sure. I'll get it tomorrow morning out of the library." She took his wanting to read as a positive sign. She patted his hand.

His face suddenly twisted into a grimace. "What's gonna happen to me, Lou?"

Ettore answered, "Nothing, big boy. You don't worry."

"The doctors have to operate," added Serafina. "But then it will be all right."

The boy looked doubtful and glanced at Lucia for confirmation. Her head bobbed in agreement. Then his tousled head sank back into the pillow as he gripped her hand. His eyes closed.

They kept silent vigil for most of the two visiting hours. A boy occupying a nearby bed whimpered softly. The laughter of a nurse chimed in the corridor.

Soon it was time to leave. Ettore and Serafina kissed their still-sleeping son. They waited in the doorway for Lucia.

She bent over to stroke his hair and his eyes fluttered open. He beckoned her closer. She placed her ear to his lips and he whispered something that made her freeze for a second. She straightened up, looked at him tenderly. Then she quickly nodded and left the room.

Serafina fixed a late snack of cantaloupe and spiced ham which they ate on the front porch as they stared through the moth-battered screens at the bay. Lucia devoured the melon slice with uncommon hunger. She had regained her appetite. Ettore yawned. Insidious languor had spun its web, softening the edges of their distress.

Lucia finished eating and patted her lips with a napkin. She watched her parents for signs that they were about to go to bed. She tried to quell the pangs of conscience caused by her secret decision. She hated to use trickery but felt compelled to resort to it that night. There was no other way.

Ettore was the first to murmur good night and slog upstairs. It was after ten—well past his normal bedtime. He had to rise at dawn to be at the construction site by eight.

Serafina remained on the porch, staring out into the night. Lucia was growing impatient. "Aren't you tired?" she finally asked, unable to contain herself. "Why don't you go to bed?"

Serafina glared at her. "I go when I want," she snapped. "Who's the mother here, anyway?"

"I'm sorry, Mamma." She lowered her eyes abjectly.

Serafina grunted and lapsed back into silent communion with whatever nocturnal ghosts then possessed her. The rocker creaked. Fifteen minutes passed before the woman spoke. "Go to bed yourself."

"Yes, Mamma."

Lucia lay awake fully dressed on top of her bed for almost an hour before she heard her mother's footsteps on the stairs. She then waited another twenty minutes or so before she dared get out of bed. Her mouth parched, she listened at the door. Not a sound. She swallowed hard as her hand touched the cool metal of the doorknob.

Nature's camouflage made it fairly easy to sneak out of the house unheard. She simply undid the back door latch and slipped into the rattling night. The air was cool on her face which, though set grimly toward her destination, betrayed some apprehension as her eyes flitted from chirring creature to crunch of brush. A craggy moon floodlit the path to Pelham Bay Park.

Lucia quickened her pace, drawn by some primal force to the shrine. Midnight was the right time, she felt. By day the site was overrun with cultists and curiosity-seekers who made it difficult to pray. So she hurried now to the place where it had all begun.

The time was ripe. Her brother lay with his spleen bloated with clustering erythrocytes, warped and run amok like blood-lusting sharks. Couldn't the Virgin with a sweep of her draper-ied arm change the course of this river of death? This was the question, phrased differently, that Mario had whispered in her ear. Now she was going to get the answer.

With pounding heart she entered the park, its green hoard silvered by the moon. Wild things skittered in the dark. She made her way across the football field toward the tree that marked the shrine, the holy bridge that once spanned the chasm between spirit and matter, where once Our Lady had walked and changed Lucia's life. They wanted a *sign* now, a palpable symbol on which to hang their fragile faith. Amen, she whispered in her stride, crossing herself with the hand that clutched her rosary. She would pray for a sign.

Soon she smelled the mingled odors of burnt tallow, laurel and box. She could just make out the rounded outline of the statue. In a few seconds she would be on her knees, hands joined in prayer.

Genuflection was a familiar posture and the ground no stranger to her knees. She prayed naturally. She grasped the essence of prayer as a state of being rather than a function, as an act of love rather than obeisance, as a kiss more than a bow. She poured her whole self into the prayer as into a cup that she tendered to the God of love. This was how our lovely candidate prayed on the night of defilement. This was how her soul opened unsuspecting to a brigand fate!

Forgive me, tribunes, for this loss of objectivity. I continue.

She was on the threshold of trance. Her eyes were fixed, her body immobile, her skin alabaster, her face beautiful. Hair strayed to her cheek and brow. Somewhere on the edge of consciousness the question rang: Will she come? Will she come?

Nearby a twig snapped.

Her vital heat plummeted, draining her face of color. Her heart slowed. She was on the brink of ecstasy. Come, My Lady, come.

A leaf rustled.

Now her body was completely still as her spirit swam in ecstasy. The bridge unraveled across the realms.

A vine bled underfoot.

She shrank into a dense mass of feeling, a white dwarf of ecstatic prayer, balled up in expectation. Waiting.

The song of crickets filled the air, futilely sounding alarm. Footsteps.

The spell broke. Joy surged within her. It had to be Our Lady. The figure drew closer, mottled by the drapery of the half-lit night. Closer.

Her face froze in its expression of happiness. Now the jeering moon illuminated the visitor, haloed the approaching form. She waggled her head, dumb with wonder. She tried to speak but as in a dream no words came out, just a low guttural sound.

Closer he came, smiling like an asp. His mouth was slack as a marionette's. Then his shadow blotted out the moon.

24

❧❧ ❧❧

Saint Augustine said, "For what is nearer to Thine ears than a confessing heart?" The licentious Numidian had a point. Sometimes confession is good for the soul of the auditor. Now, tribunes, that my protégée's death has untied the fetters of secrecy I can finally spill the sacramental beans.

It was the day of Lucia's scheduled appearance before the archdiocesan witchhunters. I sat in my basic black suit in a stifling vestibule of the Chancery. A huge pedestal fan whirred to little avail. Beads of sweat formed on my freckled brow. As I waited I read the receptionist's *Daily Mirror*. DiMaggio's successive-game hit streak stood at 54. A shake-up was wobbling the Jap Army's high command. John L. Lewis, chomping a cigar, took a couple of verbal swipes at FDR. The new tax bill required husbands and wives to file joint tax returns. U.S. bombers sat poised on the take-off strips of a naval base in Reykjavik, Iceland. The scroll of those troubled times (ah, what times aren't troubled?) unrolled before my bloodshot eyes (I had been up late the night before, imbibing with fellow alumni of Dunwoodie). I glimpsed over the top of the newspaper a round face blooming with anger.

"Where is she?" Acosta demanded. "She's an hour late."

I shrugged in wounded innocence. "Have you tried her parents?"

"Can't reach them." He paced like an angry penguin.

"This is a black mark against her. You'd better find her. And quick."

"I?"

His black eyes scorched. "As advocate, I hold you responsible for her appearance."

I stopped myself from alibiing that I had received no advance notice of this responsibility. Meekness was the best course. I rose from the chair and said, "I'll try, Father."

He glanced at his wristwatch. "It's too late for today," he grumped. "The panelists have other engagements. We'll set another date." His eyes narrowed. "In the meantime I want you to find her and lecture her sternly about this."

"Yes, Father Acosta."

"Her behavior is more than neurotic. It will go into the file."

I interrupted. "Of course, she may have a valid excuse."

He ignored the remark. "You better warn her that Church sanctions are not our only recourse. I'll be blunt, Father Fogarty. The Chancery is not without influence in the secular community. In medical and psychiatric circles, for example."

"I can well imagine."

"The panelists—in particular Dr. Andrieu—have connections in certain agencies. Agencies concerned with mental health."

Under the lid of my moral cowardice I was boiling over. Fury turned my cheeks scarlet, hampered my voice. But I kidded myself that if I bridled my rage and kept a respectful silence, things would go easier on Lucia. "I'll do my best," I said.

"See that you do." With a wave of the hand, he dismissed me.

That afternoon I finally reached Lucia's mother by telephone.

"You mean you don't know where she is?" I asked.

"I thought she was with you at the bishop's office," she said with mounting alarm. "Don't tell me she she no show up."

"That's right, Mrs. Buonfiglio. When did you last see her?"

"When she went to sleep last night. This morning I figure she go to mass, as usual. I left a note for her that I went shopping on Arthur Avenue. I take the bus. My God, what happen to her?"

"Don't worry, Mrs. Buonfiglio," I said, hiding my own concern. "She probably just got cold feet."

"Eh?"

"I mean she got scared of the inquiry and went off somewhere to think. She'll probably be home for dinner."

"She never do nothing like this before," she said stridently. "Maybe she's hurt or something."

"Now calm yourself, Mrs. Buonfiglio. I'm sure she's all right. Where's your husband?"

"Still at work."

"If she's not back by the time he gets home, phone me."

"Okay. What's your number?"

I recited the number, said a few more soothing words and hung up. I stood frowning at the telephone box mounted on the wall of the rectory vestibule. Soon Mrs. Carney, the housekeeper, was at my side, toweling her pudgy hands on her apron. "Father," she said, "there's a girl outside wants you to hear her confession." This was uttered with the frosty air of superiority she displayed toward curates.

I grumbled. "Can't she come back tonight at the regular confession hours?"

Arching an eyebrow, she didn't dignify the question with an answer. Mrs. Carney was as well versed as any seasoned Thomist in the duties of the priesthood. What if the soul whose confession I postponed hearing should die in the state of mortal sin before Saturday came? She would be plunged into hell and I would have to shoulder the blame. These thoughts seemed to flicker across the woman's disapproving pudding-wife face.

I relented. "Where is she?"

"Waiting in your box."

I nodded and went through the side door, crossed the courtyard and entered the church. It was much cooler within the vaulted interior. My footsteps echoed on the terrazzo before the premonition flashed in my mind. Quickly I drew back the curtain, entered, sat down, adjusted my maniple and slid open the panel separating confessor from confessing. My throat was parched.

The voice confirmed my suspicions. Yet her "Bless me, Father" had a disturbing vocal quality, a gloomy coloratura that sent shivers through me. I had to interrupt the litany. "Lucia, where have you been? Are you in some kind of trouble, child?"

Silence.

"Bless me, Father, for I have sinned," she finally repeated, ignoring my questions. Her tone rebuked me for disturbing the solemnity of the sacrament. "It has been six days since my last confession and . . ."

I was undeterred. "Why didn't you show up at the Chancery? Father Acosta was furious. And your mother has been worried sick."

Soft sobs floated through the grid.

My voice grew softer. "Please tell me what's the matter. I want to help you."

"My confession," she said in a faint voice, "will make everything clear."

I probed the shadows, trying to bring her face into focus. But I couldn't see her expression clearly. The dark tenor of her voice struck me with fear. I leaned forward to place my ear close to the grid. Then, couched in the rigid formalisms of the Sacrament of Penance, the ugly story emerged.

My hand shakes now from something other than the infirmities of age. I hesitate, even though she is dead, to draw open the curtain of confessional secrecy, to illumine the shadowy corners of the box where souls are bared. It seems even now a vulgar intrusion of privacy, a betrayal. And other more vague inhibitions stay my hand. In some nook of that tumbledown pumphouse I call a heart, I think I want to keep it for myself.

But my selfish wishes must yield to the cause of Lucia's vindication and subsequent beatification. I must divulge the terrible truth of her confession which—although it may not rank with those of Augustine, Merton or Rousseau—is certain to rivet the attention.

" 'Oh, my God, I am heartily sorry for having offended Thee . . .' " she prayed in conclusion.

Again I was compelled to interrupt. "But, Lucia, I can't give you absolution."

"Why not?" she asked, stricken.

"Because you've committed no sin. What happened was no fault of yours. Go in peace, child."

Although I couldn't see her face, I'm sure it was tinged with scarlet. "Please, Father, you must be mistaken."

"I'm not mistaken."

"If I was really holy," she said, "I would have followed the example of the girl saints. I would have let him kill me rather than give in. I remember reading about Saint Catherine of Alexandria, Father. I don't remember the exact words. Do you?"

" 'He is, in sooth, my God, my Lover, my Shepherd, my only Spouse.' "

"Yes, that's it. Don't you see why I'm so ashamed?"

"Dear girl, it's no sin to be less than a saint."

These words seemed to make an impact because they silenced her protests for a moment. She sobbed again, her violated body heaving. I felt so powerless and awkward. "Please don't cry," I managed to choke out.

The crying subsided and she asked, "What am I going to do now?"

"Go home to your mother. Tell her what happened. Let her comfort you." I managed to say this while still reeling under the enormity of the crime against her. She was not yet twelve. My anger was somewhat tempered by the knowledge that the culprit was a victim too, by my long immersion in the tenets of Catholic morality which held that mental incompetents—since they never reached the age of reason—were incapable of sin. Wrongdoing, according to the theologians, occurred in the mind and heart, not in the flesh. Intellectually, I agreed with this reasoning. But I still felt like throttling the boy.

"I can't tell my mother," she said. "I'm too ashamed."

"I'll tell her for you," I offered.

"No," she said, panic-stricken. "Please don't."

"You can't keep a thing like this from your own mother."

"But I have to. You see, my mother would tell my father and then he would kill him. And what good would that do?"

Anguish filled her voice. "Oh, Father Fogarty, I don't want to cause even more evil."

I was mute, for in many ways she was right. She quite simply didn't want to ignite a chain reaction of evil. But, if she snuffed the fuse, even more evil could result. I asked, "Don't you think Basil should be punished?"

"He's not responsible. He can't control himself."

"That's exactly why we can't allow him to go scot-free. Why, he might rape again."

I must have been too outspoken and direct. My explicit language seemed to release a flood of unbearable memories. I heard her crying again in the darkness, croaky like a frog.

"Please," I pleaded, the sense of impotence rising again. "Don't cry. Don't cry."

"I can't help it," she sobbed.

"There, there," I blathered.

When she had grown calmer she asked, "What should I do? My father would kill him."

"You must decide. I can't reveal your confession without your permission." Something kept me from making another pitch for it. So far my stumbling efforts had done little but increase her pain and indecisiveness.

"Oh, Father," she repeated. "I'm so ashamed."

"You have nothing to be ashamed of."

"Still, I'm so very ashamed."

"Stop beating your breast, Lucia. This guilt of yours is wrong. You know, contrition is a funny thing. It's like a dose of medicine that heals a sick person but harms a healthy one. Like quinine, it can cure you or kill you. Don't poison yourself with a dose of unnecessary contrition."

"Didn't Christ let himself get crucified even though he was innocent?"

"That's right. To save us from having to." I clucked my tongue. "You think He needs your help? Beware of pride, Lucia. Maybe you're confessing the wrong sin."

She was stunned into silence. It hurt her more deeply to think that she might be guilty of this sin of sins, the same offense that had cast down Lucifer and exiled Adam and Eve. A mere sin of the flesh paled before it. She cried again but her tears now were cathartic, filled with relief at her own imperfection. "Forgive me," she said.

I raised my hand in benediction. *"Ego te absolvo . . ."*

25

❧❧ ❧❧

A week later young Mario went under the scalpel and his spleen was removed. The doctors were still pessimistic about his future. The operation was performed merely as a holding tactic, to retard his body's perverse manufacture of misshapen red blood cells. Yet the operation seemed a positive step and ignited a spark of hope in Lucia, who somehow still found an anchor for her faith.

She visited her brother at the hospital twice a day, taking the Fordham Road bus by herself each afternoon and going by car with her parents each evening after dinner. Sometimes, but not often, Rosemary would come too.

The department store where the older sister worked was not far from the hospital and once or twice out of a sense of duty she stopped by after work at the tail end of the visiting period. She didn't like to stay long because the antiseptic odors and peevish sounds of the place depressed her. On one such occasion she arrived in Mario's semiprivate room to find Lucia staring blankly at the sleeping boy.

"Hi, Lou." The announcement of her presence was said in a half-whisper that was undermined by the clack of spiked heels. She plopped into a chair. "How's he doing?"

Rosemary's appearance had jolted Lucia from a reflective mood. She was surprised to see her. "Not so bad, I guess. He's sleeping now."

"I can see that." She crossed her plump legs, clicked open a handbag and produced a pack of chewing gum. "Want some?"

Lucia smiled and shook her head.

Rosemary popped the gum into her mouth, primped her hair and was silent. There was little rapport between them. After a while she asked, "How's things with you?"

"Me? I'm okay."

Her half-sister made a face. "Well, you look awful," she said with characteristic candor.

Lucia winced, for she too had a touch of female vanity. "Really?"

"Really. What's the matter? Aren't ya getting enough sleep or something?"

"I guess not."

"Don't take things so hard, kid."

She colored slightly. "I'll try not to." She changed the subject. "How's Peter?"

Rosemary brightened at the mention of her boyfriend. "Fine. He bought a new Pontiac the other day. You should see it—it's beautiful."

"That's nice."

"He was gonna pick me up at the hospital but he had to work late." She frowned. "We'll have to take the bus home."

"I don't mind. I take the bus a lot."

Rosemary gazed at the sleeping boy. "What are we doing here if he's not even awake?"

"I don't know," she replied, leaning tenderly toward him. "I think it helps. I think it makes him rest better, dream better."

"Oh, that's crazy . . ." She covered her mouth with embarrassment. "Sorry, kid. Didn't mean anything by it."

"That's okay."

"Let's go, huh?"

"Five more minutes."

Rosemary sighed. "All right."

Before the five minutes were up they were asked by a nurse to leave. Visiting hours were over. On the bus they were silent most of the time but Rosemary seemed preoccupied and often on the verge of speaking. She seemed to be composing her thoughts or mustering the courage to say something. She never managed to get it out.

After dinner Lucia went back to the hospital with her parents while her sister stayed home to wash her hair and listen to "Fibber McGee and Molly" on the radio. It didn't occur to her that she still hadn't seen Mario in a conscious state since the operation.

That night as Lucia was getting ready for bed Rosemary came in the room. She had knocked, but only perfunctorily and, before the younger girl knew it, was sitting cross-legged on the bed beside the flamenco doll.

Modest to a fault, Lucia was a little embarrassed because she was clothed only in underpants. Hastily she ducked her head and arms into a cotton nightgown.

"Mind if we chat?" said Rosemary, plumping a pillow against the headboard. Her abundant hair was haystacked in big rollers and she had cold cream on her face. She was barefoot and wore a low-cut nightgown that displayed the shimmering hilltops of her breasts. How different these two females were from each other! Even though they had the same father and their mothers had been sisters, they were poles apart in personality and appearance.

"I don't mind," said Lucia. "I was just about to say my prayers."

"Oh. You say prayers a lot, doncha?" Rosemary had brought a bottle of nail polish which she now uncapped and applied to her toenails.

"Yeah."

"Isn't it boring?" Her tongue was extended in concentration as she applied the nail polish.

"No, it isn't. I don't pray the way most people do, like it's a duty or a chore. I make it a chat. A conversation. Like the one we're having now."

Rosemary looked up. "You're pretty weird, you know?"

"No, I'm not," she protested, wounded by the observation.

Rosemary scrutinized her. "Why do you wear your hair so short? You didn't used to. You're getting older and you'd be sort of pretty if you fixed yourself up more."

Shyly, she touched her hair. "I . . . I don't know." The

comments had made her inarticulate. She was never so ethereal a child as to be untouched by concern for physical things. She liked the idea of being beautiful and admired, even took pleasure in the stirrings she felt in her adolescent body. But, on another level, she was frightened by this ferment and didn't want to talk about it—especially now.

Rosemary asked, "You gonna become a nun or something?"

"No," she said hesitantly. "I mean, I don't think so." She hadn't fully considered the question of a religious vocation. At bottom, despite her spiritual bent, she felt herself too finely modulated to the biological tuning fork. Her recent ordeal might have shaken this attitude but its foundations were still strong.

Rosemary fished in the pocket of her nightgown and produced a pack of Camel cigarettes. Tapping one on her knee, she raised an admonishing finger to her lips. "Don't you dare tell Daddy," she said before lighting up.

"I won't," she promised, wide-eyed at the performance of an illicit act in her room. She hadn't even been aware that her sister smoked. "When did you start smoking?"

"Oh, ages ago," she drawled, exhaling a gust of smoke that curled around her rollered hair. She offered the butt to her sister. "Wanna try?"

"No, thanks."

Rosemary shrugged. "Daddy's old-fashioned. I'm nineteen, after all, and this is 1941. Peter doesn't mind my smoking. In fact, he kinda likes it. Says it makes me look like Dorothy Lamour."

"Does Dorothy Lamour smoke?"

"Of course. All actresses smoke. She just doesn't smoke when she wears a sarong."

"What's that?"

"You know, those sexy dresses they wear on exotic islands like Tahiti or Bali. Boy—would I love to go someplace like that someday and drink rum from a pineapple while Peter fanned me with a palm leaf. Wouldn't that be great?"

"I guess so." Lucia sat on the edge of the bed. "Are you and Peter going to get married?"

Rosemary suddenly looked solemn. "We want to but . . ."

"But what?"

She looked askance at Lucia, smoking meditatively. "Well, his parents . . ."

"I thought they liked you."

"So did I. Until recently."

"What do you mean?"

"I'm not sure, exactly." She looked directly into Lucia's eyes. "They've been sort of cool to me lately. Like last week we went to the Loew's Paradise to see *The Philadelphia Story*. As usual, we went to his house for coffee after the movie. Well, as soon as we walk in the door, Mr. Giusti ups and goes to bed without so much as a 'Hi, how are ya.' "

"Maybe he was just tired."

"It ain't like him, I tell you. He's a big flirt, you know. He never misses a chance to call me his 'juicy sirloin.' " She interrupted the monologue to frown and smoke. "Mrs. Giusti stayed up with us in the kitchen, of course, just to make sure no funny business went on. But she didn't say two words to me. Just sat there pouring coffee with that Sicilian mamma scowl on her face. It was creepy."

"Maybe you're just imagining things. Did you ask Peter about it?"

"Yeah. He says it's nothing but I think he knows and just won't come clean. He doesn't want to hurt my feelings."

"What could it possibly be about?"

Rosemary narrowed her eyes. "I have a hunch."

"Huh?"

"Now don't take this the wrong way, but I think it's you."

"Me?"

"Yeah. The publicity and all." She picked a fleck of loose tobacco from her lip. "Frankly, I don't think they like the idea of their precious son getting mixed up with such a weird family."

"Our family is not weird."

After a pause she added, "Mario's sickness doesn't help matters either."

"So that's it," said Lucia.

"Can't say I blame them. They gotta think of their future grandchildren. The disease is, whatchacallit, hereditary." She flicked a long ash into the cup of her hand. "Got something I can use as an ashtray?"

Lucia looked around the room. "I don't know." Her eye caught a water glass sitting on the dresser. She went over and got it. "Here," she said. "Use this. I'll wash it out later."

"Thanks." She flicked the ash into the glass and shrugged. "No matter, though. If they don't let us get married, we're gonna elope. I got Peter twisted around my little finger." She veiled her eyes suggestively. "I got ways."

Lucia looked disconsolate. "I'm sorry."

"Forget it, kid. Ain't your fault." She took two long drags and then squashed the butt out on the edge of the glass. "Anyway, thanks for listening." She got up from the bed, still holding the glass. "I'll dump this in the toilet." As she reached the door she said, "We oughtta do this more often, you know?"

"Sure," said Lucia eagerly.

She closed the door behind her. A second later the curler-bound head poked back in. "Say a prayer for me too, huh?" You can be sure the request was not ignored.

The Dog Star rose over Eastchester Bay, heralding another fulgent August day. My elbow was resting on the mattress and my tousled head propped in my hand. I was gazing at the sky through the bedroom window and watching Sirius's progress. The day was already hot and humid, crackling with the ions of the season. I got out of bed, yawning and scratching.

I had slept poorly, disturbed by worries about Lucia, whom I had not seen since having heard her so-called confession. Brushing my teeth in the adjoining bathroom, I recalled the evening. I had escorted her home afterward for moral support. Against my advice, she had decided not to tell her parents about the assault. She wouldn't lie, so she decided to tell them nothing at all, even though silence might constitute a mute form of disobedience. By her sympathy and fear for her rapist's safety the poor girl was caught in the coils of her own scruples. Each way she turned loomed the specter of what she perceived as sin. How—my theologist tribunes—would you have advised her in these dilemmas? I took the path of least resistance and found sanctuary in the vow of confessional secrecy from which she refused to release me.

The Buonfiglios were happy enough to have their daughter back safe and sound and didn't press for a full explanation. Since she often rose earlier than they, they never realized that she had been out all night and so weren't as alarmed as they might have been. Lucia had told me that following the attack she wandered the neighborhood in a dazed state until the church doors were unlocked. Unnoticed, she sat through three masses and various other rites, praying all the while for forgiveness and purification. Finally she summoned the courage to make confession. Another confession to her parents would have drained her of all emotion. We decided to leave them with the impression that her disappearance was connected with her fear of appearing before the panel of inquiry.

Lucia had gone upstairs to bathe while I sat in the kitchen with her parents, drinking coffee spiked with anisette. I found Ettore a gruff but likable man, a no-nonsense sort who neither fawned over nor sneered at my collar as was the habit of most southern Italians (pardon the ethnic generalization). And Serafina's natural reticence and suspicious nature seemed to thaw in my company. So we got along well. I decided that the time was right to raise the subject of the inquiry and Acosta's anger over Lucia's failure to appear. As I spoke the lofty tenor of Beniamino Gigli was heard softly in the background. As usual, the kitchen radio was on.

"You have to persuade your daughter," I said, "to do her best not to alienate the panel. It's very important. These people have power. They may even be able to have her put away."

"For what?" Ettore demanded angrily, veins bulging in his neck.

I made a face of embarrassment and frustration: I was not to blame for the hypocrisies of the clergy. "They'll say she's insane. They have friends in high places."

"Would they really do this?" Serafina asked.

"It's possible," I said. "They may even rationalize that they are acting for her own good. Let's stay on their good sides. Especially Father Acosta's."

"Who is this Acosta?" Ettore asked.

"The one I told you about," said Serafina. "The one who promised to help us with Mario."

"Pah!" spat the bricklayer. "Who can help Mario now? Only the Lord above."

I looked glumly at the demitasse cup on the table. It was decorated with hand-painted alba roses that reminded me of the thornless flower Lucia had given me. Out of the corner of my eye, I saw Serafina studying my expression.

"Father," she said tentatively, "maybe it's a good thing for my daughter to see a head doctor, eh? What do you think? And maybe it's also good for her to come out of the clouds."

"You mean deny the vision?"

She nodded.

"I used to think as you do. Now I'm not so sure."

"The priest has been converted, then?"

"In a manner of speaking," I said with a smile. "Signora, your daughter is a remarkable person. In some ways she is like steel. But she is also very fragile. I constantly have to remind myself how young and vulnerable she is. Still, her faith is infectious. Maybe I'm catching it."

She eyed me closely.

I continued: "As her confessor, I'd like to say one more thing. She has passed through a tremendous ordeal. You must take pains to be especially kind to her."

Ettore looked puzzled. But a shadow of understanding had crossed his wife's umber-colored face as we sat that evening in the Buonfiglio kitchen drinking a bittersweet brew.

I remembered her expression now as I finished brushing my teeth. It conveyed not that she knew about the rape specifically, but through some maternal clairvoyance sensed the nature of Lucia's suffering. Watching the expression, I had felt like an outsider, an interloper crouching behind a pilaster in the temple of Vesta.

I went downstairs to put on the vestments for the seven o'clock mass, trying mightily to ignore the odor of bacon and coffee wafting from the kitchen. For priests who haven't yet said mass the door to breakfast lies beyond the baldachin.

A growling stomach wasn't my only problem. I had, regrettably, again promised to play golf with Tomlin this morning and was not looking forward to it.

On the way to the sacristy I ran into Mrs. Carney, who informed me that I had a phone call. It was Acosta, instructing me to tell my client that a new date three weeks off had been set for her appearance before the panel, and warning me again to make sure that she showed up. This admonition added another sour note to the new day.

I said mass in an even more distracted manner than usual. When it came time to dispense communion I was busily hatching alibis to get out of the golf date, thus heaping sacrilege upon sin by concocting lies while bestowing the consecrated host. I was reflecting on this irony when her pale cameo face, mouth open and eyes tightly shut, appeared before me. My composure was shaken.

I gave her communion and tried to catch her eye. She was too devout a guest at the Lord's table to let anything distract her. I felt, as usual in my encounters with her, chastened. During the rite of lavabo I determined to intercept her somehow before she left church. I had to tell her about the new hearing date.

As the congregation shuffled out I dashed into the sacristy and, leaving the altar boys mute with wonder, rushed back into the church by the side door. Still clothed in the mass vestments, I motioned to her, making hissings sounds. She had just reached the main portals when she heard me and turned around. All eyes followed her down the center aisle. She was an object of wonder and fascination in the neighborhood, and whispered asides rustled in her wake.

"Father?" she said.

"A word with you, please."

She nodded and followed me into the sacristy. The altar boys were waiting to help me remove the vestments. They looked at her with frank curiosity. I dismissed them.

I asked her to sit down and examined her face, a map of melancholy. Events had taken their toll. I tried hard not to think about the image of her cruel introduction to the facts of life. How, I marveled, could she still preserve her altruism? I smiled gently and said, "They've set a new date for the examination." I gave her the date.

Fear crossed her face. "I don't want to go."

"You've got to, for your own sake. They can have you put away."

"Then why should I go? Why should I play into their hands?"

It was a good question and demonstrated for once a healthy rebellious streak. Still I felt she should face the panel and vindicate herself. "You can't run away, Lucia."

"When they examine me, they'll find out what happened. And I'm ashamed."

"You have nothing to be ashamed of. Purity is in the heart, not the body."

"But will they believe I'm innocent?"

I shrugged. I had to be honest. "Maybe. Maybe not."

"What time?"

"Nine in the morning." I touched her shoulder. "Should I pick you up at your house, say, at eight?"

"No need," she said. "I can meet you here. I always come to the seven o'clock mass." She tossed her cropped head and looked at me. "What will they do to me?"

"Well—you'll get a full physical."

"I know." Her eyes searched the marble floor.

"Then the psychiatrist will ask you a lot of questions. I'm not sure what else." I tugged nervously at the edges of my fiddleback chasuble. "You're very brave to go through with this."

A familiar luster shone in her eyes. It reminded me of the way she looked that day in May when she first came to my office to tell me about the vision. "I'm not brave," she said. "I'm scared. I'm ashamed, too, of what they will find out. But I know I have to face what comes. I know Our Lady wants me to. For some reason I don't fully understand, she wants me to go through a test. This is going to sound sacrilegious, but sometimes I get mad at her. I think, 'Why me? Why can't I just pick raspberries or giggle with my girl friends?' But then I think, 'Who am I to question the plans of God's Mother?'"

She started to cry. I touched her hair in a clumsy effort to comfort her. My own emotions had been thrown into turmoil.

Was the rock of her faith eroding? Would Gibraltar now topple?

When she had mastered her emotions she said in a low voice, "Sorry, Father."

"That's okay." I removed my hand from the silky strands of her hair, the warmth of her radiating through my fingertips. I got down on one knee and shook her gently by the shoulders. "Don't be afraid to cry, Lucia. Don't despair because you're not perfect. Remember, even Christ stumbled on the road to Calvary."

She took a handkerchief from her jumper pocket and dabbed at her eyes. "I guess you're right."

"And in Gethsemane He prayed to be spared the bitter cup."

A pale smile appeared. "I remember reading about that."

I grinned.

"Will you pray for me?" she asked.

I nodded.

"And give me your blessing?"

"With pleasure." I raised my hand and sketched the ritual signs.

She bowed under the benediction. After a while she rose from the chair, looking refreshed. "Thank you, Father Fogarty," she said. "You're the best priest I ever met." And she was gone.

I was rooted to the spot for a long time. Finally I began to remove the vestments. It had hardly ever occurred to me that I might be worthy of the collar I wore. Now I smiled rather idiotically in the sunlight of her esteem and thought that maybe I had chosen the right line of work after all. When the pastor arrived to say the next mass he studied my face quizzically. I was still smiling like a dunce.

Serafina was in a foul temper as she sat on the stoop, hoping for a bay breeze to ease the heat and humidity. Not a ruffle appeared on the water's surface. *"Sacramento,"* she said, drinking beer straight from the bottle. "New York is a furnace in hell." It was never, she mused, so unbearably hot in the old country. Zephyrs always blew in northeastern Sicily and the nights were always cool. Here in August, she grumbled, there was no relief at all. Her dark brows met in a scowl.

The weather was only partly responsible for her black mood. She stared at the bay, thinking about her troubles. One child lay in a hospital bed while the other was afflicted in a more mysterious way. What had the young priest meant by Lucia's "ordeal"? The question sparked Serafina's formidable intuition. She would have a talk with the girl.

It was also time to broach another subject: Lucia's promise to consider denying the vision. Since her chat with the red-haired curate Serafina was having second thoughts about her unspoken pact with Acosta. She now doubted that any specialist could do more for Mario than the doctors at Fordham Hospital, especially at this critical stage in the disease. It seemed that with his spleen the surgeons had also removed a mother's hope. But wouldn't it still be wise to play ball with the Jesuit? There was an old saying in Catania—priests make devilish enemies.

She sighed and finished the beer as the hot sun beat down on her kerchiefed head. She sank deeper into a mood of dark contemplation, convinced that the family destiny had been sealed long ago. Then why did she continue to ferret for scraps of advantage, hunt for propitious signs? Maybe it was the rearing of family pride.

Serafina was about to go indoors when she saw Lucia coming down the street. The sight of the girl with her monkishly short hair and slender figure quickened the woman's heartbeat. Often she scarcely could believe that Lucia was her daughter, this odd offspring of her union with Ettore. Well—Serafina, a native fatalist, did not expect to understand everything.

"Hot, isn't it?" she said as the girl approached the stoop.

Lucia had been walking with her eyes down and hadn't noticed her mother. She gave a little start. Then she said, "Sure is, Mamma."

Chimes were heard. An ice-cream truck with the pitched roof of a mock bungalow came down the street, veering to avoid potholes.

"How about a Bungalow Bar?" Serafina offered.

"Okay." It was already early afternoon and she had had

little to eat, just tea and toast at the nursing home where she sometimes dropped by after mass to visit with the old people.

Serafina walked down the steps and hailed the driver. A man in a white uniform hopped out, gave them a friendly nod and placed his hand on the handle of the freezer door on the back of the truck. "What flavor?" he asked.

Serafina looked at Lucia.

"Toasted almond, please," she said.

A blast of cold vapor escaped as he opened the door and handed the ice cream to Lucia. "You, lady?"

"No, thanks."

"Why not, Mamma?" asked Lucia.

"Just had a beer." She handed him a quarter that she had fished from her apron pocket and waited for change from the change-maker that gleamed at his belt. Then he hopped into the truck and drove off chiming like a summer Santa Claus.

Lucia was already devouring the ice cream. "Thanks, Mamma," she said between bites.

"No mention it." They walked back to the house. "Let's sit on the stoop for a while."

"Sure."

They sat down on the concrete steps. "Where you been all morning?" the woman asked.

"I went over to the nursing home. They're having a paper drive and I helped them tie up bundles."

"Humph," said Serafina. "Charity begins at home."

Lucia looked wounded. "I'm sorry, Mamma. You need my help with something?"

"That's okay." Serafina was playing Mutt and Jeff with her mind, softening her up with ice cream and guilt. Of course, Lucia was eager to please. She welcomed this new moment of intimacy so shortly after the bread-baking session. Were she and her mother finally drawing close? It would be a solace to her in these hard days. Maybe she might even confide her awful secret to the woman who bore her. But she couldn't muster the courage. She finished the ice cream under the hot sun and her mother's languid gaze.

Finally she said, "I have to go to the Chancery again. I

have to be questioned by a panel of important people—doctors and priests and psychiatrists, people like that."

"When?" said Serafina resignedly.

"In three weeks."

"Who told you?"

"Father Fogarty. This morning."

"Where's the Chancery?"

"Way downtown on Madison Avenue. Remember the time Daddy took me? Father Fogarty will take me this time. He's my advocate."

She studied the girl's face. "So? How do you feel about it?"

"I'm scared."

"Why? Because they could have you put away?"

"Not only that."

Serafina was about to press her old argument about recanting the vision but an impulse restrained her. It was not only her memory of this curate's recent advice to be kind to Lucia, and not only the disconsolate way her daughter now leaned both elbows on her scrawny knees and rested her head in her hands, that stirred her sympathy. As she gazed now at the roses growing around the driveway she sensed the growth of another budlet in her neglected heart. Serafina had done nothing to cultivate this sproutling of feeling but there it was. The woman was not so remote from grace to have lost all maternal magic. Somehow she *knew*.

"Loo-chee," she said in an unusually tender tone, "what happened, eh? Tell Mamma."

The girl began to tremble. She said, "Oh, Ma, I can't."

Serafina hestiated, poised between reproach and sympathy. Finally she responded with muted feminine gallantry. She handed her daughter an embroidered white handkerchief and said, "I know, *figlia mi'*. I know."

Lucia took the hand that offered the handkerchief and kissed it.

26

❧ ❧

She spent the time before her appearance at the Chancery in the usual way, attending mass, playing solitary games, reading and visiting Mario in the hospital. His condition was unchanged and the doctors said it would be a while before he could go home. They spoke in a matter-of-fact way but the words seemed to echo with doom. But Lucia continued to hope.

Her spirits had been lifted a little by the truce with Serafina. Wounds were beginning to heal but she faced new and unknown dangers, particularly in what I felt certain was an effort by Acosta to paint her as an apostate—or worse.

The day of the inquiry was mild and less humid than usual, a welcome interlude amid the dog days. After mass I quickly divested myself of my costume and met her outside the sacristy. I flashed a chipper smile to boost her morale. "Ready to hit the road?"

She nodded and we were off.

We decided to walk the few blocks to the IRT elevated subway. Not surprisingly, her mood was subdued and reflective. But she seemed primed too, like a taut acrobat, for her appearance. After all, she was finally going to give testimony of the miracle.

Her clothes seemed consciously demure: green school beret, white blouse with peter pan collar, green cotton skirt and canvas shoes. I thought I detected even a hint of rouge on her lips.

"Are you nervous?" I asked.

"A little."

We passed a luncheonette. Since I had just given her communion I knew that she hadn't had breakfast. "We have some time. How about a bite to eat?"

"Oh, no!" she protested rather vehemently.

"Come on. Just a little something. My treat."

Her demurral was firm. "We might be late. Besides, my stomach feels funny."

I yielded. "Okay." I didn't want to push her on a trivial matter. To the extent of my feeble powers I wanted to act as her shield and scaffold, but not get in her way. I reminded myself that she was, after all, a remarkable and capable child. My role was subsidiary; the picador of the pageant; loyal Sancho Panza.

As we walked down Westchester Avenue passers-by looked at us with curiosity and groups of neighbors whispered into cupped hands. I felt uneasy and angry for her sake because she had to suffer this scrutiny every day. With an expression of scorn, I tipped my straw hat to them all, usually causing the busybodies to turn away in embarrassment. Lucia gave no sign of noticing.

Our route passed the outskirts of the park, humid and perfumed reminder of how it all began. It wore the green of late summer, rich in the season's boon of moisture. It was overpopulated with picnickers and growing things. I was not especially fond of summer. I liked early spring when the sun was like found gold and the damp of winter still trickled out of the earth. For me the girl who now walked at my side, trying to keep up her courage, epitomized this vernal mood.

"Are you nervous?" she asked me.

"Of course."

"Don't worry, Father. Somehow it all fits into her plan."

"Yeah," I said with gloomy sarcasm. "The Lord works in mysterious ways, and all that."

The blasphemous tone earned me a sharp look. "I'm serious, Father."

My face flamed. "Don't pay any attention to me. But I just don't see how you keep from becoming cynical."

"What does 'cynical' mean, exactly?"

"Sarcastic. Distrustful of life's ultimate goodness. Sour about people. Like the wine of your faith turning to vinegar."

"That's what I thought it meant. No, I don't think I'll ever get that way. Then I'd be just like Dunlop or Father Acosta, wouldn't I?"

"Or like me."

She broke her stride. "No, Father. You're not really cynical. Maybe you're sour on the outside. But I think you're sweet on the inside."

"That's a nice compliment. But I'm not sure you're right." I frowned at the ribbon of sidewalk stretching before us. "I was like you once. I felt the same way about things."

"How do you mean?"

"Seems like many lifetimes ago. When I was a kid the world was black and white. The black was there, but a weak force lurking in the background. While the white was dazzling, dominating. Now it seems the other way around."

"Do you see any gray?"

"Lots of it. Mostly in the mirror, cropping up in my hair."

"Does growing older mean you automatically lose faith?"

"Could be."

We started walking again, and she looked reflective. "Sometimes, Father, I think we know everything when we're born. And we forget as we grow older. Instead of vice versa."

"Another person had the same theory once," I said, looking at her with admiration. "He was a Greek named Plato."

"Maybe there's something to it."

"Maybe. The lucky ones like you seem to remember longer."

"When did you start forgetting?"

"In the seminary, I think. Say," I said in mock anger, "who's the confessor here anyway?"

She suppressed a smile.

We had reached the Pelham Bay Park station and the stairs to the elevated platform loomed before us. She took a deep breath and led me on the climb.

Even though it was her second visit to the Chancery, the granite and stained-glass grandeur of the place still made a deep impression on this girl of eleven for whom the trip to Manhattan in itself was a rare excursion. In addition she faced the prospect of a humiliating physical and mental probe by what seemed an olympian group of inquisitors. Gargoyles must have haunted her imagination as our footsteps echoed in the marble corridors leading to Acosta's office. She gripped my hand and sought my eyes. I tried to smile to put her at ease but the facial expression that formed was a strained parody of pleasure.

The Jesuit greeted us gruffly and directed my protégée to a chair out of earshot. Then he turned to me and said, "She goes first to the infirmary. It's on the second floor. Klewski and O'Hare are already there, waiting for her."

I nodded morosely.

He smiled. "Good thing she's on time. How did you persuade her to come?"

"It wasn't my doing," I said. "Thank the Virgin Mary."

"Eh?"

"I didn't think you'd understand."

The scorching look in his eyes made me immediately regret the remark.

I brought her to the infirmary and waited outside, dying a thousand deaths for her sake. I thumbed through a copy of the *Catholic Digest*. The exam took over an hour. No portion of her nubile body was uncharted by the two doctors and their arsenal of glittering instruments. She later told me that the physical was more thorough than any she had undergone. I was trying to concentrate on a copy of *America* when she finally emerged, her face even paler than usual. Dr. O'Hare stood by her side.

"Everything okay?" I asked.

"She's in good health, if that's what you mean. Maybe a little run down but basically sound. Some of the test results won't be in for a day or two."

"That soon?" I asked.

"Father Acosta wants no more delays."

"What's next on the agenda?"

He consulted a clipboard. "You're to take her upstairs to

the conference room where Dr. Andrieu is waiting for her."

"A head-shrinking session, eh?"

Lucia looked startled at the phrase. "What's that mean?" she asked, hollow-eyed.

"It's just an expression," I said. "Means you're going to be questioned by the psychiatrist."

"Oh."

We went upstairs. I was not allowed to participate in this part of the procedure either and was told to wait ouside. I considered objecting, but then thought better of it. I was in enough hot water with Acosta already. Lucia later sketched me the details of the psychiatric examination.

Andrieu was suitably paternal. He introduced himself with a courtly air and motioned her to a couch that occupied the center of the large room. She eyed this article of furniture suspiciously, as if it were a torture rack. Maybe it was. First of all, it stuck out like a sore thumb as an oasis of comfort in the hard Gothic decor. It obviously had been inserted in the room for the present purpose. Besides, she had never before been interviewed in the supine position and the circumstance increased her dread. Still, she complied, meek as a lamb.

"Why am I lying down?" she mustered the courage to ask.

"To relax you," he said.

"Oh," she said, fidgeting with her skirt to make sure it covered her knees. It was obvious that she didn't at all feel relaxed. She shifted her shoulders on the couch. Her face was crimson. But she didn't avoid eye contact with the psychiatrist for she was by nature candid and guileless.

Andrieu also gazed candidly through the lenses of his nose-nippers. His manner showed that the girl's aura had captivated him. "But," he said, "you don't seem relaxed."

"No," she admitted.

"Why do you think you're not relaxed?" he asked, launching his free-association technique.

She answered directly, "Because I don't know you. And because I'm lying down."

"Do you feel vulnerable?"

"Yes."

"Do you think I'll hurt you?"

"No. Not anymore."

"Then try to relax."

"Okay." Her eyes rested on the ornately molded ceiling.

"What are you thinking about?"

"How beautiful this room is," she replied. "I've never been in such a beautiful room."

"Do you like it?"

"No."

"Why not?"

"Because it's beautiful in a cold way."

He looked around. "The colors are warm."

"Still—the room seems cold."

"What does it remind you of?"

"Nothing."

"Surely if you find it cold, you associate it with something."

"No."

"Some past room you have seen? Some experience, perhaps?"

"I don't think so."

"You don't have to be embarrassed about anything with me, you know. You can say anything that comes into your head. In fact, that's exactly what I want you to do."

"I'm not embarrassed. The room reminds me of nothing but itself."

"What's cold about it?"

"I'm not sure." She glanced around her. "I think it's too big. And, somehow, impersonal."

Andrieu surveyed the room too. "How so? What would you put in here to warm the place up?"

"Framed photographs," she said without hesitation. "And flowers. Lots of flowers."

He frowned, indicating his conviction that the interview had gotten off on the wrong track. He veered in a different direction. "Do you have dreams?" he asked abruptly.

"Of course I do, Doctor."

"Do you sometimes remember the content of them? The subject?"

"Sometimes."

"Can you remember one now?"

"Not offhand."

"Take a minute or two to think about it," he coaxed, sinking deeper into the red leather chair.

Finally she said, "One night last week I had a nightmare. I dreamed that a wooden puppet was chasing me on a bicycle. If he caught me I knew he would do something terrible, maybe even kill me. Yet I couldn't move. My limbs were paralyzed."

"Interesting. Perhaps the puppet represents a real person in your life."

"Yes. I know who it is."

Avidly, he leaned forward. "You do? Who?"

She averted her eyes. "I'd rather not say."

His face twitched and the pince-nez fell to his vest, dangling from the fastening. "My dear," he said, honey-toned, "you don't have to be afraid of telling me anything. Whatever you say here remains in the strictest confidence. Think of me as a confessor."

"But you're not a priest," she protested.

"No. But my role is similar. As a psychiatrist I also take a vow of secrecy."

"Aren't you asking me these questions to make out a report about me?"

"Yes. But the report will include a general diagnosis. I won't reveal anything specific without your permission."

Lucia turned sideways and propped her elbow on the couch to rest her chin in her hand. "Isn't it possible," she asked, "to guess the specifics from the general things you say in the report? What kind of vow of secrecy is that?"

The doctor's cheeks were tinged with red. "Why not tell me?" he coaxed. "I won't judge you. It must be a terrible secret you're harboring."

"Is it a sin for me to refuse to answer, if you're not a priest?"

"I don't trade in sins or virtues. I'm a scientist."

"Aren't you a Catholic?"

"Yes."

"And isn't this . . . this inquiry a Church thing?"

"Yes, but my role is a different one."

"I don't understand."

"I mean, the ecclesiastical part does not concern me, only the psychological part. I'm not a theologian."

"But you cooperate with the other panelists, don't you?"

"Yes, yes." He became annoyed. She was asking more questions than he. "Never mind. Don't tell me who the puppet represented." Seeing that this path of inquiry was also blind, he again switched gears. "Tell me something about your parents."

"What about them?"

"Anything that pops into your head."

"I love them," she said immediately.

"So?"

"That's what popped into my head."

"I see. Well, tell me more about them, okay? What are they like?"

She knitted her brow. "I don't know what to say. They're not special or anything. At least they wouldn't seem so to you or anybody else. They're ordinary people. They're immigrants from Sicily and kind of old-fashioned."

"I'm an immigrant too," he said.

She reacted with a blank expression, not grasping the significance of the remark, this bid for solidarity.

He continued, "Do you love one of your parents more than the other?"

"No," she replied calmly. "I love them equally."

"Are you sure?"

"Sure I'm sure." Her face revealed impatience. Was he trying to extract preconceived answers? She was not easy to manipulate. "May I ask you something, Doctor?"

"Okay."

"What do all these questions have to do with the vision I had?"

"Perhaps nothing."

"Then why are you asking them?"

"I said *perhaps* nothing. I'm trying to get to know you better. These questions may or may not have relevance. Trust me, my dear. I have wide experience in these matters. Something that may seem trivial and even absurd at first, later turns out to reveal areas of conflict. A random thought may be used to bring out hidden things—what we psychiatrists call repressed desires or memories. But you shouldn't bother your head with the technicalities. Just say whatever comes into your mind and let me worry about the interpretation."

"Okay," she said. "Why do you wear those silly-looking glasses?"

He fingered the pince-nez on his vest. "Why do you ask?"

She shrugged. "It came into my head."

"I don't think they're silly," he said with a tolerant smile. "They're practical for me. I can take them on and off easily." He put them back on. "Can we get back to your parents? Why don't you like discussing them?"

"I don't mind talking about them. I just don't see the point of it."

"Leave that to me." He folded his wrinkled hands, the skin of the knuckles circled like knotholes, and rested them on the seersucker cloth of his lap. "Now—as to your parents, do you think you might have a special feeling toward your father?"

"Yes. I have a special feeling toward my mother too. They are different persons."

"Ah. In what way are they different?"

"In many ways. For one thing, one's a man and the other's a woman."

Eyes glittering, he pounced on this statement. "Exactly," he said with an air of discovery.

She peered at him.

"Go on," he urged.

"Go on where?"

"With your parents." At her uncomprehending look he threw up his hands and sighed. "Oh, never mind. Let's go back to the puppet, all right? Can't you tell me anything about him? For example, what did he look like? What role did he play in the dream?"

"He looked like an ordinary wooden puppet except that he was always grinning like a death mask. It was just a dream."

"Just a dream?" he said in a tone of condescension. "If I may paraphrase Keats, 'Was it a vision, or a waking dream?' *Herr* Freud would turn over in his grave to hear you talk."

"My vision was not a dream," she said. "It was real."

"Dreams are real, my dear. I don't agree with the poet's distinction. What is a vision but a waking dream?"

"My vision was not a dream," she said flatly.

"Just as you like, my child." He patted her hand. "Tell me, this puppet is your father, isn't he?"

"No." She looked puzzled.

His eyes narrowed under twin gray shrubs. "It's nothing to be ashamed of. What did he want to do to you?"

"I tell you, it was not my father. And, if you don't mind, I'd rather say no more about it."

"As you like."

Andrieu gave up this method and tried more classic free-association techniques. But they were inconclusive. Next he tried hypnosis. Surprisingly, she did not respond. She wouldn't surrender to trance. He was quite puzzled that such a suggestible personality—an ecstatic who had suffered a stigmatic attack—would resist hypnosis. It was clear to him that she was consciously trying to conceal something.

He asked her direct questions about the stigmata and she recounted the experience in a flat prosaic manner.

"What did it feel like?" he prodded. "The experience itself?"

"I can't remember anything except what came before and after. The attack itself is a blank."

"Of course." He scribbled something on a memo pad and asked, "In the days before you received the stigmata, did anything special happen, anything memorable?"

Her face clouded. She was silent.

"Well?"

"Yes," she said with obvious reluctance.

"Can you tell me what it was?"

"The night before I collapsed in church," she said, stammering slightly, "I had crazy dreams. I don't have a clear memory of them now, only that they were a funny mixture of things—blood and Christ and a boxing match, all blended together like in those weird modern paintings. I woke up in the middle of the night—or maybe I dreamed that I woke up—and found the wounds of Christ on my body. Then I fell asleep again. In the morning my mother discovered something."

"What?" he said impatiently.

"She discovered . . . she discovered that I had become a woman."

"You mean you menstruated?"

She studied the ornate ceiling. "Yes."

He scribbled more notes. "What was your reaction to this?"

"I felt embarrassed."

"Guilty?"

"No. Embarrassed."

"Why were you ashamed? It's a natural thing."

She flushed. "I know. But I'm only eleven."

"Shame derives from guilt feelings. Why do you have these guilt feelings?"

Her voice rose. "I don't know."

He gestured to her to calm down. "All right." After consulting a pocket watch, he said, "That will be all for now, young lady. You may get up."

As she rose from the couch she scrutinized his face but found no clue to his thinking. "Thank you, Doctor," she muttered.

"Yes, yes," he said, getting out of the chair with agility and showing her to the door. "Now take good care of yourself, and don't worry about a thing."

I met her at the door. She looked a little shaken. "Are you all right?" I asked.

She nodded, smiling to reassure me.

"What was it like?" I whispered.

"A little like confession. Only without prayers."

I laughed. "Did he give you absolution?"

"He tried. But I wouldn't accept it."

"Why not?"

She thought about this. "I'm not sure," she said. "I think it's because I can't name the sin. And I don't trust in his powers."

"He's a priest of Freud," I said in a mocking tone.

She chanted the Confiteor: " 'I believe in God, the Father almighty, Creator of heaven and earth . . .' " She broke off with a pale smile. "Father Fogarty," she said, "there's no magic without prayer."

27

❦❦ ❦❦

We left the Chancery around noon as the sun-spangled buildings of Madison Avenue disgorged a stream of office workers headed for lunch. In silence we merged with the crowd and walked down the street toward the subway. The inquiry would continue but no specific date was set for us to return. We were to await further instructions.

Lucia gazed wide-eyed at the fashionable shops and imposing buildings. She had entered the heart of the city only once before and its sights and sounds still struck her with wonder. I offered to show her around.

"Would you, really?" she said.

"Sure," I said, consulting my wristwatch. "I have over an hour to spare. Where would you like to go first? Rockefeller Center?"

She looked at the twin spires of the Gothic edifice that reared a block away. "No. Saint Patrick's."

I might have known.

We entered the cool interior of the cathedral where tourists roamed the aisles as worshippers knelt and prayed. Lucia was mute with reverence as we walked around. She seemed scandalized to hear me plunge into the role of tour guide, indicating the large rose window of stained glass and the apsidal windows portraying scenes from the parables of Jesus. She was shocked not only by my calm speech but also by the tone of my voice for she had been taught never to speak in church unless absolutely necessary and then only in a whisper.

We walked up the middle aisle to the front of the church where a new high altar and ornate baldachin were under construction. She was again stunned to see in these hallowed surroundings workmen dressed in denim and carrying tools.

I smiled at her expression. "Did you think that altars were built by angels?" I asked.

"I guess I never thought about it," she replied in a whisper. Then she noticed a stairway tucked behind the altar. "What's down there?"

'A crypt," I said.

"What's a crypt?"

"A mausoleum. A tomb."

"You mean where they bury people?"

"Uh-huh."

She hesitated, then asked, "Who's buried down there?"

"All the former archbishops of New York."

"Oh, my!"

"Someday," I said musingly with a willful dash of wickedness, "the present archbishop will be carried *down* there too. It's conveniently closer to his ultimate home."

Lucia covered her mouth with her hand.

Meanwhile, fanned by the winds of jingoism and superstition, the cult of Pelham Bay Park continued to grow. After Dunlop's article about the so-called sign appeared, the leaders laid plans for a candlelit procession to be held at dusk on an evening soon after Lucia's first appearance before the panel. She had done nothing to encourage the plans but her wishes now mattered little or not at all.

The time passed and I attended to my priestly duties one day in good spirits, the next in low. I knew that my erratic emotions and behavior were somehow based on Lucia's predicament. I spoke to her often, trying to buoy her spirits. She didn't seem to need my morale-boosting. While not exactly elated, she seemed calm and collected, in short, in better shape than I. My mood was vaguely premonitory. I couldn't shake the feeling that some dreadful event lay ahead and my apprehension grew when toward the end of the week I got a phone call from Acosta about the procession.

"But she had nothing to do with it," I protested hotly.

"Calm down," he said. "I want her to attend the devotional service. I'll be there too."

I was momentarily puzzled. Soon it all became clear.

"In fact," he continued, "I intend to use the occasion to announce some preliminary findings in the girl's case."

I knew from his triumphant tone that the results of the physical had come back from the lab. The park ritual provided the perfect chance for him to publicly brand her as a sinner, to destroy her influence over the people, subvert the cult and—I might add—probably ruin her life. He cared little how such public humiliation would hurt the girl.

"Don't do it," I urged. "You'll demolish the poor kid."

"Then you know of her condition?"

I paused. "I can't discuss it. I think you know why. Let me just say this: she's totally innocent of any wrongdoing. She's pure as snow, I tell you."

"Not according to the doctors."

"I mean in heart, not in body."

"Then why," he asked sourly, "doesn't she release you from the vow so you can defend her?"

"I can't tell you that either."

"Too bad," he said. "The facts, I'm afraid, will have to speak for themselves." Abruptly, before I had time to compose another plea, he hung up.

I later learned that he had been calling from Bishop McArdle's office. I could just picture the look of smug satisfaction on his bulbous face as he replaced the phone in the cradle and turned to face his superior.

"She'll be there," Acosta said.

"Good," the bishop replied with a laconic smile. A tendril of gray hair had strayed to his forehead, giving the prelate an incongruously boyish appearance. "This thing seems to be working out even better than we anticipated."

"Yes, Bishop," said Acosta. "After people find out just what kind of girl this 'Bernadette of the Bronx' really is, it won't be long before the whole matter is forgotten."

"What a nuisance," said McArdle, slipping a pastille into his mouth.

"Then we can quietly submit our recommendation to the archbishop that the case be shelved."

"What happens to the girl?"

"Andrieu's working on that. There's that place near Albany—Saint Agatha's. Perfect for her, I would say. They treat wayward girls with mental problems."

As usual the tall and slender prelate paced the room while the portly subaltern sat practically motionless in a comfortable chair with only the flitting movements of his beady black eyes to show he was alive. Framed by the big bay windows, McArdle turned to face the Jesuit. "It's hard to believe of that innocent-seeming child. Only eleven years old. It's disgraceful."

"Yes."

" 'Hypocrisy,' said a wise Frenchman, 'is the homage that vice pays to virtue.' "

"How true."

"Do we have Andrieu's diagnosis?"

Acosta patted a sheaf of papers in his commodious lap. "Right here. It's a, uh, Freudian interpretation."

McArdle hoisted his brows. "Can't we somehow avoid Freud's name?"

"Now that Freud is safely in his grave I think we can make use of some of his theories. I seriously doubt that this report will ever reach the eyes of the Holy Father."

"Heaven forbid!"

"In any case, the sexual emphasis in the Freudian system is tailor-made for our present purpose."

"Oh?"

"Andrieu is convinced that the stigmatic attack was a classic example of 'hysterical conversion.' In other words, the discharge of repressed sexual energy in stigmatic symptoms. This is cut-and-dried." He consulted the report. "The doctor also writes that the patient was not very forthcoming during the interview, that she refused to answer many of his questions." He leered. "Now we know why, don't we?"

McArdle looked annoyed. "Continue, please."

"The child was a bundle of repressed sexuality. 'Repressed,' that is, until recently."

McArdle asked, "There can be no mistake about this, I hope."

"The test was absolutely conclusive." His eyes turned again to the report. "Andrieu concludes that the girl suffers from a distinct psychoneurotic complex—a mental disturbance known in psychoanalytic circles as the 'Electra Complex.' "

"Which means?"

"In Freud's mythology it means the girl incestuously loves her father, wants to bear his child and hates her mother, whom she secretly desires to annihilate. A pretty little notion, isn't it?"

McArdle was struck by a sudden idea, causing his eyes to widen. "You don't think . . . ?"

Acosta shrugged. "It's always possible, although we have no proof of it."

The bishop rubbed his angular chin reflectively. "Sicilians are hot-blooded knaves," he decided.

The Andalusian winced at the slur against his racial cousins but kept silent, savoring the thought that the Celts *were* narrow-minded boobs. And soon his mind was occupied by more pleasant thoughts—visions of his imminent lunch.

I pleaded with her, "You've got to accuse him. There's no other way."

She gazed troubledly at the thicket of boat masts spiring up from the bay. We had come to the end of the wharf to talk in private. We sat on the hard planks, dangling our feet over the lapping water. I studied her sad face, looking for signs of surrender to the inevitable. I pressed the argument. "He'll disgrace you in public. You can't let him get away with it. Think of your family, Lucia."

"I can't do it," she said. "I just can't."

"You have to."

Her blue eyes now shifted from the bay to my concerned face. Her expression betrayed no real conflict. "No," she said firmly. After a pause: "I saw her again, Father."

I was stunned. "What?"

"Don't worry. I'm not saying I had another vision. I saw her in a dream."

I was visibly relieved. I grunted an inarticulate reaction.

"I'd like to share it with you, Father."

"Okay."

"Yesterday, when you told me about Father Acosta's plan to disgrace me, I had made up my mind not to show up at the procession. I decided to run away or something, anything not to face the shame. I wanted to die. Then I fell into an old habit. I started to pray. I prayed and prayed all day and night, mixing prayers and tears like a magic formula. I got very tired. I fell into a deep sleep."

The tempo of her voice quickened. "The dream was a mixed-up thing. First I saw a kindly bearded man holding a flowering cane. A dove was perched on the cane. Then this picture disappeared and I saw a handsome angel standing in a garden with a white lily in his hand. He was surrounded by jars of sparkling water. I heard a clicking sound. Near the garden wall dripping with roses, I saw a woman at a spinning wheel. She was spinning something that looked like a veil. It was her. She smiled and called me to her side. She looked straight at me and put her hand gently on my belly." She fell silent.

"And?" I asked impatiently.

"There's no more. That's the dream."

"So?"

"I don't know how to explain it, but when I woke up I didn't want to run away anymore. My shame was gone but I felt another shame: shame because I had lost faith in Mary and her protection. When the going got rough, I wanted to run. Now I know what I have to do."

"What?"

"Attend the procession and trust in Our Lady."

"What about Basil?"

"I can't accuse him. It's in God's hands."

I sighed, knowing from her demeanor that it was no use arguing. "You won't change your mind by tomorrow?"

"No." She rose and looked toward land at the end of the pier. "Thank you, Father."

"Don't mention it."

She waved shyly and walked back toward her house. I watched her slim figure recede into the landscape of trees, telephone poles and tiny houses dotting the shore. I watched and with a brisk sign of the cross resolved then and there to take certain matters into my own freckled hands.

28

꜀꜔꜀꜔

The day came, clothed like Prospero in the magic robes of the season. It was hot and humid again and the air purled with the breath of coming rain. Beneath the dampness, like wands, lay the threat of lightning.

The procession began, a giant glowworm of candles curling into the shadowy reaches of the park. The play of light and shadow lent a fabulous atmosphere to the mundane place where on other evenings footballs were thrown and old men leaned on canes, staring at the misty vista of the past or into the abyss of the future. Now, as the worshippers entered, chanting hymns to the Queen of Heaven, the park seemed transformed to a mythic forest where the borders of possibility were extended and the laws of nature suspended, instead of a patch of green in an asphalt city.

I had arrived early and chosen a seat high in the bleachers with a commanding view of the entire shrine area which I now surveyed with racetrack binoculars. The statue stood as always in the clearing where the vision was reported to have appeared. It was decorated with branches of laurel and boxwood, surrounded by crucifixes, holy pictures and other religious emblems. A brocaded blue cloak still hung on the statue's stone shoulders and roses were scattered on the wooden platform altar.

The crowd was large and still growing, the curious augmenting the ranks of the devout. I scanned the faces, some familiar, others not, encompassing all ages, both sexes and all physical types, a gallery of moods from skepticism to fascination to the kind of avidness I imagine must have marked the features of Roman spectators at the Colosseum. Here were ravenries of Italian widows clothed in black, there a legless boy in a wheelchair. Nursing mothers sat beside laborers in soft caps, their hands kneading rosary beads. A fat butcher in a gory apron stood beside a wealthy matron dressed in the dernier cri. Young girls in babushkas sat on the grass near a group of teenage boys in baseball uniforms. It was a tapestry of opposites threaded together by the shared desire to witness a miracle and maybe get a glimpse of what lies behind the veil of death.

I caught my breath. Through the binoculars I spotted on the outskirts of the crowd the boy called Basil Two-Times. He sat on his bicycle which was propped against a tree, and stared vacantly ahead.

I made a mental note of where he stood and shifted my gaze over the crowd. Weaving through the throng was the familiar figure of Albert Dunlop. He was conducting what journalists call "color" interviews. I wondered why he bothered, since his powers of invention far surpassed his skill as an interviewer.

The processionists by now had all filed into the park, and the seating area in front of the shrine resembled a giant birthday cake under the darkening sky. The worshippers sang: "'Oh, Mary, conceived without sin, pray for us, pray for us who have recourse to thee.'"

I looked at the horizon and frowned. The skies looked ominous, billowing with cumulus clouds, just like that day on the golf course. My thoughts were interrupted by the sound of my name being shouted.

I looked down from the bleachers and saw Acosta's auklike figure motioning me to descend. I turned to the person sitting next to me, a buck-toothed teenage boy who had an annoying habit of snuffling. "Would you mind this seat for me?" I asked.

"Yes, Father," he said, listless eyes widening in awe of the Roman collar. My occupation carried certain fringe benefits.

I clambered down from the bleachers, threading clumsily

through a maze of limbs, torsos and heads, leaving a muttered trail of "excuse me's" in my wake. When I finally confronted the Jesuit on terra firma, I noticed an amused glint in his eye. It pleased him to make me jump through hoops. The crowd now chanted, " 'Oh, Queen of the Holy Rosary, Oh, bless us as we pray. And offer thee our ro-oh-ses in garlands day by day.' "

"Good evening, Father Fogarty," he said with mock courtliness. "Looks like rain."

I grunted in reply.

"No matter," he said, scanning the skies. "This shouldn't take long."

I then decided to try one last appeal to the man's sympathy, to his sense of humanity, if such an attempt wasn't based on a vain assumption. "Can't you reconsider?" I asked. "She's an innocent kid. Think of what you'll do to her."

He flushed a little and stammered. Perhaps I *had* kindled a spark of humanity in the callous Spaniard. Finally he said, petulantly, "Sorry. She's nothing but a fornicator and I can't have pity for her."

"But I tell you she's innocent. Give me a little time and I'll prove it."

I glimpsed a flicker of indecision on his face. But it soon vanished. He shook his head emphatically.

It was useless. Why would he anger his superior Bishop McArdle by sabotaging his own plans to discredit Lucia? It was too much to ask. Altruism and charity were beyond the grasp of this servant of Christ. Still I pressed for the impossible. "Look—give me a little time. Give her a break." I searched the crowd for the figure of the boy on the bike. He was still there, leaning against the tree. "I have a chance to prove her innocence."

"I have a duty to perform," he said.

My eyes blazed, my hands balled into fists.

He touched my arm. "I want you to prepare her for my announcement," he said.

"She knows about it," I said.

"She's pregnant," he said.

The news hit me with sledgehammer force. I stood there

in mute surprise. "Oh, no." My voice was barely audible. "Oh, no."

"Yes." There may have been a hint of compassion in his voice now, but his manner was as inflexible as ever. He wouldn't yield to my pleading.

Fuming with anger, I left him standing there and weaved my way through the crowd. They chorused, " 'Mother dearest, Mother fairest, help us all who call on thee. Virgin purest, brightest, rarest . . .' "

There was one possibility: to persuade the boy to make a public confession of the rape and clear Lucia's name. My line of sight now was blocked by the crowd so I made my way blindly toward the spot where I had last seen him.

A ripple of excitement passed through the gathering. Then the people broke into applause. Lucia had arrived. She was standing near the statue, her frightened eyes ferreting the area. She was probably looking for me. I shoved through the crowd, calling her name. He face showed relief as she spotted me.

"Am I glad to see you," she said as I grasped her hands. "I need what they call moral support."

"You got it," I said, squeezing those cold hands. *"Dominus vobiscum."* I couldn't disguise the concern on my face.

"What's the matter?" she asked.

I looked around furtively. Everybody was watching us. Silently I led her to a sheltered spot near a group of trees. "Where're your parents?" I asked.

"They wanted to come," she replied. "Especially my father. But I convinced them to stay home."

"Good," I said, glancing at the crowd. The people were kneeling and reciting a litany of prayers. The candles flickered eerily against the menacing sky.

She studied my troubled face and said, "Don't worry, Father. Our Lady will take care of everything."

Fat chance, I thought, grimacing. How wantonly I sinned in my head. I even toyed with the idea of suggesting an abortion, considered in those days an ineffably heinous act. I grasped her slim shoulders. "Look, Lucia. I have something very important to tell you."

She waited patiently as I summoned the courage. Her eyes coaxed. I looked at the ground and my ears turned scarlet. I was certain that this news would constitute the last straw to her composure, perhaps to her very sanity. I fumbled for a way to break it to her as gently as possible. It wasn't fair that she should be haunted forever by a living reminder of that horrible night. Was this how Our Lady treated her servants? Was this how the Lord rewarded virtue? I felt like ripping off my collar and trampling on it. I looked at the statue, at the gaudy replica of the second Eve, and wondered whether she mocked my client, she with her virgin birth. Did she preserve the purity of her own pregnancy by knotting it to the umbilical of Lucia's joyless fetation? Did the cord stretch down the ages of flesh and word, word and flesh, to the First Mother who sold us down the River Styx? Was this her plan? Well, she wasn't going to get away with it.

"What is it, Father?" she asked again. "It can't be all that bad."

"It is, Lucia. Believe me. I don't know how else to tell you, except to come right out with it: Father Acosta says that you're pregnant."

A growling rose in the distant sky. A dark squall cloud tumbled over the bay, amassing power from the clash of air and water, rumbling like an animal about to pounce. The trees whispered its approach.

Nervously, I studied her face, starkly defined in the sun's absence. I steeled myself for the reaction, the collapse I was certain would come. Slowly her lips curved into a smile.

"Praise be to God," she said.

Forgive the understatement, curiales, but I was dumbfounded. Then I remembered her extreme youth. "Maybe you don't know what that means, child."

"Of course I do. I'm going to have a baby."

"Yes," I said in a rising voice. "And do you realize whose baby? That idiot's baby. That rapist's."

She smiled sweetly. "I know."

"That doesn't bother you?"

"It's God's child. All babies are."

I grew exasperated. "Lucia, listen to me. You weren't im-

218

pregnated by the Holy Ghost, you know. This is no virgin birth. This is a child of sin."

Her gaze was filled with reproach. "Don't ever say that," she said, placing her hand on her belly. "All children are born innocent."

I was petulant, unwilling to concede the moral point. "But some, dear Lucia, are conceived in sin."

Her cheeks grew rosy with argument. She seemed taller, inflated by her impassioned advocacy of the unborn. "Are the babies to blame? I'm sure they're not, Father." Her eyes glittered in the gathering twilight. "I think that pure things grow in dirt. Flowers fertilized on a battlefield are still beautiful, aren't they?"

I felt like a Talmudist getting lectured by a prodigy. "Don't ask me," I said with gruffness to mask my embarrassment, "I've lost my moorings."

"And where's the sin in this case, Father? You yourself said I wasn't to blame. Is Basil guilty? He doesn't know any better."

"Sometimes evil can be an atavistic thing."

"I don't understand those big words."

"Read the Bible," I snapped. "It says the Lord God is jealous and visits the iniquity of the fathers upon the children. Maybe you're paying for someone else's sin."

"Okay, then. I'll pay it. As long as it's not my sin. And as long as I don't have to pay it in hell." She fell silent, standing proudly under the foliage of mature summer. Nearby the crowd grew murmurous in harmony with the approaching storm. It was clear from the way the cultists looked in our direction and whispered to each other that they were becoming restless. The words "Show us a sign" and "Miracle" were distinguished amid the drone of voices.

"Listen to them," I said with disdain. "Listen to the blathering of the Mystical Body. They want their money's worth."

Lucia's lips arched and her pallor turned to wine. The crescendoing wind loosened strands of her hair and made her jumper skirt flap around her knees. Was it possible that this tidy young body contained the seed of life? Her face looked radiant as she spoke. "Don't be too harsh on them, Father. Is a miracle so much to ask for?"

I was speechless at how calm she remained, how the news of her pregnancy seemed to gladden her. I wondered at her fathomless sympathy for the people who I knew would turn against her after Acosta revealed her condition.

She touched her midsection. There beneath flesh and cartilage lay the pear-shaped muscle to which clung like a bat this fetus, at once blessed and cursed by this mystery of eternal change. Still equipped with the gills and tail of earlier times, it swam now in a state described by Wordsworth as "Not in entire forgetfulness, And not in utter nakedness, But trailing clouds of glory." She touched her belly and rejoiced. "I have a miracle."

I frowned.

She made the sign of the cross. " 'Hail Mary, full of grace, the Lord is with thee. Blessed art thou among women and blessed is the fruit of thy womb, Jesus . . .' "

No use arguing. I had to act myself to save her. I scanned the crowd and located the boy still sitting on his bike. He kept brushing locks of hair off his low forehead and staring at the shrine. I started off in his direction.

She interrupted her prayer. "Where you going, Father?"

"I'll be back," I said. I knew that I could never put out the torch of her charity and get her to agree to my plan so I kept silent about it.

Suddenly she looked afraid. "Please stay," she pleaded.

"I promise—I'll be right back."

I was about to leave when Dunlop appeared. He nodded to Lucia, who was looking at the ground. "Anything to say for my readers?" he asked.

Her face registered more pity than reproach. "No."

"Come on," he urged. "Monosyllables make lousy quotes."

I snarled, "Why don't you make it up, like everything else?"

He gave me a mocking smile. "Now, now, Padre . . ."

"I have nothing to say to you, Mr. Dunlop," she said.

"Won't you comment on your . . . uh . . . delicate condition?"

I reddened. So Acosta had already told him. "How would you like a swift kick in the ass?" I growled.

"Tut, tut," he said. "Such language, Padre." He grinned. "Can I quote you?"

"Leave us alone, Mr. Dunlop," said Lucia. "Please."

"I have only one or two questions," he persisted. "Like who's the father? Or was this a case of immaculate conception?"

"Why, you lowdown skunk," I said through clenched teeth, "I'm going to take off this collar and beat the daylights out of you."

"I wouldn't advise it," he warned with a sharp glance. "Don't let my handicap fool you: I can use one fist better than most men use two. And those black robes cut no ice with me either."

"Just go away, Mr. Dunlop," begged Lucia. "Please."

"Not until I get a useful quote or two."

Her face suddenly and incongruously radiated happiness, pink and translucent. "Okay. Tell everyone that I have a miracle inside me—a baby. Write that my body is . . . is a temple of creation." She fondled her abdomen. "Say that I'm happy to be God's cup of life. Is that enough for you?"

"Not quite. Who's the father?"

"The Lord is the Father of all," she replied.

"Don't be cute." He arched an eyebrow, prompted by a sudden inspiration. "Could it be Father Frecklepuss over here?"

I lunged at him but Lucia hurled herself between us and stopped me from bloodying his nose or maybe incurring harm to myself. Under her withering gaze, I desisted. The crowd murmured with alarm.

Lucia calmly shifted her gaze to the reporter. "I'm not going to say anything more," she informed him in a resolute tone.

He started to speak, then checked himself. A muscle in his cheek twitched. The rising wind ruffled his curly hair. He took out a notebook and cradled it against the stump of his missing arm. Then, with a lidded look at both of us, he jotted a few notes and vanished into the crowd.

I stood rooted to the spot, seething. I muttered, "Man like that makes me feel certain that Lucifer's winning the war."

"I feel sorry for him," she said.

I found it hard to share her sympathy. I glowered and said, "Why? Because he has one arm?"

"No. I think he has a more serious handicap."

"Like what?"

"Have you looked hard at his face and those shifty eyes? It's like he's haunted by something."

"Hmph. The ghosts of his lies."

"More than that," she said, staring into space. "Much more."

I scrutinized the sweet cameo face.

"He's lost more than an arm," she added. "He's lost the fight." She looked up at me with brimming blue eyes. "Hell is certain. And he knows it."

Time froze in a flare of lightning that candied the surrounding trees. A rumble grew in the gray sky. We saw umbrellas billow before the shrine and the birthday cake now resembled a patch of toadstools, swaying vanguards of the rain. Her gaze shifted to the horizon yellow with lightning. "The storm's coming fast," she said.

"Let's get out of here," I urged.

"I can't."

"What are you going to do?"

"Nothing."

I looked at the platform in front of the shrine where Acosta was ascending, gathering the folds of his cassock. He raised his arms to silence the people.

"Are you going to just stand there while he slanders you?" I asked urgently. "Let's just vamoose."

"I told you, I have to stay."

It was hopeless. I watched the Jesuit nodding gravely at the crowd. Some people called Lucia's name, demanding a sign. It made me heartsick. Suddenly I realized that I was standing alone.

She had walked out into the clearing and fallen to her knees to pray. A hush fell. Some cultists showered her with cut roses. Pats of rain.

Acosta frowned and raised his pudgy arms. "May I please have your attention," he shouted.

I had to act quickly. I looked around for the boy, but now

he had vanished. I grew frantic and began shoving my way through knots of people toward the tree near which I had last spotted him. I asked a bystander, "There was a kid on a bike standing here. Did you happen to see where he went?"

The man, a clerkish fellow with a brush mustache, looked annoyed. I had diverted his attention from the riveting tableau of girl and Jesuit. He shrugged.

I frowned and looked around again. Then I saw a bicycle lying in the grass about ten yards away. But no Basil. Acosta was speechifying about how carefully the archdiocese had investigated this case, while Lucia continued to pray in silence. The rain was light, the sky forbidding. Where was that boy? I had to find him before Acosta (thank God he was a windbag) reached the end of the speech.

I hurried over to the bicycle and examined it as if it somehow would disclose his whereabouts. There was no clue. I grimaced at the crowd and the black-garbed figure on the platform telling them, "The panel has made some shocking discoveries about Lucia Buonfiglio."

I knew there was little time to lose. Acosta was raising the tar brush. But my hands were tied. Then I heard a rustling in the branches above my head. A squirrel scrambling up the oak? I peered through the foliage and saw him. He had climbed up to a high bough for a better vantage. My heart pounded.

"Come down," I shouted. "I want to talk to you."

Our eyes met. There was panic in his glance.

"Come down," I repeated sternly. "Quickly."

Tentatively, Basil Two-Times descended monkey-fashion, hand over hand. His feet touched the ground and he shrank from me.

"I'm not going to hurt you," I said. "But you've got to listen to me."

Spittle glazed his bared teeth. He made guttural sounds.

"Only you can save her from disgrace, Basil. You must tell the truth."

His face was void of comprehension, stricken with fear.

"I promise you won't be harmed . . ."

He bolted for the bike, got a running start, leapt onto the saddle and pedaled off. I gave chase.

Drumrolls of thunder filled my ears as I ran panting after

him toward the open football field. The sky shimmered with electric activity. I ran as hard as I could. Gopher holes and other natural obstacles slowed him down. Still there seemed to be no way I could overtake him and I almost abandoned the effort. But something kept me going. The bike zigzagged across the field. He kept turning to see where I was and losing his footing. In the background talons of lightning reached from cloud to horizon and I suddenly became frightened. The bike, of course, had metal parts, and he was pedaling over a large open area. I shouted in a husky voice, "Listen, you must stop! Get off that bike!"

He ignored my commands and kept cycling. And soon it was too late.

Acosta was reaching the main point of the oration while Lucia continued to pray impassively and the onlookers grew impatient, unruly. They wanted to hear the girl speak, not this pompous Jesuit. Yet he droned on, "Mother Church cannot merely grant her liturgical honors indiscriminately. Private moral certainty of sanctity may be enough for private veneration. But it is not enough for public and common acts . . ."

The event had a certain macabre beauty. The vehicle phosphoresced as power flowed to the metal. The light shimmered, catching objects unawares, preserving them in the amber of a split second. The crackle of static foretold the finish and he fell without a sound.

I rushed to the spot and examined the body. I gazed at the now-mute sky.

Acosta continued: "The bones of the martyrs and saints are dearer to us than priceless gems, purer than gold. We cannot be too careful in such matters as identifying miracles and studying the character and background of any persons associated with claims of visions, stigmatic seizures or any spiritual phenomena." Here he cast a disdainful glance at the prayerful figure kneeling in the grass. "The Lord does not pick sinners as His pawns."

I left the body in the wet grass and walked in a dazed manner back toward the shrine, hauling the added freight of guilt.

I alone now stood between the child and scandal. And I was gagged by a vow of silence. I stumbled across the football field.

Acosta raised an accusing hand. "You see before you," he said, pointing at Lucia, "a little girl who says she has seen the Holy Mother. A girl who says she has suffered the wounds of Calvary. A girl who gives the appearance of sanctity and innocence . . ."

Lucia mumbled the garlanded formulas of the rosary, praying coolly and without cerebration. She wasn't listening to the Jesuit's words. White beads coiled around pale veined hands, knees sank into the damp grass.

His cruel oration reached my burning ears as I neared the shrine. Still dumbfounded and tottering on my feet, I elbowed aside one or two persons and hurtled toward the platform, drawing scalding glances on my black-robed back. In that instant, with full consent of the will, I chose to sin. I made up my mind to break my vow and save her reputation, tribunes. *Mea culpa, mea culpa, mea maxima culpa.* So sue me. But I couldn't stand idly by while he blackened her name.

"Wait," I croaked.

My sin never passed from the realm of thought to deed. What happened next throttled both my own words and Acosta's speech.

Three fingers of Irish, please, before continuing the narrative. The pause that refreshes the spirit, if not the memory.

Here God sprang from the machine, so to speak, and wrested matters from my hands. Acosta was about to lower the boom when the crowd let out a collective gasp. People dropped to their knees. I looked around me, puzzled at this sudden display of wonder and reverence. The crowd buzzed. Then I saw it too.

The whole thing lasted less than half a minute. How long did it take the Saviour to rebuke the wind at Galilee? A bluish halo of light formed around the crown on the head of the statue, glowing unmistakably amid strands of mist. Then it was gone.

For a full minute the people knelt in stunned silence. Soon a rustle of whispers swept through the gathering. A woman shouted, "Praise be the Lord!" Tears and rain mingled on the cheeks of some. An old man with a pickled nose danced a jig of joy. Now everyone stood up in a tumult of shouts and prayers. "A sign, a sign" was heard on all sides.

The crowd rushed toward the figure of Lucia, still kneeling, mute with wonder. A group of men scooped her up and carried her on their sturdy shoulders in triumph through the park. Her eyes grew wide with fear and awe.

I saw Dunlop shake his head and mutter, "What a story. What a helluva story!"

At last the heavens opened and buckets of rain fell, scattering the crowd, except for those who carried Lucia toward her home. I glanced around, looking for a policeman or someone to whom I could report the electrocution. I saw Acosta still standing speechless on the platform. Oblivious to the rain that poured on his head and soaked him to the skin, he glowered blackly into space.

I spat on the ground and went and got a cop.

29

In late September as President Roosevelt rattled the saber over errant German torpedoes and as the first portentous snowflake fluttered over Moscow's onion skyline, Serafina Buonfiglio sat in the kitchen reading a scrapbook of news stories about her daughter. As Japanese troops marched through China and DiMaggio belted the horsehide, Serafina thumbed through the scrapbook that was held together with brown shoelaces. And her buckthorn heart was yielding.

As she closed the book a rare thing happened to her: a tear glistened in the corner of her eye. She went to the cabinet, produced a bottle of Marsala and poured a dollop into a tumbler. The wine warmed her stomach and strengthened her resolve. She went to the coat closet, donned a cardigan sweater and tied a kerchief around her head. Heaving a sigh, she left the house.

Seated at my bedroom window, I read a newspaper, and watched evening skulk over the bay. The nights were cooler now but the unceasing murmur of summer lingered. I was reading an article about a bill before Congress designed to extend the service of Army draftees. The story quoted the usual squabblings between hawks and isolationists. There was a rap at the door.

Behind the door was planted Mrs. Carney's dumpy form.

"Some lady it is," she announced in the reproachful tone that for some reason she often used with me. "Wants ya ta hear her confession, Faa-ther." She peered at me. Did she think I took some sly pleasure from hearing the lurid secrets of women? I nodded curtly and went to get my vestments.

As I entered the church I dimly saw the figure of a woman lighting a candle before the side altar. I coughed to disclose my presence and walked under the transept to the last aisle, my heels clicking rather too ostentatiously on the tiles. Discreetly averting my face, I swept down the colonnaded aisle until I reached the confessional box to which my name card was affixed. I went inside and sat down.

I rested my elbow on the ledge and cradled my chin in my hand in the pose priests use to convey meditation while masking boredom at the old penance stand. Confessions are usually monotonous and predictable affairs, more like tabulations of petty infractions than the bouts of breast-beating and soul-baring they are cracked up to be. So I was prepared for the worst.

This confession was different. The penitent was Serafina Buonfiglio.

I recognized her voice right away. It had been over twelve years since her last confession, she related, according to the formula.

I had to interrupt. "Please, forgive me, signora . . ."

"It's me who come for forgiveness," she said.

"I mean, forgive me for interrupting. But I must know, how is she?"

"Okay."

"I'm glad. And the boy?"

"He's out of the hospital. The rest, we don't know."

"I'll pray for him. I'll pray for the whole family."

"Can I continue?"

"Of course."

I settled in to hear this occupational oddity—a truly epiphanic confession. Since, tribunes, I know that the penitent passed away seven years ago, I feel no compunction about disclosing it here. Come with me, tribunes, to the siren that was Sicily twelve years before the Miracle of Pelham Bay Park. Fall with me under Morgana's spell at the place where Charybdis spouted death.

It is night. The air is scented with jasmine and orange blossoms, the shoreline washed by the sea. The night lamps of fishermen stud the Strait of Messina. The stars glow, and Aphrodite laughs at the crescent moon.

A slim figure darts along the rocky shoreline, avoiding beached dories in the sand. She reaches a fisherman's shack and goes inside. He is there waiting for her. They embrace hungrily, savoring the taste of forbidden fruit. Soon they make love under a canopy of mended nets.

That night on a beach somewhere outside Messina Lucia Buonfiglio was conceived. This was the sin that Serafina confessed to me. She had made love to Ettore while he was still married to her sister who was then dying of tuberculosis. So Lucia, herself lily-pure, was, like her own child, conceived in sin.

Over the years guilt had embittered Serafina until it soured her completely, against her husband and life in general. The sin, she felt, brought a curse on the family which ultimately resulted in Mario's affliction with a blood disease. Do I subscribe to this atavistic view? I merely record it here to put the portrait of my client in perspective. I leave you to your own devices.

Serafina's remorse was genuine. I readily gave her absolution and no penance. Guilt had flagellated her enough. When she left the box, I sat there and let feeling wash over me. My throat was constricted with emotion. I had done my priestly duty and for once it made me proud.

When Serafina got home Ettore was sitting on the porch, smoking a cigarette. He greeted her with an inarticulate sound and gave her a quick furtive look, lips clamped sullenly on the butt. The tip glowed as he puffed. She said nothing and sat beside him on the couch, a wicker piece from the Salvation Army store on Westchester Avenue. The cushions were decorated with palm-tree graphics on which she now fastened her eyes in the awkward silence.

The cigarette glowed in the darkness. Somewhere a frog

croaked. She looked at his face in profile, etched in moonlight. An automobile purred past the house. She heard the even rhythm of his breathing.

Her fingers traced the fur on the back of his hand. His eyes widened in surprise as the fingers, soft as butterflies, touched his stubbly cheek. They embraced.

30

The rising sun made a glaze of sea and sky. Waves crashed on drowsy Waikiki, its sands gleaming in the new light. Sentries prowled the retaining wall at Fort De Russy overlooking shallow waters where wading natives speared fish for Sunday breakfast. The fleet bobbed peacefully in the landlocked harbor. In downtown Honolulu a boozed-up sailor leaned against the trunk of a palm tree and gazed at the clock on the Aloha Tower. It read 7:55.

The planes came from the southeast over the emerald Pacific, over the gaping mouth of Diamond Head where the ancient idolators buried their dead. More than three hundred aircraft hummed like dragonflies over the vast expanse of sea and headed for the harbor that nestled like a pearl in the shell of Oahu.

Along with the rest of the world, I read and heard the gory details the next day—December 8, 1941, when the United States Congress declared war on the Japanese Empire.

All the residents of the rectory huddled around the radio in the sitting room. The pounding of Sam Rayburn's gavel echoed in the House chamber. Then came President Roosevelt's voice: "Yesterday, December 7, 1941—a day which will live in infamy—the United States was suddenly and deliberately attacked by the naval and air forces of the Empire of Japan . . ."

I soon received the expected greetings from my local draft board and for the next four years got a lot of practice in dispensing the Sacrament of Extreme Unction. Don't worry, tribunes, I won't digress to the point of boring you with war stories. Suffice to say that my military tour, served mostly in North Africa and Italy, tended to sharpen my cynicism and increase my girth (ah, Satan in the guise of *pizza rustica* and *spaghetti alle vongole*).

On mustering out I was assigned to a curacy at a parish in suburban Larchmont, where I toiled in benighted bliss for four years. Then, somehow or other, my intellectual gifts won recognition in the form of an assignment to teach philosophy and theology in the seminary at Dunwoodie.

In the intervening years I heard nothing of and thought seldom about the Buonfiglio family. The memory of that summer soon faded like a yellowing photograph in an album, an accessible memento that I rarely bothered to look at. Yet, somehow, I knew that these events of 1941 had exerted a seminal influence on my future life. The Buonfiglio episode lay in a dusty corner of my memory, ignored, perhaps, but ticking like a time bomb. Until 1952.

He showed up at the freshman tryout for the basketball squad of which I was assistant coach. He was a rarity among seminarian candidates for the team: he was a fine athlete. He had deceptive moves and a quick release on his one-hander. He was also a deft ball handler with the ability to dribble and pass behind his back in an era when such skills were rare. Only ten minutes into the drill he had me and the coach salivating. He was star guard material.

"Blow the whistle," said Father Mitchell, the coach, with this greedy look in his eye.

I blew. "Take a breather," I yelled.

Mitchell and I looked at each other and then walked over for a closer appraisal. He was a handsome kid with dark wavy hair and almond-shaped hazel eyes. He was somewhat fragile-looking but cords of muscles rippled in his arms and legs as he continued to dribble the leather basketball. Apparently, he was still wired up for the tryout.

"What's your name, young man?" asked the coach.

"Mario," he replied. "Mario Buonfiglio."

I took a deep breath.

After the drill I took him to the cafeteria for sugar doughnuts and coffee. When I told him who I was, a glimmer of recognition crossed his face. "I remember you now," he said, inspecting my waistline. "You've changed a lot."

"So have you," I observed, smiling. He was the picture of health. "You were ill."

"Terminally."

"And?"

He shrugged and raised his eyes skyward. "The Lord seems to have decreed a postponement." He bared bright white teeth.

"Remission?"

"That's what the doctors called it." He batted his eyes in a disarming way and looked at me with candor. Something about his demeanor reminded me of her.

"Are remissions from thalassemia rare?"

"Unprecedented, Father."

"Well, well, well."

Tranquilly, he nibbled on the doughnut and washed it down with gulps of coffee. He ate with the concentration of a young animal at the trough.

I rubbed my chin and observed this coltish boy, thinking that he embodied in his wholesome flesh the prodigy of love's power. "Your sister must be happy about this," I said. "How is she?"

A shadow crossed his face. He looked guarded. "Okay. It's been pretty rough on her."

"Where is she? I'd like to see her. She's a young woman by now."

"Yeah."

A disturbing thought came to me. "Was everything all right? I mean the baby."

"Oh, sure. Eddie's fine. He's ten now."

"A boy. She had a boy."

233

"Yes, Father. Born May 1, 1942, in the month of Our Lady." He chuckled. "Funny how things turn out."

"He's not . . . not sick, or anything?" I asked sheepishly.

"If you mean is he retarded, quite the contrary. He's a very bright little boy."

"I'm glad."

"We moved, you know. Around Christmas 1941. Papa sold the house and we moved to a neighborhood in Queens where nobody knew us from Adam."

"To avoid talk."

"That's right. Lucia didn't care for her own sake, but she didn't want to raise the kid in an atmosphere of gossip or scandal."

"I understand."

"He's being raised in the family like a younger brother." Doubt lurked in his eyes. "It's not a lie, is it, Father? We'll tell him the truth when he grows up."

"It's the whitest of lies. Don't worry about it, son."

He looked sad. "You know, it's hard for her to pretend she's his older sister. But she's got so much love, I guess it doesn't matter."

"Is she married?" I asked hesitantly.

"No. She's living at home. She'll never get married."

"How do you know?"

He shrugged. "I just know."

"How are things going for her?"

"I don't know. She doesn't have much of a life. Had to quit school when the baby came. But I think she's happy in an odd sort of way."

"What's she do for a living?"

"She's a secretary at the Botanical Garden. Doesn't pay much. But she seems to love being around greenery and flowers. She's had a bunch of odd jobs over the years. She seems happiest with this one." He drained his coffee cup.

"Want more?" I asked.

"No, thanks."

"How are your parents?"

"Pretty good. Pop was promoted to foreman."

"That's great. Wasn't there an older sister?"

"Rosemary. She married the butcher's son and moved to Great Neck. Has three kids now."

"That's nice." I eyed him nervously. "I'd like to see Lucia. Just to say hello."

He looked dubious and shook his head. "I don't know about that, Father. She keeps to herself a lot."

"Will you ask her for me?"

"All she does is work, take care of the kid, go to church. She doesn't like to see people."

"Just ask her, okay?"

Finally he nodded. "Okay."

We shook hands and he left me nibbling on a doughnut and the thought that the baby had been born in May, the month of miracles.

After this meeting, I didn't run into Mario again until a week later at the first practice session with the new squad members. Naturally, he had made the team. I bided time, watching him work out. He excelled in the fast-break drill and piled up assists with his sharp passing during the scrimmage. He didn't score much but his shot selection was good and his percentage high. He wound up with eight points and his performance impressed the coach.

I ran out of patience and yanked him out of a lay-up line to ask, "Well?"

He lowered his eyes to the hardwood floor. His olive skin glistened with perspiration. "Sorry, Father."

"What do you mean?"

"She doesn't want to see you."

"Why not?"

He shrugged. "I don't know. But she gave me a letter for you. It's in my locker."

I tore open the envelope with slightly trembling hands. The girl still exerted a powerful effect on me. I had to remind myself that the author of the letter I was about to read was now a full-grown woman of twenty-two. In my mind and heart she was frozen in time at the age when I knew her. I pictured her now as she looked then, with the pearly complexion of an eleven-year-old. I read the letter:

Dear Father Fogarty,

How lovely to have word of you after all these years! I'm glad that you are well, although my brother informs me that you have grown a little stouter, shall we say? I guess you still have a fondness for doughnuts. Well—as vices go—it's a fairly innocent one.

Please try to understand that I can't see you. I have no clear idea why. My instinct, rather than my reason, tells me not to. Maybe it would be like Lot's wife looking back at fiery Sodom. Something like that, I think. In any case, I know I shouldn't see you. Let me add that a part of me wants to very much, and that thinking about you brings a lump to my throat. I'm so grateful to you for your kindness and guidance in my time of need.

If you ever do, don't worry about me. I'm a little lonely now and then, but happy enough with my life. My boy and my family keep me busy. Oh, I lose heart sometimes, when I think about the old days and the glory of my vision. I am reminded of the words of Saint Bernadette to a young nun at the convent of Notre Dame de Nevers: "What do you do with a broom when you've finished using it?" "You put it in a corner." "Yes, indeed. And that's what the Virgin has done with me."

But most of the time I'm content. The world is still largely a faithless place, but I think I did my best to carry out the mission I received in Pelham Bay Park. Did I succeed? When I look at the son who knows me as a sister, I believe so. Have you read Milton's Paradise Lost? *I'll quote a few lines:*

> *This further consolation yet secure*
> *I carry hence; though all by me is lost,*
> *Such favour I, unworthy, am vouchsafed,*
> *By me the Promised Seed shall all restore.*

That sort of sums it up for me. I hope you don't think I'm presumptuous. Maybe Sister Mary Rachel was right when she said I had hubris.

Mario must have told you that I work as a secretary in the Bronx Botanical Garden. I love it there; it's an Eden of beauty. Do you know that plants have the unique ability to transform carbon dioxide and water into starches and sugars for their own sustenance, and then return oxygen to the air to boot? All life on this earth depends on the daily miracles performed by humble blades of grass. A flower can turn stones into bread effortlessly and man, who poisons the air with diesel fumes and atom bombs but cannot duplicate this simple feat, has so much false pride.

No, Father, I haven't become cynical. I've merely grown older and wiser. I hope. Keep the flame burning and please remember me in your prayers.

Yours affectionately,
Lucia

The letter was the last communication (except perhaps in the realm of prayer) between me and her. The years paraded by. Mario was ordained and sent to Rome to study. We lost touch. After eighteen years at Dunwoodie I was assigned again to parish work as assistant pastor of a congregation in Yorkville. In the eyes of my sacerdotal peers, my career was a dismal failure since I never rose above the aide-de-camp rank in the hierarchy, even after the winter of age had covered my carrot patch with snow. Yet I was happy enough to shun the rubber-chicken circuit and spend more time on golf and private scholarship. Ambition was never my strong suit, as I have already noted.

In my dotage as a chronic newspaper reader, I of course became a devotee of the obituary pages where I learned the fate of some of the people whose lives touched my client's in the spring and summer of 1941. With a bow to the compulsive Stagirite who advised tying things together (although here nature imitates art instead of the other way around) I sketch their finales for the learned tribunal.

Sister Mary Rachel met a sordid end. She apparently committed suicide by taking an overdose of barbiturates while vacationing in Atlantic City in 1962. Many details of her death were shrouded in mystery, hushed up by the hierarchy. The full story is left to your imaginations.

Albert Dunlop landed a job with the Associated Press after the *Home News* was absorbed by the *New York Post*. When the wire service assigned him to cover the Korean War he decided to quit the news business and took a job as a City Hall press relations aide in which capacity his talent for lying was exploited to the hilt. At age sixty-five he died in his sleep of a cerebral hemorrhage.

Father Eugenio Acosta was assigned by the Vatican as an aide of the papal nuncio to the Franco regime. After the war he remained in Spain, serving in Ibiza as an envoy of the Jesuit provincial—ever the crafty subaltern. In 1959 he was dispatched to the former Belgian Congo. Two years later he was killed in Katanga province by a leopard-skinned animist rebel who ate the priest's liver and heart.

The destinies of other figures in Lucia's life are unknown to me. Her own death—which prompted this narrative—was far from a dramatic event. She was traveling with a group of women to a religious retreat in the Adirondacks when the chartered bus was disabled near a curve. The driver left the passengers sitting in the vehicle on the side of the road and went to get help. Soon a truck came barreling around the curve and hit the bus. Four women were injured. Only Lucia was killed.

This shepherd was put out to pasture five years ago when he doddered into his seventieth year. I then went to live with my widowed sister in Bayshore, Long Island, where I continue to spin out my days, trying not to make too much of a nuisance of myself as I battle the hydras of gluttony and sloth.

31

✥ ✥

Positio Super Virtutibus

The cobwebs of an afternoon nap still cling to my thoughts as I sit in the coppery light of the scriptorium. I have just written the covering letter to my nephew, the auxiliary bishop, and begin with a mixture of sentiment and trepidation the conclusion of the brief for the beatification and subsequent canonization of Lucia Buonfiglio.

First another *Confiteor:* two minutes ago I drank a Harp and Bushmills boilermaker to steady my mottled hand. I make this disclosure not to win absolution from the worthy jurists but simply to put into perspective my emotional state at the end of the case. It is with more than a dash of rue that I lay down the quill, for it signals a final adieu to my beloved client. *Dominus vobiscum,* Lucia. Pray for this old witch doctor.

Before summarizing the evidence, I offer for your edification another personal observation. In the cloister of writers I am but an aged novice and thus beg absolution for the literary excesses I have doubtless committed. I hope that devotion to the cause compensates for my lack of skill. As for the literal truth of every point in the story, I confess to an exercise of creative faculties only when it was absolutely necessary to capture the prismatic colorings of life. Veracity is a mosaic of such grandeur that its overall beauty is hardly undermined by the presence of a few chipped tiles.

Now it is customary in such documents to list the miracles

inspired by the servant of God who is proposed for veneration—in the hope of obtaining a decree authorizing further action (*quod in causa procedi possit ad ulteriora*). Before doing so I must first clarify a fundamental difference between my own and the classic scholastic definition of a miracle. Feeling more kinship with Plato and Augustine than Aristotle and Aquinas, I favor the more mystic interpretations that put me, if not in the mainstream, at least paddling in some pretty strong backwaters of Catholic theology. Saint Anselm's motto was *fides quaerens intelligentiam* (faith seeking understanding), underscoring the power of reason to illuminate the content of belief. I am more concerned with the ontology of the heart.

A miracle, say the red hats, is an extraordinary or prodigious event perceptible to the external senses, beyond the power of nature and intended as a divine sign. They spout a lot of hocus-pocus distinguishing three classes (*miracula quoad substantiam, miracula quoad subjectum, miracula quoad modum*), but it all adds up to the talking dog and the flying nun.

I agree with the "divine sign" business but when it comes to "beyond the power of nature," we part company. Behold the starfish. Need we look beyond nature for our divine signs? The scent of lemon trees conveys the presence of God. When neolithic woman first observed grain sprouting out of the earth where she had scattered seed as an offering to some god of the kitchen midden, didn't she regard it as a miracle? And wasn't she right?" "It is the folly of the simple disciple," wrote H. G. Wells, "which demands miraculous frippery on the majesty of truth and immaculate conceptions for righteousness."

Yet the apologists of the canonical inquiry demand miracles. Smiling dolphins and daybreaks are not enough. Think, then, of Serafina's act of contrition. When a heart melts on this mean disfigured earth, isn't that a kind of miracle? Lourdes—mecca of marvels—is known as the heaven of penitents. Let's put Pelham Bay Park on the same map.

The ancients considered lightning a miracle, a forked weapon of Zeus. Thanks to Ben Franklin, we know these fulminations of nature as electrical discharges. Does this make them less marvelous? While moralizing man with his vaunted technology strips the land, dispossesses the beasts and upsets the equilibrium of things, these storms keep a balance of electrical discharge between earth and sky. Through the tongue of killer lightning flow tons upon tons of nitrogen from the atmosphere into the soil, providing a vital link in the food chain, breathing life into man, beast and flower. And Lucia's green beauties return the gift to the air.

Life and destruction are wonderfully commingled. Consider, tribunes, the fate of Basil Two-Times: having bequeathed his genes in an act of violence, he is struck down by life-giving lightning—an accident, by the way, that is not all that uncommon. I looked it up. Each year in the United States about four hundred persons are struck by lightning. The Lord's contrivances would make a dramatist blush.

At last we come to the question of the "halo" that glowed around the head of the statue as Lucia prayed. Wasn't that a humdinger? I anticipate the objection: it was merely a manifestation of a common physical phenomenon that takes its name from the patron saint of Mediterranean sailors, Saint Elmo's fire. The sign from God is reduced to mere static electricity. Yet the same luminous ions in 1519 calmed the fears of Magellan's crew, making possible the first voyage around the world. Was it static or the good bishop's ghost that changed the course of history? As in Pelham Bay Park, perhaps the miracle was in the timing rather than the event.

I could mention all the miraculous cures of paralytics, cancer victims and the like, but the record of these is already replete and they could doubtless be rebutted as psychosomatic recoveries, as if this too made them less marvelous. Speaking of cures, I add one more fact to buttress the case. Lucia's son, named Ettore for his grandfather, is now almost forty years old. He studied medicine and entered cancer research where he has distinguished himself. In fact, I recently read in the newspaper that his experiments in immunotherapy against cancer-causing viruses have made him a top candidate for the Nobel Prize. Thus, even with the simpleton's son, good is adumbrated in evil, life in death.

Cardinals of the Congregation of Rites, I near the end of my plainsong text. Please consider my candidate's exemplary and holy life. Did she have a true vision? Were the stigmata real or bogus? I shrug. Must you always have loaves and fishes multiplied? Why are you dazzled when somebody walks on water but unstirred by the miracles of faith and love?

Allow me a parting swat at the neo-gnostics, determinists and cynics. The last laugh's on them who have estranged themselves from the sweep of life from the primordial lagoons to the vastness of space, divorced themselves from the fundamental miracle of reproduction. Consider the biblical miracles—the multiplication of loaves, the raising of Lazarus—all symbols of renewal, resurrection, fecundity. They are shadows of the truth in the lantern show staged for us who are still imprisoned in the flesh. Lucia is free now and, I submit, beholds the face of God.

I'm tired. The rubric ends. And I am old. Forgive me for closing with a sermon but I am, after all, still a priest.

Dusk is gathering and I hear my sister's dinner call. I gaze now through the window at the guttering sun. How fascinating it all is, how stately and mysterious, like the dance of the bee. How can one remain unmoved by such spectacle?

As the liturgy requires, I have lit two candles. I need a relic. I fumble in my desk drawer. It is still there, pressed between the dog-eared pages of my breviary. I look at the brittle remains of the rose and see what Dante called "the saintly throng" etched in the petals. I smile at the final miracle—my own faith restored.

Catherine calls me again, her voice sharp with impatience. Keep your corset on, old girl, I'm coming. Bring on the corned beef and cabbage and break out the beer. And don't order me not to drink. I'm a priest, not a saint. Not yet anyway. I feel chilly. Where's my yellow cardigan?